RESILIENCE

Maya Gospel

Contents

Chapter 1

Shock, loss and grief, morbid pre-occupation, damaged self-esteem, self-doubt, anger. That is just some of the effects betrayal has on someone's life.

Dwelling obsessively on how you were wronged. Feeling exultant in your self-righteous pain. Turning your pain into an ongoing drama. Acting erratic and scattered, with no plan on getting better.

That's how the effects of betrayal is described, but experiencing it firsthand feels so much more complex.

When life doesn't grant you the opportunity to go through all those emotions in order to heal, you become set in being someone you're not, and sometimes someone you don't even recognize anymore. It produces life-altering changes to one's personality and your outlook on life.

Like every day is an act to protect yourself from the world outside your circle of people that you actually do trust. That's when protecting yourself becomes like a second job, almost like a burden at times.

I am taken out of my wandering thoughts by a voice in my office doorway.

"Doctor Harris, the patient you operated on this morning in 208, is experiencing a stiff neck and pain. Can I administer anything to alleviate the pain or do you want to check up on him first?" Ingrid, the lovely middle-aged nurse assigned to work with me since I've been here, informs me as she stood arms folded over her chest and with her shoulder leaning against the door frame.

"No worries, I'm almost done here, then I'll go check up on him. Will you meet me there in 15 minutes, please?" I asked as I completed my last batch of paperwork and files. Who said being a doctor doesn't entail lots of paperwork?

"I will wait for you at the nurses station, then we can walk to him together" she said smiling at me.

Ingrid has been kind and helpful since the day I stepped foot here. She is the only person I would care to talk more than five words not relating to work.

Oh, and did i hear the stuff being talked about me by the staff, when I first started working here exactly one year ago.

As the Doctors would say, I slept my way up the ranks that's why I am at senior level at such a young age, but they are proven wrong with my skill and way of thinking when it's comes to problem solving almost impossible surgeries, saving many lives that would have been lost if not tended to.

Nurses think I'm unkind and have no personally, but I make sure to thank them and give them recognition when things are done well. Even with my emotionless face, I still thank where thanks are due. Besides, a hospital is where people come that need help, so it isn't a place where you go play buddy-buddy for people to like you.

I also don't do emotions because emotions equals attachment and that creates room for disappointment when betrayed. It's not a question of, if betrayal will happen, but when it will.

At the end of the day I really do not care what people think of me, because I'm here to help people get a second chance at life.

Today is my last day here in Germany and it's a little bitter sweet saying goodbye to another place that has been helping me grow in my field of expertise, but I'm excited to see my family at home.

I am what many would call an intellectual genius. I graduated high school at the age of 16, studied at the best Medical school in America and travelled the world giving hope while healing people and learning so much.

I am a Neurosurgeon, people in a private capacity or hospitals would hire me to come in and deal with difficult cases. I'm also not permanently contracted which gives me the flexibility to be involved in the lives of my family. That's why the longest contract would be no longer then 1 year.

Any doctor would tell you, that to become the best in your field, you have to gain the experience and knowledge in the field.

That is why I decided to stay up to 6 months, or a year at most in each country to gain the expertise, because each country teach differently and come with different opportunities to learn new skills.

Traveling to some of the poorest to do surgeries for free, also to some of the richest countries gaining a wealth of knowledge doing so.

I have been to countries no doctor would prefer to go to due to the poverty, but what they don't realize is that you gain the most experience in those places.

I have also been approached by many rich people that would hire me where doctors either refused or didn't want to take the risk.

Which brings me to my next challenge. I have been contacted by a hospital at home one month prior, to come and help with a few special cases for the next six months.

They want me on a permanent basis, but I declined because want to live my life and not be tied down. I want to dictate my own path, that's why I only work on a consultancy basis.

How could I refuse being near my family? I jumped at the opportunity because I feel that I've gained enough knowledge and experience to be able to settle in one place, and which better place then home?

And before you say it's an opportunity to make more money, my parents are wealthy, but my world does not revolve around wealth.

They never flaunt their wealth and always made sure we are aware of how hard they earned their money.

I have two brothers, to which I'm the middle child of. Chase is 29 who took over from dad last year when he retired.

Daniel is 24 and an Engineer, also for the family business and serves as one of the directors.

Then myself who is 25, turning 26 soon.

All of us are single as can be. Chase doesn't have time to date and Daniel is too much of a nerd to attempt to ask a girl out.

Me on the other hand, I don't believe in relationships because I won't be able to trust anyone....ever, besides my family.

All of us still lives at home and dad made sure to build a huge house out of the city on a 14 acre piece of land, and for everyone to have their own separate living quarters. We don't mind because we love them.

I finished adding notes and signing the last file then proceeded to head out to the nurse's station to get Ingrid. As soon as she saw me she followed me to room 208, where the patient resides.

"Are you excited to see your family" she asked.

"I cant wait. It's been six months too long" I said as we headed to the elevator.

I will surely miss you" she said, making me glance over in her direction seeing the emotional side that she always tend to show me.

I get attached to no-one besides my family, but i do get comfortable enough to have a conversation with them and this nurse is one of them.

"I have to say, I've worked in a lot of countries and have met some cruel, heartless people in this field, but you have a heart of gold. Please protect it" I say as I face the front entering the lift with her following behind with a shocked expression. This was the first time she saw me giving a human like response.

I can see from the corner of my eyes, her wiping the glossiness from her eyes "I knew there was a person with a heart inside that body" she says while chuckling at her own comment.

I just smile as we exit and finally enter the patient's room.

"Good Evening Mr. Hans, how are we feeling?" I ask as Mr. Hans as I look at his monitor, then proceed to pick up his file glancing through his stats.

He answers me in English with his thick Germán accent "Not so good, this pain in my neck and I'm unable to move my neck.

"That is totally normal after having a big tumor removed from your neck. The nurse here will give you something for the pain as I don't see any further issues with your stats.

After explaining to Mr. Hans what is to be expected as time goes by, i also explained the medication and why we're not able to give too much.

leaving the patient's room after Mr. Hans was satisfied with my answers, I head to my office gathering all my personal belongings to head to the airport for my flight back home.

Ingrid came in a few minutes before I left, bringing me a cupcake to celebrate the time we spent together.

I gave her a gold necklace with a pendant of a brain, with the words saying "Thank you - DH" inscribed on it.

That was followed with a lot of tears from her, but I eventually made it to the airport. That's also why I hate emotions, the vulnerability that accompany it sometimes.

Once I boarded the plain and got settled, I messaged my dad to let him know that I have boarded and that he should not forget to come and pick me up at the airport in nine long hours.

It's already 12:30 at night when we took off as I settled and got some shut eye so the time could go by quicker.

I slept the whole nine hours through not removing my seatbelt or going for a toilet break. Getting this amount of sleep is a luxury.

I was woken by someone touching my shoulder to wake me up. I opened and saw it's the airhostess waking me up. We are probably going to land I thought.

"Dr. Harris?" she asked bending down almost unsure if it's me.

"Yes" I answer her with a questioning look on my face.

"The captain just informed that there's medical emergency and requested your help at the airport when we land. The person needing the help is high profile and you are the only person nearest to the airport with the level of medical expertise that could help. The medical staff they have there are only the paramedic because the doctor is late for duty and an hour away from the airport" She explained.

I just nod in response as she thank me with a smile and made her way to the front of the plane again. A few minutes later the Captain started to speak.

"Good Morning everyone, Welcome to New York city. We will be landing in exactly five minutes. I would like to ask everyone to remain seated when we land and for Dr. Harris to disembark first. She will be helping us with a have a medical emergency on the ground. Once again, thank you for flying with us"

Five minutes later all eyes were on me as I'm the only one able to grab my backpack and exit the plain. Awkward.....

I am ushered into a black SUV that does not belong to the airport. Once we reach the building that only serve private clients on opposite side of the airfield, we exit and is shown to a small medical room.

A bulky man in a black suite with black shirt and tie stretch his hand in my direction for me to shake.

After the formalities are over he starts to explain the situation as we head into the room where his boss is situated.

I glance to my side and see about 15 men also dressed in black scattered around. How high-profile is this guy?

"Dr. Harris, thank you for agreeing to help. My boss, Mr. Giordano complained on the flight of head ache and nausea. He threw up and then fainted shortly after" he explain as we made our way to the room where his boss is.

I only nod as he hold the door open for me to enter first. As I enter I can see a middle-aged woman, a man, probably her son and a girl her daughter because they both look like her.

They stood to the side observing me intently, but I ignore them as one of the only medical staff i see approaches me.

"Good Day Dr. Harris" the guys which I assume is medic from his attire. I respond with a nod.

After glancing at the person on the bed, I froze as soon as I see the person's face in front of me.

I am so use to masking my emotions in difficult or surprising situations, that I don't think anyone would be able to read the thoughts through my expressions, because there is none.

How is this possible and how can there be more then two of these faces in the world. This can't be.

I start to panic internally at the meaning of that face. This can't be possible, the man is married with big kids.

Never, I say to myself as I force my mind into believing that it's just a coincidence.

I am however taken out of my reverie as the paramedic starts to talk.

"We have a male, 53 years of age, blood pressure 180/120, unresponsive" he says.

I just nod as I approach the table where the man is laying and start to measure his pulse with my finger. I stretch my hand out "Statoscope?" because mine was packed with my luggage and i won't be able to rummage through it now.

As soon as I feel one being placed in my hand, I place it in my ears to listen to the functioning of the organs when I look up at the man's face, notice a clear fluid running out of the patient's nose.

I look at his wife cause she would be able to give me better answers to my questions I'm about to ask as I continue listening to his organ function.

"Does he have flu or any illnesses such as hypertension, diabetes?" I ask her waiting for her to respond.

"No, he's a very healthy man. He loves to eat, but goes to the gym regularly" she says as she shake her head.

"Did you check his sugar levels?" I ask the paramedic ignoring her response she just gave as i start to feel his ribcage and the rest of his body.

Most of the time family don't notice things about their loved ones and other times family members hide stuff such as illnesses and so on.

"Normal Doc" he says.

"Did he fall or bump his head, complain of head aches, drowsiness" I ask as I lay the statoscope on my neck looking at her again waiting for a response as my hands move to his head feeling for any bumps or lesions indicating any trauma.

"He complained on the flight of a headache for the first time and that was on our way here, that's when he started to feel unwell" she says with tears in her eyes. You can see she's trying to stay strong for all of them.

I could feel the bump under my fingers as my suspicions is confirmed.

I look at the medic who's the only one on duty "we have to do a trepanation to the scull plate" I say looking at him and his eyes bulge out of his sockets. I know he knew what I was referring to by his expression.

"A What!?" the son asks as the mother starts to cry into her hands.

"I have to drill into your father's scull to alleviate the pressure to his brain" I said.

"No! Just make him stable enough so that we can take him to the hospital" the guy says as his sister move to her dad's side side in shock looking at him in disbelief.

"Your father has" I lift my arm to check the time on my watch "15 minutes then he will go into cardiac arrest due to the pressure preventing his his heart from functioning. A hospital is 30 minutes away from here, not taking into account the fact that he has to be loaded, then driven to one and the morning traffic" I say as I wait for them to respond.

"Have you had any exposure to the procedure before?" I ask the paramedic totally ignoring their shocked faces and continuing to save their dad's life..

"No doc, this will be the first time seeing something like this being performed" he says.

"Ok, lets get ready. We have a husband and dad to save" I say.

Chapter 2

Third Person POV

Isaac Giordano 53, his wife Amanda 50, son Julian 22 and daughter Alessia 20 are on their private jet, on route back home to New York, after attending a charity event of one of Isaac's friends was hosting last night.

They had such a lovely time there, that they did not keep track of time and only got back to the hotel at 2:00 in the morning. Just in time to change and gather their belongings to leave. They boarded at 3:00 to be back in New York by 9:00 the morning. Just enough time for Alessia to shower and head to campus.

Alessia was writing an exam at 11:00 and left the event earlier than the rest to get some sleep and to study before they had to leave for home. Everyone decided to return with her, instead of her having to travel home alone.

Julian had to sort a few things for the business, so he was more than happy to return with his parents.

Almost at the end of their flight home Isaac was hit with a wave of nausea accompanied with an irritating headache and excessive perspiration.

He's currently bent over the toilet on the plane with his wife standing in the doorway, keeping an eye on him while rubbing his back every now and again.

He threw up a few times but had to go back to his seat after thirty minutes because the plane was about to land.

Amanda helped her husband get settled with the assistance of their son and two of the guards that normally travel with them. Once seated and strapped in everyone was waiting for the plane to land in order for their dad to receive medical attention.

They already asked the airport staff, through the captain to arrange help for when they land.

Amanda was concerned but had to keep a level head in order for her daughter not to freak out. She's a true daddy's girl in every sense.

She's also the one with the softest heart of the three siblings. They've always tried to shield her from the life the rest of them are accustomed to even though she's aware of the family business and the dangers it entails.

The ones we try to shield from the world are often the ones that are better equipped to handle the world we live in. Death always is just a heartbeat away.

"Isaac how are you feeling? "Amanda asked as she rubbed his one hand that is situated in her palm.

"Not good Honey. I don't feel well. The pressure in my head is unbearable. Can I get some water please, my throat is parched?" Isaac asks as the sweat is dripping off his forehead holding his head between his hands.

Amanda wipes his forehead with a towel as Julian sat on the opposite chairs with his sister looking at their dad.

"We'll be landing shortly, then we can take you to the hospital, but I don't think you should drink anything. It might come up again or you might choke" she said trying to reassure and calm him.

Amanda thought that he must have eaten something that didn't agree with him but didn't want to assume anything because he doesn't have any allergies or food aversions, she was aware of.

He might just be experiencing a heavy case of heartburn, or his gallbladder might be acting up due to all the foods he was served and ate at the party. He's not someone that can hold back when it comes to food even though he's not overweight, he exercises and tries to lead an active life, even after he's retirement from the business.

As they were landing Isaac was complaining of a headache that was becoming unbearable to the point where it was becoming too painful to even keep his eyes open.

Julian and Alessia, their children, could only hope they got medical help in time. They did inform the pilot of their father's condition and he did alert the staff at the airport to get medical staff ready for when they land.

Amanda nodded in response because she knew her husband required help urgently as his breathing has become more labored.

The hand that was gripping hers a minute ago is now laying lifeless in her palm with his head now slumped forward due to him losing consciousness.

"Julian" is the only word Amanda utters to her twenty-two-year-old son, as both sit with concern and panic written all over their faces. Alessia immediately starts to sob and the airhostess then proceeds to calm her down.

As soon as they landed Amanda saw her husband's face was very pale and his breathing was strained. She was afraid that they would not make it in time for the hospital as his health was deteriorating rapidly.

Once the plane landed, Julian gave Jessica, the airhostess that always work on their flights, instruction to contact the airport and confirm help will be waiting.

They have men that will be waiting for them when they arrive that work for them in the Mafia, but they are not doctors.

They landed on the opposite side of the normal airport that is used strictly for private planes.

Jessica informed them that they had a doctor on another flight that's about to land, that would be able to help their dad.

She's on the other side of the airport and that his men will get her to the medical side.

They didn't want to waste any time, so Julian and the three guards that travel with them for security purposes helped load his dad onto the awaiting vehicle that would drive them over to the doctor.

Once they reach the medical center, they are welcomed by the paramedic on duty that also helped to unload Isaac onto a gurney. He's then wheeled into a private room where he attached Isaac onto different machines that monitor his vitals.

The room is equipped to deal with minimal medical situations just to stabilize patients to be able to travel to the hospital.

Amanda and the kids stood out of the way to the side of the room as the paramedic busied himself by helping Isaac.

They are stood in the corner experiencing a hundred emotions at once. They hope and pray that their dad and husband would be fine.

"Julian, did you call your brother?" Amanda asked her son.

"I made contact with him as soon as dad went to the bathroom on the flight. He's on his way and should be here in four hours" he answers his mother.

"Good" is the only response she gives when the door of the room is held open by one of the guys that work for them.

A few seconds later a woman entered the door with a long dark-haired braid cascading down the middle of her back, almost reaching her behind as she glanced across the room assessing the situation an reading the people.

Normally family of patients are to wait outside, but the rich get what they want and how they want it, always. They made it clear that they will stay in this room until Isaac is fine and out of danger.

She looked almost out of place as her eyes scanned the room. She was dressed in a pair of indigo denim jeans, black t-shirt underneath the black puffer jacket, with a backpack on her back.

The woman in their circle is always dressed to the nines in designer, but it could be seen she's not a materialistic person from the way she is dressed, to the make-up less face.

What stood out the most for them was her untouched beauty that captivated them that they forgot their dad is busy fighting for his life, lying unconscious on the table. No hint of make-up or surgeries. Her eyes are pools of turquoise with an innocence that could be seen to hold a past....pain.

Her cheeks had a rosy tint as her eyes fell on their father and husband. A sense of recognition, maybe? She stood there for a minute then the paramedic took her out of her reverie introducing himself and thanking her for helping.

"What do we have?" she asked as she scanned over Isaac with her eyes.

"We have a male, 53 years of age, blood pressure 180/120, unresponsive" he said.

She immediately went to work on Isaac, checking over his body, then listening at his organs trying to establish what the cause of his illness is.

She looked at Amanda "Does he have flu or any illnesses such as hypertension, diabetes?" She asked and Amanda answered all her questions to the best of her knowledge.

They had no clue what the doctor was looking for and had to endure the beeping of the machines they were quite familiar with. They watched her every move to make sure she does not try anything with him.

They didn't know her and this was the first time they met her and, in their industry, no-one could be trusted.

The doctor mentioned something to the medic about doing something to Isaac's scull plate and that's when Julian lost it

"A What!?" Julian asked as the Amanda started to cry, unable to contain her emotions. She loves him so much and couldn't imagine anything happening to him or being without him.

They have been married a very long time due to an alliance between Mafias. Her father was the head of the Spanish Mafia and she had to get married to Isaac. They learnt to love each other and never looked back because they were doing it for their families.

"I have to drill into your father's scull to alleviate the pressure to his brain" she said.

"No! Just make him stable enough so that we can take him to the hospital" Julian said as Alessia moved to her dad's side in shock looking at him in disbelief.

"Your father has" She lifted her arm to check the time on my watch "15 minutes then he will go into cardiac arrest due to the pressure preventing his heart from functioning optimally. A hospital is 30 minutes away from here, not taking into account the fact that he has to be loaded, then driven to one and the morning traffic" she said as I waited a few seconds for them to respond.

Nobody could respond because they could see Isaac needed to be saved. They've never seen him like this before.

The doctor just went ahead doing what she thought was best to save Isaac's life and pretended that they were not there. If she were to wait for them to respond Isaac would not make it and time was of the essence.

"Have you had any exposure to the procedure before?" she asked the paramedic, totally ignoring their shocked faces and continuing to save Isaac's life.

"No doc, this will be the first time seeing something like this being performed" he said.

"Ok, let's get ready. We have a husband and dad to save" she said.

Amanda took Alessia's hand and pulled her out of the room and went to wait outside the room until the whole procedure was done. Everything was just too much for them to witness

Julian's eyes didn't leave the doctor's hands as he just stood there powerless looking at the doctor's every move. He could not understand how someone with such an innocent face could just drill into a person's head without flinching or second guessing her actions.

It also told him that she was a professional and knew what she was doing.

He knows better than anyone which emotions someone goes through you when you cut, shoot, stab, beat another human being.

After the cutting, drilling, patching and injecting, the machines made a little less noise. That was also the time that the doctor that was supposed to come in earlier decided to rock up.

He stumbled through the door and his eyes fell on the doctor "the famous doctor Harris?" he asked as he made his way to the table where Dr. Harris was busy finishing up with his dad.

She briefly glanced his way ignoring what he said and gave instructions on what to do next "now that you're here. The patient is stable enough to go to the hospital. You will travel with him and before you leave get the airport to get sufficient staff here. Make sure they do a head CT and MRI to check for underlying issues" she said as she removed her bloodied gloves and threw it into the bin.

"Doctor" the medic stopped her before she could head to her bag to exit the room "it was an honor working with you" he said.

"You should become a doctor. You have the skill" she said without smiling smirking or any expression for that matter.

She picked her bag up and glanced at Julian, who still stood there with his mouth halfway open, gave him a curt nod and left without uttering another word.

Amanda approached the doctor at the door and she said the same to her that she told the doctor and proceeded to leave.

When the Giordano's reached the hospital, they sent Isaac for tests and were visited by the Chief of the hospital as they were prominent figures in New York.

The chief informed her that they are waiting for the results and that they would advise what is wrong with Isaac as soon as his results come back.

Isaac out of danger....for now.

Chapter 3

Matteo's POV

I just reached my hotel room after bidding my parents a safe flight and having to find the right opportunity to get away from the crowd downstairs.

All of us attended the event Gina's dad was hosting here at the hotel. I would have stayed in New York if it was up to me, but it seems my life is still being dictated by my parents until I'm officially married.

Thus, I can only fly back home tomorrow as I'm having breakfast with my fiancé and her parents to discuss the wedding.

I sat on the couch with my head resting on the backrest of the couch. With my eyes closed in thought about my life and the direction it is being forced in.

Not that I had any choice in the decision to marry Gina Russo in about six months. You can call it an arranged marriage, the same as my parents.

They don't care if I'm happy and they think that because it worked for them that it would work for me.

I don't love her at all, on the other hand, I find her annoying and pretentious with fake everything. Her character matches her exterior. Fake!

Unfortunately, in the Mafia, when you take over, you are only afforded a certain amount of time to settle and marry to produce offspring that can carry forward the next generation of mafia leaders.

My time to remain single was over, so my parents decided to make the decision to marry me off to their friend and business partner's daughter.

It's already 3:00 in the morning and I should head to bed because I'm way pass tired.

My elevator dinged and a few seconds later, just as i was about to head to the bedroom. I heard heels clicking against the marble floor.

It can only be one person. As I turned my head, I saw the very fiancé making her way over in my direction.

She situated herself next to me as I sat there staring at her with a questioning look on my face, not lifting my head.

Her perfume always made me want to puke. It's just too loud and sweet.

"Can I sleep here tonight?" she asked looking at me expectantly.

"I don't mind, but it will have to be the couch" I said as I stood up and made my way to my room.

"Matteo! We are going to be married in six months. We might as well start living together now instead of waiting" she said as she followed me waiting for an answer.

I turned and walked in her direction, meeting her halfway. In a split second I gripped her by the throat and slammed her back against the wall as my anger and frustration with this whole situation is on full display. I Didn't even cared that I have hurt her.

"I have told you countless times and I will remind you for the very last time. I do not love you and I don't have any interest in fucking you ever again. We will get married, but we will live separate lives and sleep in separate rooms. You got me drunk once and seduced me and that was your first and last time. Now get the fuck away from me before I kill you" I said, making

her eyes glass over with unshed tears about to fall any second.

"Why are you making things so difficult for me and yourself!? Why can't you get it in your head that this is a marriage of convenience and nothing else!" I shout as I made my way to my room and locked my door. I don't' trust that bitch at all.

I undressed and walked into the shower as my mind drifted to the face that has been haunting me for years. I don't know why I still think about her, but that's a face that haunts me to this day.

It became like a favorite memory that you constantly replay in your mind when you have nothing else to think of.

But this was not a memory, more like a nightmare because I don't know the extent of damage I've caused to that innocent soul.

I stood there for a solid hour feeling more miserable than before. I came to the realization a few years ago that my life serves no purpose of its own. It only serves others.

I stepped out of the shower and dried myself, then slipped into a pair of crisp white Calvin Klein boxers.

I got under the cool sheets about to close my eyes when my phone started to vibrate.

I lift my head to look at my screen and frown when I see my brother's name popping up on the screen.

I decide to answer, "What's up?"

"Matteo, I've been trying to get hold of you for the last hour" he said, sounding a little panicked.

"Sorry I was in the shower. What's going on?"

"Dad...something big is wrong with dad. He's sick and just fainted on the flight after throwing up"

That was the last Julian said as I interrupted him midway "I'm on my way".

I got dressed in less than five minutes and piled all my possessions in my bag and walked out of the bedroom to find Gina sitting on the couch sipping on a glass of whiskey.

She turned her head in my direction, waiting for me to say something.

"My dad got sick on the way home and he's in the hospital, so I'm heading back now" I said, making my way to the elevator. I don't really care what her thoughts or response are and I thank the heavens I don't have to sit and have breakfast with them tomorrow.

The plane was refueled and ready to leave once I reached the airport. I decided to get some sleep for the next 4 hours because I don't know what will be waiting for me once I land.

The airhostess woke me just before we were about to land. I got strapped in quickly and headed straight to the hospital where dad was held.

When I arrived at the hospital, my family was sitting in the lounge area of the private suite my dad was placed in.

"Thank goodness you came" mom says as she got up from her seat embracing me with swollen eyes. Alessia was sleeping on the other couch in the room as Julian was pacing up and down.

"What is wrong with dad?" I ask, starting to panic after seeing how tired and stressed all of them look.

"Dad started to get headaches onboard the flight home and threw up, then he passed out. We asked the airport staff to get help once we land. Luckily, we found a doctor on another flight that just landed to help. She drilled dad's scull there at the airport. She said something about head trauma and pressure. I was too stressed to make out the rest, but she actually saved dad's life" Julian rambles.

"She what?" I asked in disbelief when I heard about dad's scull being drilled into. How serious is his condition is she had to go to that level to save him.

"Yes, bro. We are just waiting for the test results to find out what is wrong with dad" Julian said as the door of the room dad was in opened and a male doctor and nurse make their appearance.

"Doc, what's the matter with my dad" I ask looking at him for an answer.

"The doctor that did the Trephination saved your dad's life. The hospital director will come shortly and explain what's the matter with your dad, but for now, you can head in and accompany your father. He's awake and waiting for you" the doctor said, then point in the direction of the door.

"Thank you doctor" mom said, as we all made our way inside.

Dad sat there with a frown on his face, but when he saw us, it lit up immediately.

"Why did it take so long for you guys to come in?" he asked.

"We had to get all clear from the medical staff" mom said as she took in the seat next to him and we stood spread out in the room. Alessia also made an appearance and wrapped her arms around my torso giving me a hug, then head right over to dad.

"When will I find out what's wrong with me?" dad asks as he rubs Alessia's head that is now situated on his chest.

I knock was heard before we were able to answer him.

Julian opened the door as the Director of the hospital, Dr. Williams walked in with his expensive Armani suit and glasses resting on the tip of his nose, followed by a nurse.

He came around and shook all our hands then cleared his throat. Can this guy start talking already. I internally groan at him trying to buy time, but for what?

"The test results just came in and it seems you have a tumor on your brain" he explained, as my mom sucked in a breath.

"What does this mean for my dad? Is it operable? What can be done to save my dad's life?" I fire question after question as dad just sat there looking shocked as he heard the revelation.

The doctor held up his hands indicating I have to stop with the questions in order for him to answer. As he was about to talk another knock was heard and the nurse opened the door for the person that knocked.

In walk the most beautiful woman I have ever seen with the exact same face that has been haunting me for the past ten years.

My brain struggled to register that the face I've been dreaming of was standing here in front of me. Is it even her?

I have to try and find out more about her. She looks a little more mature now then 10 years ago, but that face is the same.

The moment she caught me staring at her she stood there in an unrecognizable expression splayed across her face. We stood there staring at each other until Dr. Williams cleared his throat gaining both of our attention.

"Thank you for joining us Dr. Harris and thank you so much for coming in so soon" he said to her as he heads over in her directions shaking her hand. She nods without giving him any further response. Strange creature.

"She's the doctor that drilled dad's head at the airport" Julian said, with excitement in in voice.

"She did what?" dad asked in a shocked expression.

Dr. Williams spoke up again "Yes, Dr Harris happened to fly in from Germany the same time you landed. She had to alleviate the pressure the tumor was putting on your brain.

Mom walked over to her taking her hand in hers "Thank you very much for saving my husband's life. I cannot thank you enough. We appreciate what you've done" Mom said as the doctor looked dazed and in her own world, but eventually gave mom a nod. She stepped back and retracted her hand as if the contact with mom was making her uncomfortable.

"Dr. Harris is our head of Neurology for the next six months and I must say we are honored to have the best Neurosurgeon in the world helping us out" he said almost licking this woman's ass.

For someone that works with brains she is a little strange or maybe we are just used to people throwing themselves at us and she's not doing it.

The nurse hands her my dad's file as she takes a seat in a seat in the corner of the room going through the thick file.

I stood there in a daze as I watched at her every action. She was busy twirling a loose strand of her hair in her finger, then she looked up, as if going over everything in her head then she continued reading through the file.

After all of us stood there for 15 minutes in a trance not saying a word, she spoke, but not to us, to the nurse.

"Get the OR ready in 20 minutes, the tumor has to be removed right away" she said as my mother gasped and Alessia started to cry.

"Why so soon? He just woke up" mom said, as her head snapped in mom's direction.

"There's a slight drop in his vitals every minute. His brain is hemorrhaging, though very slow, any brain bleed is dangerous. In order to save his life, the tumor would have to be removed and the bleeding stopped "she explained like it is just another surgery with a detached emotion on her face. Isn't she perfect for the Mafia?

Could she be out for revenge and want to kill my dad? I immediately shake that thought off.

She rambled off a list of medication the nurse should administer after dad gave his authorization to be operated on and then she left as if she was never in the room a few seconds ago.

Meanwhile I'm standing there shocked with a magnitude of emotions coursing through me.

"Dr. Williams, is everything alright with that doctor?" Julian asked out of curiosity because everyone could see how detached she was.

"That is how she is. That's why she is the best at what she does and has been hired all over the world. We have been trying to get her help for more than a year now and eventually got her to agree to help us. With her expertise we are able to give so many a second chance that doctors with more the 30 years' experience were unable to help with. She has saved so many lives in her short time being a doctor and we are truly honored to have her here." he re-assured us, as the nurse standing beside him shook her head in agreement.

"Where do I sign" dad asked making my eyes bulge out of my eye sockets. The man that trust nobody, is willing to sign paperwork to let someone cut open his head?

The nurse handed him the documents and explained to him where to sign as mom stood there in a daze with Alessia in her arms stroking her hair.

"Dr Harris will meet you in front of the OR waiting rooms once your dad is prepped for surgery" Dr. Williams ends off the conversation and bids us good luck, then proceeding to head out.

I was too stunned to utter another word, not being able to process what just happened. I need to talk to her after the surgery to confirm it's her.

We stood outside in the waiting area as Dr. Harris came in with her emotionless face dressed in blue scrubs and cap ready to cut my dad's head open.

"Do you have any questions for me?" she asks.

"How long will the surgery take?" Alessia asked.

"It will take 4-6 hours, but I'll send the nurse to update you regularly" she said and headed over to perform my dad's surgery.

Chapter 4

Daniella's POV

Once I finished saving that man's life, I headed straight to baggage claim collecting my bags, then proceeded to go to where my dad would be waiting for me.

It's true what they say, your mind is your own worst enemy. That man's face played over and over in my head. As soon as I was done saving his life, I had to leave as quickly as possible to keep my mental health in check.

Almost like running away from the possibility of the truth.

"Danny! Here!" Dad stood there and waved with an excited expression.

Once I reached him, we hugged for a few seconds before he reluctantly let me go.

"Come on old man, I know you love me, but this is too much" I chuckle at his eyes that became glossy in a matter of seconds.

"How dare you? Do you know how much I missed my favorite girl? Dad asks as he tucks away stray hair behind my ear.

"Don't let mom hear you" I chuckled as I glanced around, as he catches on.

"They are at home. We wanted your homecoming to be a surprise for them. On another note, why did you take so long to come out? I thought your plane landed 30 minutes ago?" Dad asked, taking over from me and pushing my luggage to the car.

"There was a man on a private flight that also came at the same time our plane landed that required medical help" I say not wanting to go into that much detail with dad.

"If you saved him, which I know you did, then that's good" dad said and didn't interrogate any further.

We drove home through the horrible morning traffic and only reached home after an hour. Dad told me to sneak in through the garage and that he will go through the front door and pretend he came from his morning drive to from the shop.

Dad was already inside the house talking to all of them in the kitchen as I took my time strolling to the kitchen where they were all sitting around the huge kitchen island.

It seems they are baking something from the tray loaded in the oven. Mom is always baking or making something to feed all of us. Bless her heart.

I peeked around the corner and could see my mom preparing another bake tray to go into the oven while my brother Daniel was wiping the counter and Max and Dylan were busy eating some scones. They have grown so much since the last time I've seen them.

I decided to make my presence know, so I clear my throat as I stood against the wall arms folded over my chest "So, this is what you guys like to do on a Saturday morning?" I asked as all of them snapped their heads in my direction, minus dad.

"Ma!?" was the only thing my boys said as they jumped to their feet and rushed in my direction throwing their arms around me. Damn why did I leave them for so long. Six months was too long.

One in each arm like we've spent so many nights.

How they were conceived made me who I am today but having them is like the consolation I received for going through hell while being pregnant, raising them and through my studies. Pure love and I wouldn't trade them for anything.

They came to visit me during the summer holiday with my parents and had to leave when it was time for school again. When they were smaller, I travelled with them and hired a full-time nanny to travel with, but I had to give them some stability, so when they started school, they only came to visit holidays and my parents made sure to bring them every holiday.

They are the main reason I decided on settling. They are at an age where they need their mother more than ever. I hope that they will one day understand that I had to create a solid career in order to raise them and give them the best they deserve.

"Hey guys, make room for me" Daniel, my younger brother says as he plucked the boys off me.

"Have you been good?" he asks hugging me, looking down at me with such love in his eyes.

"As good as I'll ever be" I said as I pat him on the back. I made my way over to my mother who still stood there with the tray in her hands and I proud smile splayed on her face.

"Mother, I have missed you the most" I said as I took her into my embrace. She says nothing and just stroked my hair.

"Ma, will you be staying this time?" Dylan the wild one of the two asked.

"Yup, Forever and ever, or until you get girlfriends and get married" I tease as I go over and rub their heads.

"Mom, we're really very happy you're staying, but you're the only woman we want in our lives besides grandma" Max says, making me want to cry at their cuteness.

"Do you guys want to make me cry? How did you grow up so fast?" I say, wiping the wetness from my eyes.

"Do you guys have practice today?" I asked Dylan and Max who go to Judo practice three times a week religiously. They are both on brown belts and can only advance once they turn fifteen. Chase introduced them to the sport as he has been practicing since a little boy as well and he says it's a way to drain them of their hyperactive-ness.

"Yes Ma, Practice is at 13:00" Dylan says while stealing Max's last piece of scone from him plate.

As all of us sit at the kitchen counter in silence taking in the peaceful environment even though the tv is playing in the background. Dylan and Max bicker back and forth about the scones of all things. I missed all of them.

I glanced over at Daniel, my brother who everyone outside my family always thought was my twin because of the similarities in our names "Daniel and Daniella" and looks.

Mom always wanted twins after giving birth to chase so they made sure to give Daniel a name similar to mine seeing that we were born a year apart, to give the family the twin effect. Whatever they meant by that.

At least I decided to make their dreams come true and grace them with real twins, they sure did help raise them like their own. Sometimes they feel like my brothers instead of kids.

When I discovered my pregnancy and explained how it happened, my family didn't shun me or scold me. They stood by me through thick and thin while also allowing me to complete my studies while helping to raise the boys.

They knew the type of daughter they raised and knew even though they were disappointed, I was feeling way worse, and it was no use they piled more stress on me.

My first thought was "abortion" because I didn't want the shame associated with being pregnant at 16 to affect my life, or my studies that I was looking forward to, to end before it even started.

Thank the heavens my parents immediately said no without even thinking about it, giving me the true Christian talk and simultaneously motivating me every step of the way.

That is what you call true Christians. They didn't judge me because they believed in the type of person they raised and made sure I was reminded of my potential, always.

Dad always made sure to remind all his children, that bad experiences or situations teach you how to be a better human being.

My brothers were pissed and wanted to hunt the person down, but when I explained everything in detail, they understood.

My children don't lack any paternal figures, that's for sure. Their uncles love them like their own and constantly spoil them.

Making up for my failures and being the best mother was my main motivation in life. I studied my but off and made sure to graduate top of my class and advancing as quickly as possible, to thank my parents for standing behind me and not shunning me when I made a mistake as a form of repayment.

My parents cut off some family members when they gossiped about me and always made sure to defend me. That's why they don't attend any family gatherings anymore as both their parents have passed away so they didn't care about those who judged them for standing by their daughter.

"Is Chase at the office today?" I asked, sipping my cup of coffee.

"He should be back before the boys go to practice. He normally takes them Saturdays" Dad said.

I gave a nod in acknowledgement, when my phone on the counter starts to buzz. I frown when I see the name of Dr. Williams flashing.

"Hi Dr. Williams, how may I help you?"

"Good day Dr. Harris, I'm so sorry for bothering you. I know you are only supposed to start on Monday, but the patient you helped this morning has a tumor and it is for your department" he says.

I close my eyes and internally groan I continue listening to his plea.

"He is a very important businessman, and I don't want to take any chances and assign someone else on his case. Would you be able to come in now, if possible, please?" he asks as a glance at the faces of my family looking at me expectantly.

"Ok, I'll be there in" I look at the time on my wristwatch "30 minutes"

I ended the call explaining to my parents and sons that I had to leave and the reasons why. They obviously understood and the boys had practice, but I promised them that I'll see them later tonight for supper.

I took a quick shower and got into my matt-black Range Rover Sport with matt black rims "damn I missed this car".

Once I got to the hospital, the staff processed me, provided me with access cards and explained how I would be able to get to the VIP section of the hospital.

From what the Director told me, they have everything of their own, theatres, recovery rooms, suites, waiting rooms and ICU.

It seems the rich gets everything they want.

I reached the room of the patient where the director is also waiting in less then five minutes.

As soon as I enter, my eyes fell on a face that looks identical to my sons and the exact same as the man who's life I saved.

I know I've tried to ignore their father's face, but this is too much for my own brain to process even though my specialty is brains. I need to get out of here and quick.

What if It's him? Focus, focus, focus Daniella! I internally shout at myself. I have worked so hard on my mental health, I can't let this get to me.

I can't have a panic attack here and it's been years since I had one. I motivate myself to look past this hurdle that I don't really want to deal with and try to answer all the family's questions after introductions was done.

The son, I presume, watched me like a Hawke, so I decided after the formalities was over to take the file and check all the results.

A lovely tumor, an Astrocytoma to be exact and one of the most common glioma's. Malignant, so no danger there and I've removed this countless times, the only issue is that it's huge that's why it impacted the pressure in the brain making it very dangerous for a guy his age regardless of his health.

I explain to the family my next plan of action and as soon as the patient agreed, I was out of there. I went to my office to have my panic attack in peace.

Chapter 5

I rushed to my assigned office that was situated on the floor below the VIP floor. How convenient.

People looked at me as if I was a crazy person, probably because I looked out of sorts as I navigate my way there.

I really didn't care, I just needed to be out of sight in order to pull myself together and prevent people from seeing my vulnerable side.

I locked the door as soon as I entered and went to sit on the couch with my mind running a million miles per second, making me hyperventilate.

I kept muttering "this can't be" under the deep breaths I was struggling to take, whilst gripping and tugging at my hair.

Suddenly, the long-sleeved t-shirt I was wearing underneath the bomber jacket, was too tight around my chest and arms. I took it off and sat there in a strappy vest and bra.

A rush of anxiety, fear and a tight, painful chest flooded my senses. I know it's a panic attack, and I know I'd be unable to stop it as my hands start to tremble.

My heart was beating so fast that it felt like I was on the brink of a heart attack. I could hear the continuous thumping in my ears clouding my ability to control my mind from thinking of that night.

I try to look for something that I could use as a distraction and see a pen on my desk, a clicking pen to be exact.

My legs felt like jelly as I got up and stumbled to my desk. I started clicking and focusing on the clicks, and only the clicks as I started to count and try to get my breathing under control.

I sat on the cold floor cross legged, swaying back and forth. Obviously, the events that I've been trying so hard to forget would start to flood my memories as if it all just happened.

I was never able to run away from those memories that violated my thoughts with the vivid reminder of the past.

I tried my best to suppress it all these years, but never being fully able to forget it as it followed me around like footprints in the sand.

Flashback

"My family and I had a celebratory lunch in celebration of me graduating high school. The day was awesome with dad gifting me a brand-new car seeing that I would be heading off to college in a few weeks.

Afterwards I headed off to a party my parents reluctantly agreed I could attend.

My first party ever to be exact. I was the only girl, so my parents were very protective of me, sometimes a little overprotective, but I loved them regardless.

My parents thought I was way too young to attend that type of party, because I would most probably be the youngest in attendance according to them.

They eventually agreed because it was my senior year, and the fact that the girls would be there should anything happen, made them change their minds.

I also did a lot of begging to convince them and told them that I would be back before 11:00.

I had three friends, Kimberley 18, Tracey 17 and Amber who was also 18 at the time.

They were the popular girls in school, and everyone wanted to be in their friend group. They were also hanging out with some of the guys on the football team. U can imagine how excited I was when they approached me a month before graduation and asked me to be part of their group.

That in itself should have been a major red flag. Who makes friends with the nerd a month before the school year ends?

I was always the odd one in the group, doing as they said, wearing make-up, body hugging clothes, you name it. I wanted to be friends with them so bad that I even ran errands for the girls and made sure everyone got Starbucks every morning.

We only hung out at school and the night of the party was the first night I was invited out by them.

They picked me up at 19:00 and we headed over to the house where the party was held.

Once we got there all eyes were on us and just thinking back to that time made me realize how I dropped my standards just to fit in.

We headed to the kitchen and Kimberley made sure I was served punch. The stupid I was at the time, thought it was a fruit juice punch with no alcohol, just to start feeling the buzz after the very first drink.

By the time I was served a second drink, I could barely stand on my own two feet. I just knew I was given something in that punch, and I thought the girls had something to do with it, because I watched them pour that drink.

Though I didn't want to believe my subconscious at the time because I didn't want to accept the harsh truth.

My vision became blurry, and my stomach started feeling funny. I felt very strange and literally had no control over my actions as I was led to a bedroom upstairs.

I was thrown on a bed or something very soft, because by then my eyes were shut, but I could still hear and feel.

I could hear the girls giggle and say, "see you later dork, enjoy!" It was like my eye lids were too heavy to remain open. I wanted to sleep but could feel movement next to me.

Someone started to kiss me down my neck and it stirred up unknown feelings that I've never experienced before. I know that person was already in the room when I went in there.

I wanted more. My lower half was throbbing for attention as I went with the flow.

As the person started to touch me. I knew what was happening was not what I wanted, but I couldn't bring myself to stop the person because my body was on fire and in need of relief of some sort.

So, I let him and when we were done, I blacked out.

The next morning when I woke up, I saw bloodied sheets after discovering I was naked. I knew someone shared the bed with me, but I didn't dare look at the person out of shame and anger.

Shame for the stain on the sheets, but most of all for causing a stain on my life.

My virginity that I planned to one day lose with the person I loved or married was now taken by someone that I don't even want to know because knowing would be a reminder of how I lost it.

I got dressed as quickly as possible and left. Luckily, when I exited the house there was no soul in sight.

When I got home, my parents were not at home, where they were I wasn't sure, but I was so thankful I didn't have to face them while going through a mental battle of myself.

I took the longest shower of my life, but I couldn't wash the shame away.

I also got a call from the girls the next morning to ask me "where the fuck I was" because Kyle was looking for me in the room, they left me. They apparently thought that it was another couple rolling around in the sheets.

Then the cat was let out the bag when Amber mentioned in the background that they worked for a whole month to get me ready for one of the boys thinking I didn't hear her.

I was too hungry to fit in that I didn't realize I was the target to be deflowered, because that was what the footballers did with the virgins in school, but I never thought I would become their target.

They give the girls big amounts of libido enhancers and sometimes mixed with alcohol could be dangerous dependent on what it is.

That also makes sense because my brain said no but my body wanted it so badly.

That is what the rumors at the school always were about, but I never thought that it would happen to me.

Luckily, I didn't have to see any of the school kids again. I stayed at home and became a different person. My parents told everyone that I left the country for the holidays.

This experience changed my whole perspective on humanity. Two months after I became sick and then I discovered that I was pregnant.

When you're 16-years-old, you think you are grown and you just want to do adult things and want to make your own decisions, but in fact you are still very immature mentally.

I never understood that until I became a mother eight months after my 16th birthday. Even then, I wasn't mature enough to handle motherhood on my own without the help of my family.

Most teens buckle under peer pressure with the desire to fit in or to be part of groups then you land yourself with permanent responsibilities, like myself.

Never once did my family scold, shun or punish me for the pregnancy, because they knew the mental struggle, I was going through was bigger than them punishing me.

My parents were pissed because I didn't tell them what happened the moment it did. They wanted to take matters further and sue the girls for their deeds, but I stopped them. I told them that the girls were under the impression I left and if they were going to pursue matters then they would find out what really happened, and I would become the talk of the town.

I knew I couldn't blame the boy, whom I didn't know from a bar of soap, but I don't think the boy was from our school because the cat would have been out the bag already.

I wanted to end my life, go for an abortion, but my parents stuck by me and motivated me to take responsibility and give birth.

When the extended family found out and made me out to be a bad person, my parents cut them off. I couldn't be more thankful for them standing 1000% behind me, but I also felt bad for causing the divide between family.

Everyone was told that I left the country but in fact, I did my first year online. I stayed at home and studied my butt off to achieve good grades.

Also, if it weren't for my parents' donating money to Harvard, I wouldn't have been able to do my first year online at all.

It's crazy how money can fix most things, but what it couldn't fix was my mental health.

As my pregnancy progressed, I became heavily depressed and wanted to end my life more than once.

I had to be admitted at 7 months gestation because I started to bleed. I had placenta previa and had to remain in hospital until I delivered. That was when I met a girl named Dahlia who didn't have anyone.

She was raised in an orphanage and the orphanage owner's husband raped her. The sad part was that she passed away during childbirth, leaving her daughter behind.

That made me even more depressed, thinking of all the girls that go through similar situations. Some, like me, don't want to report it because of the shame associated with it or not having any support.

That's why I am beyond thankful for my parents because their support meant a lot.

I gave birth two weeks after being admitted. Both boys were premature, and I instantly fell in love with them. They are my life.

The baby blues started shortly after the birth and didn't go away for a whole year. I started to experience panic attacks, suffered from ptsd and kept it away from my family until one of my brothers caught me having a panic attack.

That was also when my journey with therapists started. They motivated me to put all that energy into my studies, but I never dealt with the underlying problems.

That was when I became an unfriendly, cold person towards strangers and never made friends ever again".

End of Flashback

I was now laying on my back on the cold floor as I contemplate what this man will do if he finds out there are two human beings that look exactly like him. As a doctor the possibility of people looking that similar without being related is slim.

Why did my babies have to look like that men!!!!!

That is if he remembered that night. Or could I deny I remember and live my life as if nothing happened? Is it even him?

The looks he gave me said he might know?

For now, I need to get his father's operation over and done with and him out of this hospital. I'll deny until fate remind me it is time.

Chapter 6

Hi Guys,

I'm so sorry for taking so long to update. Work was hectic this week and unfortunately that sometimes happens.

I will try my best to post another chapter in a few hours and thank you for all your love and support

Ps. the Italian/ English translation is from google translate, so don't kill me please

Be good Always

That was the longest five minutes of my life.

Any person that has experienced panic attacks will tell you how emotionally draining and tiring they are. This one was up there with the bad ones even though it was short.

It has been a few years since I got the last one and was most probably triggered by the faces of today. That's the only reason that could explain the sudden re-appearance of the attacks again.

I still have to do a possible six-hour surgery, which I don't consider hard work because I love my career, but when you have to see those faces the task becomes a little more daunting.

Surgeons and doctors in general are used to functioning while being tired and overworked. You are conditioned that way, through hours and sometimes days being on call.

When my phone started to buzz, I saw that it was the hospital calling, probably to remind me of the OR being ready, and I still need to take the patient through the procedure.

Damn! That totally slipped my mind and Its policy for all doctors to give a rundown of what you are going to do and advise of the risks involved with doing the surgery.

"Hallo Dr. Harris speaking"

"Hi, Dr. Harris, I'm Nurse Anderson here. I'm just letting you know that the OR is ready, and that Dr. Mitchell will be waiting for you to go over the procedure with the patient. He will meet you at the nurse's station outside the patient's suite"

"Noted, thank you" I say then drop the call.

If it is something I know I'm good at, it is to mask my emotions. This will be a hard one though, because I have to be in the vicinity of the person that looks just like my kids and then also operate on an older version of them.

Since meeting these people, I have wondered what they do that makes them so important. Everyone seems to tiptoe around them, and they obviously have money to be renting out the biggest suite on the private floor.

I will have to do some snooping on the internet, normally all rich people can be found there.

I have never been interested in people, but there are too many similarities between them and my son's.

My babies are identical twins and I love them with all my heart with their beautiful turquoise eyes and dark brown hair like mine. I swear the hair and eyes are the only signs that they belong to me. Born at 7 months via c-section. They left the nicu after staying for 3 weeks and a few months later I left for Harvard but took the short flight home every Friday, then flew back early Monday mornings.

When exam times flew around, I normally stayed on campus and used that time to study, but mom and dad made sure to video call me and give me a rundown of their day.

My determination to be a better version of myself for them pushed me to excel in school and graduate top of my class with the time I had to spend away from them.

They also had a nanny to help, and I fully understand raising two kids is hard. Once the boys became bigger, the nanny was not required anymore.

I'm blessed with the most amazing parents that took charge and helped every step of the way.

It pains me to say, but Max and Dylan look just like those men. Oval faces with the same facial features, dark hair, straight nose accompanied by thin lips and tanned skin.

I have to shake these thoughts off cause now it's time to get into doctor mode.

I packed a backpack with scrubs and necessities just before I left home and brought it with me.

It literally took me 2 minutes to get dressed in a pair of light blue scrubs with the top tucked in my pants, the same color cap and a pair of high-top powder blue and white Nike's.

For a mom of twins, I am a little on the skinny side, but have been working on some weight training to tone my body and give my body a more natural defined shape.

I guess it's time to get ready and get this operation over and done with. Hopefully I won't see them after their dad is discharged soon, if all goes well.

I take in a huge breath of air to calm myself before I exit my office and make my way upstairs with the lift.

Once I reach the nurse's station, I see a beautiful African American woman with a figure to die for, whom I presume to be Nurse Anderson, who sticks her hand out to greet me as soon as she sees me.

"Hi Dr. Harris, I'm Nurse Anderson and this is Dr. Mitchell that would be assisting you" she points to guy with ginger hair, blue eyes and sharp nose, who was busy on his phone finishing off a call.

I give her a friendly nod and smile as I shake her hand "Nice to meet you Nurse Anderson"

Dr. Mitchell saw me and immediately ended his call and stuck out his hand "Hi, I'm Doctor Mitchell. It is so nice to meet the famous Dr. Harris" he says.

"Famous?" I question him to try and find out what he's referring to.

"Yes, you were on the news for saving the conjoined twins in Argentina. The news reached the medical world here. That was amazing what you did, and I hope to learn a lot from you" he says.

"Oh, that surgery. "No, I'm not famous, I only did my job and helped when everyone sent the parents of those babies away and were too scared to at least try and save them" I say, as he stood there looking at me with stars in his eyes.

Damn, I hate that look. I hate it when people treat humans like idols.

"Shall we head in?" I ask ending the conversation there and both nodded as Nurse Anderson knocked on the door of the suite and it's opened by a tall man with an expressionless face, dressed in black from head to toe, that looks like business.

The guy held the door open for us to step inside, but once I set my foot inside, we were met with a lot of stares from people whose attention was now focused on us. Let me tell you, they do not look friendly at all.

There were probably about fifteen people in this room, including his wife and kids and there's still space for more. If they are family, they sure are a huge one and this man is definitely important to them.

There are men and woman of all ages, and everyone is looking at me like I'm the new animal in the zoo to admire.

His wife sad on his one side stroking his hand while another woman sat on a seat on the other side of him.

I try to snap out of the prying eyes and focus on the reason I came here for, and that is Mr. Giordano's surgery.

"Good afternoon, everyone" I say as I awkwardly walked to the patient's bed with Anderson and Mitchell following behind me not waiting for an answer from the people. "Good afternoon Mr. and Mrs. Giordano, this is Nurse Anderson, and this is Dr. Mitchell, that will be assisting me with the surgery" I say pointing in their direction. "Are you ready for your surgery?" I ask with no trace of a smile on my face, but at least I sound friendly. I think.

"As ready as I'll ever be. I just want it over and done with" he responds, and I nod.

"È lei la dottoressa che ti opererà, fratello?" An older woman standing next to his bed ask him in Italian from what i could make out.

(Is she the doctor who's going to operate on you?)

"Sì, sorellina, è anche lo stesso dottore che ha perforato il mio cranio all'aeroporto per salvarmi la vita" Mr. Giodano respond to the woman.

(Yes, sis she's also the very same doctor that drilled into my scull at the airport to save my life)

I wonder what she told him because as they were speaking all eyes were on them, but when he responded their eyes snapped in my direction.

I ignore all the stares as i head over to his chart and scan through his stats. Then the very same woman decided to speak again, but this time in English's.

"How many of these operations have you done before? I mean, you look very young" the woman starts to ask.

"This will probably be my 950th tumor removal surgery since becoming a surgeon. Give or take, I stopped counting after surgery number 600.

I continue to go over the things that I should check and ask permission to shine the small light in his eyes to check his pupils to which he nods "and to answer your question about my age, I graduated high school at the age of 16" that's probably why I look so young" I say as a shrug my shoulders an continue checking my patient.

"Mr. Giordano, I will have to explain the procedure in a little more detail so you can understand what I'm about to do. Can I go ahead?" I ask as I quickly glance over the staring eyes in the room. Some were chatting to the side while others sat and watched me the whole time making me feel Hella awkward. He probably understood my dilemma.

"You may continue, everyone in this room is famiglia" (family)

I nod and I'm handed an I-pad by Anderson and I connect it to the tv screen in the room.

I ran through everything that a normal person would understand, from opening his scull to the removal of the tumor. I also explained the possible complications that could occur.

"Any questions?" I asked when I was done.

"Can I speak to you after the surgery, please" the one person I dreaded speaking to. The person who's staring I've been trying to avoid, decided to ask me a question. The guy that is another version of my boys.

I looked up and all eyes were on us.

"Yeah sure" is the only response I can give to divert the attention.

"The OR staff will be here any second to come and wheel you to the OR"

"Nurse Anderson, could you please administer another dose of Dexamethasone before they wheel the patient out" she nods and goes right ahead.

"That is to prevent swelling to the brain" I reassure him. "I will get ready, and I will see you in a few minutes in the OR. Your family are welcome to wait outside in the waiting section" I say and make a swift exit not waiting for a response, heading to the other side of the floor where the OR is situated.

Chapter 7

A N: Double Update

Matteo's POV

"Teo, do you know her? The Doctor?" my dad asked, looking at me expectantly. All eyes were now immediately focused on me.

I looked in the direction of my dad and asked "no, why?" I asked as I kept my facial expression as normal as possible. My dad could smell a rat a mile away and I wouldn't want him to become suspicious of my deeds.

"You asked if you could talk to her. What is your reason for wanting to speak to her when everything was discussed in detail?" dad asked not missing a beat.

Nothing important, she just looks familiar. That's all" I answered as I took out my phone to start scrolling through it as a way of getting the attention off me.

Luckily, everyone proceeded to chat up a storm, leaving me to my own devices. I glanced up from my phone searching for Vito and we instantly locked our eyes.

He knows somethings up, but I'll fill him in later.

My mind has never failed me before and I don't believe it ever will.

That's the very same face that has been haunting my dreams, giving me nightmares and feelings of guilt, for the past ten years.

I never could get her out of my mind. Life went on, but that face kept on making its appearance as if being a reminder of a past mistake made.

Her eyes are very unique, and I've only ever seen those eyes on her, that is if she's the woman, which I strongly believed her to be. That's the biggest reason I still remembered her, because of those eyes.

The painful expression that I saw on her face had been etched in my memory since that day.

Flashback

"Hey Teo!" I heard someone shout my name in the school hall as I tried to navigate my way through the hundreds of high school kids, who's also trying to head home after an exhausting week at school.

I thought I could make a fast exit to my car to avoid some people, but being popular can sometimes be a real curse.

It just becomes too much at times.

Some people thrive on attention, whilst I just want people to treat me for who I am, a normal person. Even though I'm next in line to take over the Mafia, for now I want everything to remain...as normal as a teen's life could be.

Though in today's society, popularity is heavily dependent on looks, wealth and status.

As I turned to check who's calling, I saw my cousin Vitello "aka Vito" making his way over in my direction. I internally thank the heavens its him instead of anyone else.

I don't have the energy to deal with people, I'm too tired. Dad made us train early every weekday for the last few weeks. When it comes to Fridays, I am dead tired.

I decided to indicate with a head nod that he should follow me outside, cause the quicker I can get off the school property, the better.

I've got a headache that's killing me, and I want to relax before the party later tonight.

Once I reached my car, it took Vito a few seconds to reach me.

"Hey Teo, what's up?" he asked as he gave me a fist bump.

"Hey man, could we get out of here before that Dana chick starts pestering the shit out of me again?" I asked as I turned my head in all directions, checking if she was in the vicinity.

Dana was a blonde, innocent looking girl, with huge tits and curves in all the right places. She's a senior and is innocent until she opens that sweet mouth of hers, then you know she's not really that innocent and the things that mouth of hers can do, damn.

"Nah, you're safe, relax. She left school earlier today" Vito said as he saw the expression on my face.

"How sure are you? That bitch is like a magician. You never know where she might pop up with her deep hunger for dick" I say as I got into the driver seat of my black mustang and Vito got into the passenger seat as he chuckled at my comment.

"Who told you to constantly ride the town bus?" he asked, referring to the girl in question.

"Shut up man. I'm weak and she's good at her craft and besides, she's always ready and available when I want some" I said as I drove out the school gates in the direction of my home.

"You better be ready when your dick falls off too" he said, shaking his head then continue "Nah man, that bitch is sick in the head and possessive. She's under the impression you guys are a thing. She beat up every girl you fuck with. One day the right girl will come along, and you will miss that opportunity because she will be the one to block it"

"I know man, I know, but I'm only seventeen. You make it sound like I have to marry someone soon" I told him, as I rolled my eyes at his rant.

Vito lived 3 houses away from me and our school was only a few blocks away, so we reached home quickly.

After I dropped him off, I headed home and straight to my room to take a shower. I had to wash off the last remnants of fucking Dana in the genitor's closet earlier today.

I should stop fucking Dana before she become a bigger problem. She's already under the impression we're together and telling her the opposite doesn't faze her. It's like talking to a brick.

After taking my shower, I went downstairs to get something to eat and headed to bed to take a nap.

Mom and dad are out for the day to my aunt that's in hospital and by the time they're back I'll be off to the party.

My alarm woke me 3 hours later. I did all the necessary stuff and headed out to pick Vito up.

We were invited by his cousin on his mom's side whose girlfriend attended school on the other side of the city.

Once we reached the party it was already 21:00 because Vito had to run errands for his mom.

This was another rich side of town with huge mansions and spoilt kids, not a lot of houses around for neighbors to complain.

Two hours into the party and who do I see? None other than Dana. Fuck! I was chatting with some of the friends we made here and then she had to appear. I think this is what Vito meant with her becoming a problem. She will most probably cock block me tonight, but I'll have to put her in her place.

I could see her making her way towards me as I continued talking to this guy named Bryce about football, not making it obvious that I saw her approaching.

"Hey Matteo, what are you doing here?" she said, as she came to stand in front of me waiting for an answer as if she's, my owner.

I turn and look in her direction "oh hey Dana. What are you doing here?" I asked with a surprised expression splayed across my face.

"I was invited by some friends" she said as she stroked my chest looking into my eyes.

"It's good to know" I say as I gave her a friendly smile.

"Bryce, meet Dana and Dana this is Bryce" I say pointing in between them. Bryce stuck his hand out for her to shake but she totally ignored his hand as she stood there looking at me.

This Bitch!

"I need to get something to drink. Please excuse me" I said, not waiting for anyone to respond as I headed back to the kitchen to fill my cup with some Vodka.

"Matteo! Wait! Let me get that for you" Dana was shouting over the music, a little too loud from behind while gripping my arm.

The fuck! I came here to enjoy myself and get away from the usual scene, meet different people, maybe get to fuck someone new instead of the same psychotic Dana who follows me around everywhere.

Though I'm not even thinking about fucking anyone. I just want to enjoy good company with people I don't know from a bar of soap. Kids that won't look at me as the rich Mafia boss's son.

Though the only place she's unable to step foot in is my house, because my dad will put a bullet through her skull no questions asked, so she'll never attempt to go that far. Her hounding my ass has to stop now and if it means I have to stop fucking her for fun, then so be it.

"Dana! I'm done fucking you. I've had enough. We were never dating, but you cock block me every opportunity you get, and this stops here and now. I'm done with whatever this was between us" I said, as I turned around about to head to the kitchen.

"What's wrong with you? Do you think you will be fucking any of these bitched here? That will be the last fuck you take" she says threatening me.

Her words only pissed me off more.

I gave her a sadistic smirk "I won't mind putting a bullet in between your eyes and give you an early send off. Stay the fuck away from me" I said in the calmest voice possible.

She gulped and stood there frustrated balling her fists at her sides.

This time I didn't look back as I proceeded to walk to the kitchen. I need to drink something to calm down.

I took a cup out of someone's hand not giving a shit who's drink it was. The girl looked at me shocked with a shocked expression and eyes bulging out of Its sockets. I gave her one of my meanest looks as I grabbed a can of beer from the cooler situated on the floor and headed to the dance floor.

I Stood to the side with my back against the wall, my vision started to become blurry, and I knew exactly what the fuck happened, to make me feel this way.

That cup I took from that girl was spiked. Fuck!

I took my phone out to contact Vito who went off with a girl earlier. My vision was a little blurry, but I managed to dial his number.

He answered after the fourth ring. Thank the fuck we made that a rule to always pick phones up regardless how angry we might be at each other.

Before he could speak, I spoke before I passed out "I drank a spiked drink. I'm on the dance floor in the corner" I said, as I felt my body go limp, but I don't hit the floor. Someone caught me.

I could feel myself being carried upstairs as it felt like I was levitating in the air. My face hit something soft.

I could hear muffled voices and I knew I had to sleep this one off, but I couldn't bring my heart to slow down in order for me to fall asleep.

I smoked weed every now and then, and drank alcohol, but never took any other substance before. My dad would have my head.

I started to become horny as hell and it got to the point of feeling unbearable and my body needing a release.

I felt movement next to me. I tried to look but my eyesight was too blurry. I tried to touch the person as I took in the shapes in front of me. It was a girl as I could make out from the long hair and boobs.

At this point I was too horny to stop myself and started to touch her and rubbed her boobs as my hand went down to her lower half as she started to moan.

She moved to my side, and I still don't know how we started to kiss, but we kissed.

The rest I'm unable to remember because my mind blacked out

The next morning, I woke up and saw the most beautiful person lying beside me. She was lying with the sheet covering only the lower half of her body, leaving her breasts exposed.

I must say, everything I've seen about her has been beautiful.

I moved the sheet to cover her body just in case someone might walk in and see her exposed, because the sun is up already, though It's still very early.

She started to move and rub her face as I'm lying there watching her every move through the slits of my eyes, pretending to be asleep like the coward I was. Not wanting her to think any more of what happened

Thinking she might become a Dana, though her facial expression told another story as she glanced under the sheet and saw herself naked.

She glanced in my direction and thought I was still sleeping. She got out of bed and started to look for her clothes. I could hear and feel a pause in her movement with her being out of my line of sight.

When she moved to where I was able to see her again, she had a distraught look on her face. There were more emotions that I was unable to read at the time.

She then proceeded to get dressed and left as quickly as she possibly could. I could hear the thumping of her footsteps down the stairs.

When I moved my leg, I could feel a sticky wet spot. When my eyes moved in that direction, I saw what the reason thereof, which was also the reason for the thousand facial expressions I could make out and none of them portrayed anything good.

One thing I knew I was certain of was that she was not in this bed by choice. The pain that I saw on her face made me feel like a piece of shit.

End Of Flashback

"Matteo" I hear my mom say as she touches my shoulder bringing me out of my thoughts.

I glanced up at her "come son, your dad has been wheeled out already. We will be waiting in the waiting rooms near the theatre.

I gave her a nod as I followed her.

Chapter 8

AN: Second Update for today

Matteo's POV

We are an hour into waiting as most of my family are sitting here hoping for the best. Even though the doctor explained everything in detail and assured us that It's a straightforward surgery, we will only be calm once we see dad come out of surgery.

I sat there thinking about earlier before the past flooded my thoughts, the moment she walked back into my dad's room to discuss the surgery.

When the doctor and her colleagues entered my dad's room earlier, you could see her being little intimidated with all staring eyes focused on her. I do admit that some of the people in this room may come across as scary if you don't know them on a personal level.

My family was very shocked at the fact that she's the one that saved dad at the airport and the fact that she's still so young, but she's the head of neurology, so they hired her, as the hospital director mentioned. Apparently, she's the best out there and a big deal in their industry.

She sure comes across as a little awkward, like she's not used to interacting with people. The facial expressions seem a little forced at times.

I felt bad for her when Aunt Paola bombarded the doctor with questions, but I must say she handled my aunt well. Aunt Paola isn't someone to be messed with.

My dad has five siblings, and everyone rushed here with their spouses as soon as they heard about my dad being hospitalized. Our family are tight knit and Its family above all else.

A few of my cousins also came with their parents. Vito my right-hand man, Gio and Romeo.

My father was the oldest of the six siblings at 53 and that's also the reason he took over the Mafia from my grandpa, which was passed down to me after he retired. Both Grandma and Grandpa unfortunately passed away within two years of each other from old age.

Then we have my dad's brother Aldo 51, his wife Natalia 50 and they have three sons Vito 25, Vincenzo 21 and Alessio 23.

His other brother Luigi, who was 50, with his wife Theresa 49. They have a son named Gio 24 and daughter Emma 22.

His Sister Elena, who was 42, with her husband Alessandro 45 and they have one son called Dominique.

His other sister, Catherine, who was 45, with her husband Douglas 48. They have two sons together Marco 24 and Andrea 21.

The oldest sister Paola 48, her husband Antonio 49. They have a son and daughter together, Romeo 24 and Gemma 18. Aunt Paola is the straightforward aunt that would come off as a rude bitter pill if you don't know her, but who she is comes from a place of love and protection for her family.

I think the reason she asked so many questions were because she wanted to make sure the doctor knew about her business, and she wanted assurance that her brother would make it through alive.

I cringed the moment she asked the doctor questions about her age. I know she did it out of concern for dad and all of us understood that, but you could see Doc became uncomfortable with her questioning at times.

My dad and his siblings are very close. They grew up in the Family business and had it hard from the start when our grandpa still ran the Mafia.

All of them wanted to be here for dad. They might fight now and again, but they love each other and always have each other's backs.

Part of what I've been taught since the age of ten was to be really good at remembering faces as a way of remembering who your enemies are.

By the time I was seventeen I had been the cause of a few people losing their lives and the emotional damage you feel when taking a life doesn't compare to the expression on her innocent face. The regret, hurt and betrayal I saw that morning made me want to do anything in my power to correct that.

Once thing I know, is that she didn't stop me or even attempt to stop me. She kissed me back, which made me believe she was either heavily intoxicated or ...drugged, like I was. Fuck!

My head was leaning against the wall and my eyes were closed. I know my dad will make it through.

We are all taken out of our thoughts as the quiet was interrupted with the clicking of heels.

As I glanced up in the direction where it came from, I could see my fiancé Gina, her dad Victor and her mother Dahlia, making her way in our direction.

I internally roll my eyes at Gina who's pretending to be the best fiancé ever, meanwhile I don't feel anything for her.

I stood up and shook both her parents, Victor and Dahlia's hands and just gave her a nod. Her dad is a cool guy, but my dislike started when he also jumped on the bandwagon for me to marry his daughter.

Now he's under the impression he can tell me to love his daughter or show affection when I don't feel anything for her.

We grew up together because our families have been friends since forever, but I'm just looking for a reason to not marry her.

I have my men keep a close eye on her and I'm just waiting for her to slip up.

Luckily, there was a bathroom and a corner with refreshments, so there was no need for us to leave the space.

After having my 3rd cup, I stopped and decided to respond to some e-mails and sort some work out.

Mom was sitting there while Julian rubbed her back. Allessia just sat there staring out the window. Everything has been the hardest on my sister.

I know everyone always thinks the best of their sisters, but mine are really the sweetest with a heart of gold like my mom.

After waiting a solid 7 hours, the surgery was done as the doctor came out of the door which leads to the OR.

You could see how tired she was, but damn, she's gorgeous.

She made her way to the middle of the room as mom got up and made her way towards the doctor with Aunt Paola next to mom.

"Mr. Giordano is in recovery, but will be moved to the ICU, a few doors down" she said as she subtly rubbed her hands against each other.

"Why is he being moved there?" mom asked.

"This type of surgery is normally done within 4-6 hours with minimal complications, but the tumor was much bigger than the tests revealed. We had a brain bleed that we struggled to get under control, but we eventually did" she said as Uncle Aldo interrupted her.

"Will he be fine? Will he make it through?" he asked stress evident on all their faces.

"Yes, he will, but I have to keep him sedated for a few days until the swelling of his brain goes down. I can assure you that there's nothing to be alarmed about as It's very normal after such a big surgery. We will be treating the swelling with some steroids, and we should be able to wake him up soon" she informed everyone.

"Aunt Elena, who was quiet since she arrived here, decided to also ask a question "Will he make a full recovery?"

"With all surgeries there are risks, but I believe he will" he said, as she gave a nod.

Mom took her hands into her's "Thank you so much Doctor, I appreciate everything you did for my husband" Mom said with teary eyes.

"No need to thank me Mam, this is my job" she said as she patted mom back. Mom gave her a nod as she slyly retracted her hands from Mom's grip.

"After Mr. Giordano comes from recovery, you can visit him two at a time" she finished, then left the room.

I stared at her back but could feel eyes boring into the side of my skull as Gina looked at me with a pissed expression.

At this point, I really do not care.

Chapter 9

A N: My apologies for not posting in a while. I promise to make up. Here is chapter 1 of 3 being posted today. Consider it my apology

Daniella's Pov

1 Week later.....

I groan in pure delight as I feel my face being pummeled with sweet wet kisses. It can only be the two most important little men in my life, as I gather from the giggles accompanying the kisses.

I chuckled as I opened my eyes scurrying to stop them from running out of the room. Grabbing Max by his arm and Dylan by the back of his pajama pants, I pulled them into my chest.

"You silly kids" I playfully scolded them, as both were a giggling mess as I started to smother them back with kisses and tickles.

"I love you two so much" I said, as I sighed and squeezed the living daylight out of them. Falling back on my mattress with them still nestled in my arms, I soaked in their cuddles, that I never could get enough of.

How did they grow up so fast? I internally question myself. It felt like they were born just yesterday. I thought to myself.

They were both just as greedy for my affection as I was for theirs. They wrapped their arms around my torso as I gave them both a peck each on top of their heads.

Resting my cheek on Max's head, Dylan starts to talk "Ma, we have a competition in two months. Will you come and watch us compete?" Dylan asked as they both looked up at me waiting for an answer. It's times like these that make me realize just how much I've missed out while being away from them.

I missed those looks they gave me. The simultaneous snapping of their heads when I asked them something or when they don't like something I say then they scrunch their noses in protest.

I love my babies and I sometimes wish they never grow up into this cruel world, even though the beginning of their existence was the toughest time for me. It was still worth it though.

Besides, the time spent away from them was never done in vain. What type of parental example would I be if I just accepted money from my parents to sustain our lives? What lessons and morals would I instill in my sons, who one day will have their own families that they should be the providers of? What type of men would I be raising?

Exactly, horribly spoilt men.

I think every parent just wants their children to be successful in life and being a great example is beneficial to their growth.

"You know" I start off "one of the reason's I came back, was to spend more time with you"

"Really?" Both asked simultaneously with shocked, but happy expressions. That just makes my stomach churn when they do that.

"Yup, and I'm only working for six months and after that I'll spend more time with you guys. We could maybe do a few trips, or whatever comes up"

"Will you never work again?" Max questioned.

"I don't know. I don't want to plan that far ahead. Maybe I'll work on a case-to-case basis like I am now, but just less. Who knows what the future holds, but for now I want to be here for you two"

"We've missed you too Mom. Some kids asked why Grandma and Grandpa always comes to pick us up and if we were orphans" Dylan said.

"And what was your response to them?" I asked.

"We tell them that your busy saving lives all over the world, but now that you're here, will you come and pick us up after school every day?" Max asked.

"Yes, I will schedule my patients around your schedules, but there will be times where I won't be able to, but it won't happen that much. I will be dropping you off, picking you up and taking you to all your extra-curricular activities"

"Yes!" Dylan says as he's punching the air, making me chuckle.

"Come get up, go brush your teeth and get dressed. I will be spoiling you both today" I say as I get out of their grips.

"What are you planning Mom?" Dylan asked.

"You'll see. Go get dressed before I change my mind" I say making them rush out to their rooms.

I also headed to my bathroom and took a comforting hot shower, then decided to get dressed in a pair of indigo jeans, beige hoody, sneakers, a cropped leather jacket and small leather backpack to carry my necessities in.

40 Minutes later I was headed downstairs to my mom's kitchen where all of us normally gathered. We do have our own small kitchens and lounges in our sections of the house, but we barely make use of them because mom still makes sure we all eat and theirs are just way cozier.

As I enter the kitchen, I see the whole family gathered around the huge kitchen island scarfing down their breakfast, my son's included.

"Morning Family of mine" I say as I give mom a kiss on her cheek.

"Hallo Sis" Chase says as he made his way in my direction with bare chest.

"Hey Brother bear. How have you been?" I asked as he engulfed me in a hug.

"Better now that you're back" he says.

"The boys said your headed out?" dad asked.

"Yes, I'm taking them out for a fun day. Anyone want to join?" I extend an invitation to all of them.

"I would love to, but I have to sort out some stuff for work, but next time I'm in" Chase said. I look at him for a few seconds and see he has bulked up and is well built, sitting there bare chested with his tall beyond 6-foot frame at the breakfast table.

"I will be going to a book club meeting today, so I'm out too, but you must enjoy my dear" mom said.

"I will be fixing a few things around the house today" dad said, as if he would be doing so. He probably just wants to laze around the house.

I looked at my last sibling expectantly "I've got your back big Sis. I have nothing planned for today, but I have to get dressed first" Daniel said as he took the last bite of his pancake, then headed upstairs.

"I knew someone loved me in this family" I say as I dish some fruit with yogurt.

"How did the surgery of yesterday go?" dad asked.

"It went well, but he must remain sedated for now. He has too much swelling on his brain"

"Who's the person you were operating on?" Chase asked as Daniel got up and left the kitchen to get dressed.

"I think he's a businessman, but I'm not sure. All I know is he's rich if he's able to afford the private side of the hospital" I answer, not wanting to give the name of my patient.

He just gave a nod and continued to eat his plate of my mother's lovely cooking.

"Is that all you're going to eat?" mom asked me.

"Yes Mom, I'm not that hungry"

"You are way too thin, for a doctor you should know in order to be healthy you should eat more" Mom scold and I just roll my eyes at her antics this early in the morning.

"I'm ready to go" Daniel said as he entered the kitchen after his 15 minutes spent getting dressed. Men always has it easy when it comes to getting ready.

I gave Mom a kiss on the cheek "I know Mom, Love you"

"Love you too honey"

"Bye folks" I say in greeting as I made my way to the door to head on out with my minions following behind me.

"See you later old people" Dylan said, making everyone laugh.

Chapter 10

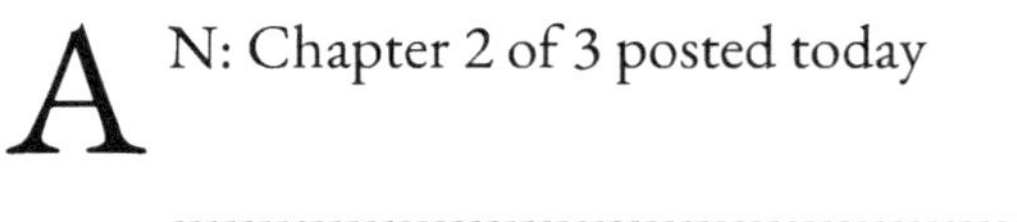

A N: Chapter 2 of 3 posted today

We left and went to a fun park with lots of rides, mini-indoor ice rink and activities for kids and adults. After an hour of enjoying the rides and laughing our buts off, Daniel and I went to sit to the side on some chairs with small round tables and watched as the boys played on some of the rides.

"So, no-one special yet?" he asked, looking at me waiting for an answer.

I gazed between him and my cup "I don't think I will ever be able to allow a man near me, ever again" I said, with my eyes now solely focused on the cup of coffee in my grip. Using It as distraction to get over the un-comfortability of the topic my brother decided to bring up.

"I know it's hard to hear your brother utter this, but you shouldn't let the past define you as a person. You are beautiful, inside out, you have such a good heart and will help anyone that's in need, regardless of who they are" Daniel said as he reached over the table taking my one empty hand into his firm grip as a form of distraction to end the uncomfortable air.

He is my younger brother, but also the most mature out of the three of us.

"A perfect man could enter your life and change your whole perspective on men, but you would miss the chance of real happiness if you don't allow yourself to grab life by the horns. You constantly isolate yourself from the world in the hopes of not getting hurt again, but that is not how life should be" he sighed and ran his one hand through his hair as frustration about the matter is clearly displayed on his face.

I remain quiet, taking in what my brother just said, even though I know in my heart that I won't do what he just said, because I'm walking around with a scar that never healed.

"If you think about it" he continues with his rant "you mentioned that it wasn't the guy's fault because you did not stop him, not that you could though. You were under the influence, but he didn't know. It was the people that were your so-called friends that set you up, so don't sell yourself short my sister, you deserve to be loved. To get your fair share of happiness and more babies" he says as he gives me a sly smirk when he mentioned the last part. To which I smiled back at him while giving him a smack on the head for his stupidity he dared to utter.

"Heck no!" I exclaimed, shaking my head at the more kids' part "even though I love those two with my whole heart, I don't think I have the stamina for more kids"

"They were very naughty, I agree, but so worth it" he said as we both glanced in the direction of them chasing each other playing tag with some other kids.

"Besides, that bitches will get what they deserve, one way or the other" Daniel said while patting my hand, almost assuring me of it.

"I know, but it is hard to think differently if you don't know any different" I respond glancing his way "If your whole existence was to protect yourself, so that the past doesn't happen again" I said.

"You won't know any different if you don't take a chance and try" He said while rolling his eyes at me "We know what you went through better than anyone else. The physical struggle was minuscule compared to the mental struggle you had, but also keep in mind that everyone goes through some sort of battle the next person knows nothing about. Our battle as a family was to keep you on this earth, that your life is so worth every day you're in it and prove to you that we stood behind you 100%, no questions asked, but it is time Sis.

"Who would have thought my little brother would give me better life lessons than our parents?" I said, chuckling at the crying mess I became in just a few seconds.

"Can I tell you something?" I asked, looking at him expectantly. He gave a nod indicating that I could continue.

"You know the patient I mentioned that I operated on when I got here?" I asked as he nodded his head in acknowledgement.

"He's an exact copy of the boys" I said looking at him as he snapped his head in my direction.

"Do you know the guy or anything about his background?" he asked.

"No, I don't know him, but you are aware that I don't know a lot of people in general. I don't know what he does, but he seems Important because the whole hospital is walking on eggshells around him and his family. There are guards dressed in black stationed outside and on the whole floor"

"What's his name? Do you think he could be linked to their dad?" he asked while biting his nails in anticipation. He always does that when he's nervous or excited.

"Isaac...Giordano...and he's 53 years old" I said squinting my eyes and scrunching my face, waiting for his reaction.

His eyes go wide in disbelief "you are freaking kidding me. Do you remember anything about him? Wait! Why is he old?"

"No, relax Dan. I don't think it was him, but the scary part is..." before I could continue, he decides to interrupt me again.

"Wait, there's a scary part?"

At this point this boy is fueling my frustration "Little brother, shut it!" I say rolling my eyes at him as I cross my arms and legs while shaking my head at his impatience.

"The son also looks like him and the looks he gives me are plain creepy. He also asked me last week if he could speak to me, but I made sure to dodge him every time I saw him at the hospital and don't ask me why, because I don't know why I'm avoiding him" I exhale then continue "I don't think it could be him, even though he's an identical older version, but I think it's fear more than anything else. What if he is related or connected to the boys and decides to take them from me? They look like influential powerful people.

"I think we should look into these people if they look like your ducklings. What if the son is the father? And you don't remember the guy, so it's best to check"

"Hey! My babies are no ducklings, but on a serious note, what if he turns out to be the father and decide to take the boys from me?" I re-iterate.

Daniel now rolled his eyes and shook his head in disagreement "Our family might be quiet and try our best to stay out of the spotlight like the rest of the family, but you know our influence in this city. No-one will try to take the boys from you, because then they will have to deal with the Harris clan"

I wanted to respond, but we were interrupted by the boys. Their cheeks were pink from running around since we got here.

We decided to eat lunch and continue with the rides and games then left for home a few hours later. Both boys took a shower then headed to mom and dad to watch a movie with them. I don't know how long that movie will last because they were both pooped by the time, I left the house.

I headed to the hospital, to go check on Mr. Giordano, as I didn't do any rounds this morning. I asked Dr. Mitchell and Nurse Anderson to do the rounds this morning and make sure that he remains comfortable and so far, I've heard nothing from either of them.

I woke him up two days ago, after the swelling decreased and it was safe enough to wake him up. He still has to remain here for another week, just so we can keep an eye on his recovery.

It is 18:00 on a chilly Sunday night and I'm now on my way to Mr. Giordano's room after checking up on another patient that I operated on in the week, that had a head and spinal injury.

I gave a slight knock then proceeded to enter. Once I stepped inside, I saw Mr. Giordano asleep with his Wife and children sitting scattered across the room.

The one son was seated on the couch in the corner with his sister next to him discussing something on their phones, but they stopped as soon as I entered. Now the attention is on me, which I hate.

"Good evening" I said, ignoring the look I'm getting from the man I've been dodging this whole week. Luckily the rest of their family is not present tonight because they surely love this man and has been here every single day.

"How are things here?" I asked Mr. Giordano's wife who was looking at me with a smile on her face as I made my way over to the side of Mr. Giordano.

"He has been sleeping a lot since he woke up after the sedation. Is that normal?" the wife asked with concern written on her face.

"That is totally normal. That's the brain trying to heal itself, so he will get tired much quicker than normal, but it should get better as the week progresses and if all goes well, he might be able to go home by Friday" I said as I look at the one machine print out.

I then took his file and read through it. Everything is perfect as expected.

"So, my dad will get through this?" the girl who I presume to be their daughter asked.

"Yes, if he rest as required of him and let us do the rest then I see no issues with him being able to leave Friday morning" I said internally smirking at the girl because expressions with strangers are hard when you see everyone as a threat.

The son who saw me drill into his dad's head clear's his throat as he rubs the back of his head. You can see the naughtiness oozing out of his demeanor "So, doc, I meant to ask you, are you single?"

"That's so inappropriate to ask, Julian" the mom said

"What Ma? I was just asking a question" he said giving his morning a sly smirk then focusing his attention on me again as I stood there with my hands in my coat pockets.

"I unfortunately do" I said, telling him a huge lie, but that's my only defense mechanism to ward off hungry boys.

"So, your married?" he asked.

I just shook my head "Well, you should have a lovely evening. Good night" I said as I tried to tun and walk out, but I'm stopped by the one that sat quietly watching me this whole time.

"Dr. Harris, can I have a word with you please?"

I gave a nod and was waiting for him to continue, but he got up from his seat and walked out the door. Probably expecting me to follow, so I do just that.

Let's get this over and done with.

Chapter 11

I followed this man out of the room until he stopped in the hallway and turned around to look at me with his scrutinizing gaze fixed on me. I lift my eyebrows as if questioning him what he wanted to speak to me about.

I was trying to ignore this man this whole week, but it seems as though he is relentless and won't give up until he gets to speak to me.

"Is there somewhere we could talk in private?" he asked, looking around for any people that might be listening to our conversation, other than the guards in the hallway.

Strange...

"Would my office work?" I asked, as that is the only private place I could think of. The floors were quiet because it's evening and you don't get a lot of traffic on this floor in general due to the type of people that come here for treatment.

He gave a subtle nod. I then proceeded to direct him to my office on the floor below. Feeling hella uncomfortable as I walked ahead, feeling his stare burning at the back of my head.

I decided to take the stairway instead of the lift and tried to keep my eyes on the floor doing so. I refuse to be in such a tight space with this man with his intimidating stare and the fact that I don't know him makes it worse.

We reached my office, I unlocked the door, stood to the side allowing him to walk first, but he refused. I didn't argue and proceeded to walk inside. I got situated on my office chair in front of my desk as I pointed to the seat on the opposite side for him to take in.

After he glanced around my office enough, I decided to start the conversation to get all this over and done with. Whatever this is "So, Mr. Giordano, how may I help you?" I asked, with my blank face on full display.

"Did you forget about my request to speak to you after my father's surgery the other day?" he asked me in a scolding fashion, as if I'm his child.

"Oh, I totally forgot about that, I'm so sorry" I lie like it's second nature, but who is he to scold me like I'm a child? "You can imagine how tired I was after flying here through the night and then having to go into surgery to help your dad" I answered him "but I'm here now. How may I help you?" I question again.

Internally I felt a little pissed having to explain myself to him. I glanced at my wristwatch and saw it was 19:55 already. Still early, but I had to get some rest for the surgery I have tomorrow morning at 8:00, that would take 7 hours of my day.

"Well, I only need a few minutes of your time. If that's ok with you?" he questioned in response to me glancing at the time on my watch. Obviously, he caught on to the idea that I don't have time to waste.

I gave a nod prompting him to continue with whatever he wants to discuss.

He got comfortable, placing one leg over the other as his arms rested on the armrests as he cleared his throat. I must admit he's attractive with his tall, muscular but lean frame, tanned skin with sleeked back hair, thin lips and straight nose.

We'll I'm not dead, so I still notice these things. I just don't want everything that comes with men, not that I'm interested in women, because I'm not.

I have burned and I have learned.

"First off, I want to personally thank you for saving my father's life and also for performing the surgery after wards" he said as he looked my straight in the eyes.

"It's my job Mr. Giordano, it's what I do, so no need to thank me" I said, not showing any trace of being intimidated by his stare. To be honest he looks like a dangerous man, now that I'm taking a good look at him.

He gave a nod then proceeded "Please call me Matteo. Mr. Giordano sounds so... formal"

I didn't respond to that request because I don't have the energy to argue about what to call him and he doesn't make decisions for me.

"You look really familiar Doc; did you perhaps go to Fairmont High?" he asked as his eyes went from the floor, then to me.

I took a few seconds looking at him before answering "yes, I did, but I don't remember you" I said, trying to get behind the reason why this guy is asking me this.

Does he know what happened? Does he know about the boys? He looks dangerous, so what if he investigated me? Why would he want to do it? My overthinking mind will kill me one day.

"I did not go there, but I knew someone that went there. Did you also attend the parties when you were at that school?" he asked.

Fuck! It could be possible. Fuck! Now I really need to investigate this guy.

"You probably know all high school kids went to parties on a regular basis, so I don't understand why you would ask me that?" I asked back.

"It is just" he rubbed his jaw, and it looked like he's contemplating if he should spill the beans "you look familiar" he said.

In my sudden panic, I interrupted him "Mr. Giordano, I don't want to come off as rude, but I don't feel comfortable discussing my personal life with anyone. If there's no questions with regards to your father, then I don't think we have anything to talk about "I said, snapping him out of his dazed look he's sporting "and besides, why are you so interested in knowing if I went to any parties?" I question.

"It's just, you look like someone I met at the party. That I had some history with, sort of"

"That surely is not me, I was not one for parties really and only went to one, but that was it"

"She had the exact same eyes as you. I do remember that, and I've never seen someone with your eye color ever before or after that"

Now this guy is starting to piss me off and I don't have time for this. I just need to be alone to process the huge possibility that he could be, or probably is, my children's father. I'm not stupid or ignorant, but I need time to process this and figure it out in my head.

The only thing that is coming up in my mind is, deny...deny...deny.

"Well, Mr. Giordano, you hooking up with anyone has nothing to do with me. I am not the one you were looking..." before I was able to continue my answer my phone started to vibrate, and I could see on my watch that it was home calling.

"Apologies Mr. Giordano, I need to take this" I said, as I got up from my chair and took my phone out of my jacket pocket. I stood in front of the window glancing over the city with the lights twinkling"

"Hallo?"

"Hey sis, when are you coming home?" Chase asked over the phone.

"I should be there soon. Why? What's wrong?" I asked.

"Can you bring some Tylenol; we ran out and Max has a fever that's not going down" he said, making me instantly panic as a wave of shock goes through my body because of the news. I'm a doctor, but my babies are my everything.

"Ok, I'll be right there. Can you give him a sponge bath in the meantime please, to help bring his temperature down. I'll be there in about 20 min-utes" I said.

I turned around and saw that this man is still sitting in the chair looking at me and he heard everything.

"I'm sorry Mr..."

Before I could finish, he interrupted me "Matteo" he corrected me.

"I'm Sorry Matteo, I have an emergency that I have to attend to. I hope you find the person you were looking for" I said, as I put my phone back into my pocket and made my way to the door while waiting for him to exit.

He got up and made his way to me while I held the door open for him so he could exit, and I could lock it up. He stepped out and I immediately locked up when I heard a female voice.

"Oh, here you are babe" A very beautiful woman dressed in a short royal-blue provocative dress approached us. Nothing about her seems cheap. Not even the over filled Botox and fillers that have taken over on her face making it look a little stiff. She's still pretty though.

"Gina, what are you doing here?" he asked her in a very irritated tone, almost cold.

"Oh, I came to see how your dad was doing and also to pick you up for dinner with my parents. We still have to sort out a few details for the wedding" she said glancing in my direction as if I'm a hinderance "you are?" She questioned.

"I am Doctor Harris" I say without bothering to stretch a hand to greet her because I know she won't shake it. She just looks like 'that type', bitchy.

So, they are getting married, but lady, what's your problem with me? She's giving me the nastiest glare.

"I told you that I would meet you there when I am done here" he said, sounding more irritated with her.

The look this woman is giving to me indicates that she thinks...heck no.

I cleared my throat and they both glanced in my direction "I will see you again Mr. Giordano, I can assure you your dad will be fine to leave Friday" I said, trying to make it sound as if we're discussing his dad, because I don't think she would be happy if she knew he was busy interrogating me about my past.

I don't give them time to respond and head out, because the last thing I want to do is get involved in the personal business of anyone and I have this ugly habit of saying goodbye to people and then leave the room. Horrible etiquette, I know, but who cares.

Let me leave this man and his soon to be wife that looks like she will kill me and go fix my baby....

Chapter 12

Hearing the shrill blaring of my alarm, serves as my reminder that a new day is upon us.

My heart is filled with thankfulness as I open my eyes, being able to see another day. Not all were granted the privilege or opportunity to open their eyes this morning.

Even though there was a time I thought my life was ruined and that life was just not worth living. Being scared that people would find out that I've become a mother at such a young age, of not just one child, but two. The stigma associated with teenage pregnancy is ridiculous while also dealing with the shame you feel for the situation you are in.

Everyone makes mistakes, but it is how you overcome those mistakes is what count. No-one is perfect, nobody. Everyone on this earth is walking around with some sort of skeleton in their closet that they don't want the world to know about.

Even though my life only consists of family and work, I won't allow anyone to ever betray me again, so there's no place for friends. I know that it is a shitty way to limit myself, but I must admit that I was and still am too traumatized to give social life or new people in general a chance.

I know it pains my family that I close myself off to the world by making safe choices or choices I feel comfortable with, but they are the only ones that matter to me right now.

Funnily enough though, I do take risks, but that is only when I perform surgeries. Which some would deem as playing with people's lives, but I have to disagree there though, because finding the solution to intricate problems with regards to the brain and nervous system excites me beyond belief. That also doesn't mean that I don't know when to stop because when the risk out whey the solution. I will never put anyone's life in danger just to feed my curiosity.

I was able to get at least two hours sleep last night, after making sure Max's fever eventually went down. He has always been the one to catch a cold or infection first when seasons changed, and the weather is starting to get very cold as we're headed into winter.

He has all the symptoms of an infection, that should pass in a day or two. I won't be able to stay at home with him because today's surgeries are important and took a lot of preparation. If I re-schedule, I would be wasting a lot of people's time and we're not going to do that.

Luckily, I can depend on Mom and Dad to look after him until I get home later today.

I got out of bed feeling so tired, as I took a lovely stretch until the joints in my body decided to protest and made some cracking noises. Once I am fully awake, the tiredness will be gone. I just need to get moving.

I went to Dylan's room to wake him up and then went to check on Max who was snoring his butt off. Clearly, he's tired and needs all the rest he can get.

Dylan went to his bathroom to get ready for the day and after I set out some clothes for him, I did exactly the same.

I stripped and got into the shower. Feeling the hot water run from the top of my head to my feet. This was just what I needed. It immediately released the tension I had in my body.

Thinking back to my interaction with Mr. Giordano's son last night at the hospital, the possibility of him being their dad seems to be something I need to confirm with a DNA test. I still need to find out how without compromising my medical license.

The are just too many coincidences. They look exactly the same, that's a huge one and him mentioning the very party where everything happened. So, what other explanation could there be?

I mean, am I ready to share them? Or have interactions with outside people? How will his soon-to-be wife treat my kids if he is the father?

He remembered my eyes. I know the eyes I've inherited from my grandma are unique, very unique to say the least. I've only seen 1 person with these eyes besides Gran and that person lives in Portugal. It was an 8-year-old boy, who came to the hospital with a broken arm.

The way he asked if I was the girl of that night was like something was bothering him. Maybe it was the remnants I left behind in the bed or the fact that I left without him knowing.

I remember picking my clothes up, getting dressed and leaving without even glancing in his direction. So, I'm not sure if he was awake or anything. I just wanted to get out of there and was way too ashamed to look the guy in the face.

The barbie doll that came and looked for him at my office of all places, is his fiancé, but their relationship seems...strange. The way he spoke to her was a little disrespectful and his tone as well. Like he was irritated with the fact that she came looking for him.

It also seemed as though she thought there was something going on be-tween us because I could sense her jealousy. I chuckle at the thought, silly woman.

I know I said deny, deny, deny, but for how long? I just hope that he doesn't snoop into my life. People with money can get their hands on any information with just a few dollars.

I will just take everything as it comes and deal with it as it happens.

I am performing 14 scheduled surgeries this week alone, from Monday to Friday. All of them are backlogs from the hospital that I'm trying to clear.

People with issues that received treatment to alleviate the symptoms until surgeries could be performed. There are a few that are urgent, so I will start with those today.

I just hope I don't run into anyone of Giordano's today. I still have to try and get some information about them somehow, but I will do that in my free time.

I head a few doors down to Dylan's bedroom "Dyll?"

"Yeah Mom?" he shouts from the other side of the door.

"I'm heading down. Should I wait for you?" I asked.

The door opened and there stood my handsome boy with that man's face. He gave me the loveliest smile that could break hearts for days. I do have handsome sons; I think to myself.

"I'm ready Ma" he said giving me a hug.

"Let me just say goodbye to your brother then we can head down" I say as I opened his door heading inside.

I gave him a peck on his head as he's still snoring his life away then headed out again.

"Come let's go have some breakfast before I drop you off at school" I said as I held the door open for him to exit.

We headed downstairs and my senses were assaulted with the smell of something baking and bacon.

The whole family were seated around the huge kitchen Island as we entered "Morning family" I chirped, trying to sound more refreshing than I actually feel.

We do have a huge dining area in the house, but mostly use it when we get guests or on really special occasions.

Good morning choruses rang around the room.

"Morning dear, how's Max doing?" mom asked, as she's busy taking a tray of croissants out of the oven.

"It looks like an infection and his fever went down a few hours ago, but he'll be fine in a day or two" I said, as I dished a small helping of bacon and eggs to get me going for the day.

"That's good" Dad says, as he's stabbing his bacon on his plate.

All of us continued eating our breakfast in silence when Chase decided to interrupt our silence.

"Daniella" I glanced up at my oldest brother who was sitting bare chested next to the other one who's also bare chested, giving him the indication that he could go ahead with whatever he wanted to ask me. They have been like that since birth and still don't mind walking around with only boxers in the house. Wild kids my mother have, besides me though. I get myself into life altering situations.

"Mhmm?"

"I need a date for an event in a week. Will you please go with me?" he asked, looking at me with a pleading face.

I looked towards him with a frown on my face "and you decided to ask the person who doesn't really like human interaction?" I asked looking annoyed because he's already aware what the answer will be. I don't do events. I know my brother has made an even bigger name for himself than dad in the industry, but it's time he finds someone or a girlfriend.

"Daniella" I turn and look at my dad

"Yes dad?"

"Don't you think it's time you get out there a little?" he asked, looking at me expectantly.

"Dad, I just don't feel like doing events. Too many people make me nervous and besides, don't you think it's time that Mr. GQ finds himself a life partner" I say as I gulp down the last bit of my food and is met with silence. Dylan is the only one in his own world busy chewing and minding his business.

"What?" I asked.

Daniel just shakes his head in disappointment while buttering his toast, but I ignore him and answer dad.

"You are being very heartless towards me and what if your hospital decides to have events? Are you still going to hide from the world?" Chase asked, with sadness written all over his face making me instantly regret my words. Sometimes I don't think before uttering nonsense.

"Fine!" I say rolling my eyes at him as his face changed from sad to happy in seconds. I don't like disappointing any of them.

"Dylan, are you ready to leave?"

"Yeah Ma"

"Go get your bag, so we can leave"

After greeting everyone and heading outside, I reminded Dylan that I'd be picking him up after his Judo practice.

I reached the hospital and did my first surgery for the day, that took me approximately two hours. I then decided to do my rounds before I take a break to re-energize for the big surgery I'm about to do.

Mr. Giordano was the last patient I did round at and as usual, his wife and two sons were there with a few other people.

He looked much better than the day before, chatting and smiling with the people in the room. The eldest son's eyes were on me the whole time, but I have not had an issue showing people I'm ignoring them.

So, the day flew by, and the rest of the week followed suit. By Friday, I discharged Mr. Giordano, and his family came to get him, and this time Matteo also came along with his fiancé.

She looked at me as if I'm a piece of cow poop, but I continued on paying her no mind.

When my Friday was over and done with, I decided to head to bed with my boys early, because all of us were clearly very tired. Max has also fully recovered. Saturday, I took them to practice and afterward, we played Xbox, ate everything sweet we could get out hands on.

I know I still have to look into Giordano's, but I feel I would be opening a hornet's nest of things I'm not ready to accept.

I don't have to worry about seeing any of them because the man was discharged and what are the chances of us meeting each other again.

My boys are all that matter in this world.

Chapter 13

M atteo's POV

"We were thinking about white orchids for the church. What do you think of the venue at the hotel, being white with gold detail as the theme of the hall, Matteo?" Dahlia asked, trying to involve me in the decision making of the farce called a wedding, between her daughter and myself.

I couldn't continue using the excuse of dad being sick anymore, as dad was out of danger now and I had no choice but to meet them to discuss the final details of the wedding.

The only reason I'm sitting here with them for breakfast is out of respect for her parents' relationship with mine. All of them are aware that I'm not that reluctant to marry Giana, but they keep on pushing me and my patience is wearing thin already.

At this point I'm scared of what my own reaction will be when I eventually combust. It takes a lot to piss me off and I'm almost there. My parents of fully aware of the monster I could be, so why they're forcing me, I have no clue.

It's Friday today and dad's getting discharged in a few hours, so I better get this breakfast over and done with because I still have to do a few things before then.

"I will go with whatever decisions are made by you. I don't know anything about weddings for that matter" I honestly answer her question, while Giana is sitting there with stars in her eyes looking like a wooden doll salivating over the non-existent dick she will be getting once we tie the knot.

"Matteo, son" Vincent says next to me and clears his throat before continuing to speak, gaining my full attention for me not to look at his wife who's sitting across from me at the table. She's just as gullible as her daughter "I know this is not easy for you, marrying someone you don't love, but you and Giana know enough about each other seeing you both grew up together. It will only be a matter of time before you fall in love with each other" he said with a glint of hope reflected in his eyes.

"Let's hope for the best" I answer him honestly, because he's clearly just as delusional as his wife and daughter. I just need proof that she's fucking around. I know she is; I just need proof. That's why my guys are always tailing her just in case she slips up.

"The cake tasting is tomorrow at 14:00. Your mom will be there with your sister. Will you please make time to join us?" Giana asked, obviously in front of her parents, so that I don't decline.

I gave her a nod instead of responding verbally. The more I look at her, the more I want to choke the last breath out of her.

I glanced at my wristwatch and decided to end the breakfast there "I have business to attend to, if you'll excuse me, I have to leave" I said as I got up from my chair.

Vincent stretched his hand out for me to shake "see you soon, son and thank you for joining us on such short notice"

After the formalities were over and done with, I left. Once I got into my car, I dialed Vito. After the third ring he picked up "Hey Teo, What's Up"

"Where are you?" I asked.

"My place, why?"

I'll be there in 10 minutes" I said and ended the call, than headed to his house.

Once I stood in front of the door, Vito opened it, and I headed inside to the lounge area, where we also frequent.

"What's wrong with you?" he questioned, as I loosened the tie around my neck and started to run my hands through my hair and blowing out deep breaths.

"I'm telling you now, either I kill her and dump her body in acid to get rid of her or shoot her in the fucking head, but I'm not marrying Giana! Could the guys find anything on her yet?" I questioned as I rubbed my face and scalp.

"And i sure as hell will help you eliminate that one" he said and i just gave him a look. We have been ride or die since birth and he always had my back and vice versa.

The frustration about this whole situation is getting to me and It's becoming too much. I don't think my sanity would last 5 and a half months.

"The bitch is covering her tracks like the fox she is, but it will only be a matter of time before she slips up and we catch her. You just have to keep your cool, man" he said, as he's pacing around the room agitating me more.

"Give me something strong to drink before I shoot all your windows out" I said, trying to get a reaction out of him.

"The fuck you will! Don't go all crazy on me or I'll kill that bitch myself" a few minutes later minutes later, I sat sipping on the glass of rum that was shoved in my hands to cool down.

"Do you remember when we were both in high school, the night I got drugged and slept with that girl?" I asked, as I leaned with my head on the backrest of the couch.

"Yup, bloody sheets? That one?" he asked, and I gave a nod.

"Are you still obsessed finding out about the girl? I thought you forgot about her and moved on already. You don't even know her name" he said, taking in the seat on the opposite side of me.

"I Found her, or I think I found her" I said, looking at him, waiting for a reaction. As expected, he was stunned that all the years of talking about a ghost that he's now sitting with his mouth agape.

"Where did you find her?" he questioned, now more than eager to know more as his arms are now resting on his knees waiting for the details.

"It's Dr. Harris, or I think it's her from the way she reacted when I confronted her'.

"You mean to tell me... that the crazy doctor...who drilled into your dad's head...at the airport... and who also removed a tumor from your dad's brain... is the girl of that night? Fuck me sideways and call me Susan" Vito said, as he slumped backwards.

"I believe it's her. The eyes, the face I remember very clearly, and when I asked her about it, though she tried to keep her cool, she was panicking when I mentioned the school she went to, and she confirmed she went there"

"But the doctor mentioned that day of your dad's surgery that she graduated at 16"

"The party we attended was a graduation party after all. That school had theirs that day. That was why she was there" I explained.

"Ok, now you've found her and now what? She doesn't look like a people person in any case" he said, rolling his eyes. Giving me the urge to smack him at the back of the head.

"I know, I just wanted to let you know that I think I found her. Now let me get out of here and go pick up my dad" I said, getting up and tucking my tie in my suit jacket's pocket.

"He's getting out today?"

"Yup, the Doc said that he will be able to go home today" I said, heading to the door.

"You sure fuck all the beautiful one's" he said, giving his last commentary.

I didn't respond to his last comment and left heading to the hospital. I still had stuff to do, but the whole breakfast saga pissed me off and threw me off my game. I'll catch up later after picking dad up.

When i reached the hospital dad was all ready to leave.

"What's the hold up" dad asked the blonde nurse that came into the room to check if he's read.

"Dr. Harris just finished a surgery and is on her way here to sign you out and explain a few things.

Not long after the doctor came in with her light blue scrubs. She looks enchanting with those light turquoise eyes of hers.

My stare followed her the whole time, entranced by her mere existence.

I engaged and even if Giana's a bitch, i will never cheat on her. I just have to get this doctor out of my head.

This was the last day at this hospital, now I'm able to close that chapter of my life that has been haunting me.

Only time will tell if the chapter is truly closed.

Chapter 14

Matteo's POV.

"What time do you think the rest of the guys will be here" Gio asked Vito as he's pouring us some drinks from the table that is stacked with different hard liquors and beers.

"They should be here any moment now" he answered, while glancing at the time on his wristwatch.

We're sitting in the private lounge area of one of my clubs waiting for a few of my cousins that's joining us soon.

The one side of the lounge has a glass wall that overlooks the dancefloor downstairs. The whole private floor we're on is decked out with leather couches and a private bar that serves anything you could think of. This floor can be accessed by members and obviously people with money that don't want to mingle with the crowd downstairs.

As I'm sitting there staring down at the bodies moving to the beat of the music, my mind starts to drift off to earlier today when I saw the doctor. She didn't even look my way or acknowledge my existence when she walked into dad's room.

Julian was staring at her like a lost puppy that had stars in his eyes. I wanted to smack him but didn't want to put the Giordano name in a bad light in front of the doctor.

She gave dad some instructions and explained a few things in detail, then she bid everyone goodbye and left. I looked at her hands while she was talking, checking for a wedding ring or a wedding band mark that would indicate that she's married, but I saw nothing. I understand that most people don't wear wedding rings, and, in her profession, I could understand why she's not wearing one.

The call she received when I visited her in her office seemed as though she was talking to a man from the deep voice that could be heard coming through. She said she would be home soon and about sponging someone off, which did sound like they were talking about a child.

So, she's married and has a child. That's why her expression changed so suddenly. She's a doctor, and doctors don't sound that panicked when it comes to just anyone.

Why does that whole scenario put a bitter taste in my mouth and make my chest so uncomfortable? I don't know this woman from a bar of soap, but I feel connected to her. Why? I have no clue.

She has been haunting my thoughts and the fact that she denies that night ever happened, does not sit well with me. I just know in my gut it's her, but it's also time to let go for obvious reasons. Life goes on and I'm about to get married to my plastic barbie doll whom I'll never love. Sad life, isn't it?

Maybe life throws me a solution and one of my men can find something on the woman so that I don't have to marry her. I know I will find a solution.

30 Minutes into the guys chilling and chatting, we were joined by Alessio, Marco, Julian, Romeo and Dominique.

We try to get together at least once a month to catch up on life and just spend time complaining ab1qout shit in life, or shall I rather say, they complain, and I listen. Because what type of Capo would I be if I'm being like a pussy in front of the guys.

"I heard your dad came home today" Romeo said, bumping his knee against mine to get me out of my daze.

I took a sip of my whiskey and glanced in his direction and looked down at the liquid in my glass before attempting to answer him, but Julian decided to get in on the conversation.

"Yeah, and I would have loved to bring his doctor home as well" Julian said while licking his lips.

"I Agree, she is damn beautiful, and those eyes. Imagine looking into them while she's on top?" Gio said as the rest started to laugh, making me internally pissed at the thought of any of them having thoughts of that nature about her.

"She's married, with a child" I inform them, cause if I were to insult them for their thoughts about her in particular, they would know something's up.

"Yeah, she did mention there's someone in her life. What a pity, but where did the child come from? And how are you so informed?" Julian questioned, as if he's not aware that I spoke to her last Sunday.

"I overheard her talking to her husband on the phone at the hospital"

Vito just gave me a knowing look but didn't say anything because he already knew what's up.

About an hour later, my nightmare came walking in, with Gio's sister Emma, and two other friends, Scarlett and Chloe, also part of their social circle. She thinks befriending my cousin to get into spaces that I frequent would soften me up towards her the more she's in my vicinity, but she's so damn wrong. It makes me want to choke the shit out of her.

I have never lifted a hand toward a woman that's not a threat to me and I never indented to. Choking her that night was the result of her constant torment and forcing herself into my life, that pushed me to my limit. The fact that I'm forced to marry her added greatly to my frustration with her.

But I was wrong to treat her that way, that I can admit, and I will have to apologize to her, but I hope she doesn't take it as an indication of me accepting her into my life, so I'll have to make everything clear when I do speak to her.

They came walking in our direction, their attire screaming designer from head to toe.

"Good evening, boys" Emma said, making their presence known.

"Hey Cousin, how have you been?" Romeo asked, with slurred speech and we weren't even halfway through the night.

"Ooh, someone had a little too much to drink, it seems" she said ruffling his hair as all of them got situated on the empty seats available, without us offering them to join.

"Nah, I'm still good. Oh, hey Gina, didn't see you" he said, then whispered into Emma's ear pointing to one of her other friends.

Emma sat in between Romeo and me. Chloe sat next to Gio and the other chick in between Alessio and Marco.

"How have you been Matteo? It's been a minute since I last saw you" Emma asked, and I could already see where this conversation is headed.

"Dad had a health scare, as you know by now, but he's much better and at home now and then there's work" I told her.

"Aah yes, I heard about your dad. I was in Spain on holiday when my mom told me. I'm glad he's better" she said, but in the same breath she continued "how are things between you and Gina? Are you trying with her?"

Bingo!

"I've made it clear to her where we stand, and I don't appreciate you allowing her to use you for her own selfish purpose to get to me. I also think, you of all people should know better" I calmly state, not showing her how pissed I am. I have never been that close with her and she's aware that I won't take orders or advice from her.

"I understand" are the only words she utters, because she saw that she was not getting anywhere with me and started a conversation with the group, leaving me to cool off, but I was not satisfied and had to talk to Gina and get everything straightened out, once and for all.

I got up and indicated for Giana to follow me to my office on the floor. Her face lit up with joy, probably thinking I'm about to fuck her in my office.

The rest of the guys didn't pay no mind, but I could see Emma looking a little panicked.

I walked ahead as she followed behind, heals clicking on the tiled floor. Once we reached my office, I held the door open for her and she walked inside with a smirk on her face.

I pointed to the seat in front of my desk, while I went and sat on the opposite side of the desk. It's better to have something separating us, you never know, she might just decide to jump me.

"Gina, I would like to apologize to you for the other night in Vegas" her eyes sparkled with delight at my attempt at an apology "my behavior was disgusting, and no woman should have been manhandled like I did you. That was the first time I am a lot of things, but a woman beater I'm far from and you have known me for long enough to know that I am speaking the truth" I said, as she gave me the biggest smile "I hope you can forgive me?"

"I do accept your apology, Matteo. I don't want any issues between us to fester and create problems in our relationship"

Hold up! Relationship? Which one? Where? Earth to fucking Gina. It's time I bring her back.

I clear my throat "Uhm Gina, you are aware that we are entering into an arranged marriage because of our parents. We do not have any relationship with each other. I would like us to remain civil when you do move in with me. You will have your own bedroom" I say to her, and her face fell.

"Can you at least give our marriage a try when we eventually do get married?" she asked, with hope clearly displayed across her features.

"I cannot promise anything to you, Gina and you cannot expect that of me either. I can promise you that I will remain faithful to you the agreement and not fool around with another woman because that's just who I am. Loyal. I wouldn't want you to bow your head in shame in public because of my escapades. I just want peace from you, I have enough to deal with on a daily basis already. This is what our parents and you want, but this is not what I want" I say, looking at her hopeful that she would accept it"

"I understand" she said, with a sad look in her eyes and got up and left.

Why do I get the feeling she will still continue to try her shit?

Chapter 15

- -

Daniella's POV

I have been trying to psych myself up for the event I'm attending with Chase tonight. If I don't do that then I'll have a nervous breakdown very soon into the night. He's a big shot property developer and has been expanding the current family business ranging from investments to partnerships and more.

He's also very respected in the business industry, which I don't care to know about.

He was invited to some type of business event and now I am the unlucky one to accompany him because he hasn't had time to find a date because he's too busy with work all the time. He did mention that we won't be staying very long as he's aware of my anxiety when it comes to big crowds of people.

The stylist my family normally hires when attending events will be arriving in a hour so I still have time to lounge around.

It's Sunday today and I did my rounds very early this morning. Luckily, I only do surgeries during the week and rounds and on weekends, but emergencies can happen anytime. You do get those drunk drivers or home injuries coming through now and then, that's why I'm always on stand-by until my contract is over.

I decided to go check on the boys while I'm still here and took them a snack as well. They are spending some time in the games room before they have to head back to studying for their test tomorrow.

"Boys" I said, announcing my presence.

"Hey Mom" both of them said simultaneously giving me a brief glance, as they refocused their attention on the X-box.

"Here are some sandwiches, fruit and juice. You better pause the game and eat something before you have to continue studying" I said, placing the tray on the coffee table in front of them.

They instantly paused the game and started to devour their food. They are the sweetest and most obedient kids, but also very protective of their mamma and will eat anything I put before them. Which makes me appreciate them even more.

"Mom, can we ask you something?" Max asked, as he placed his empty plate back on the tray while glancing between his brother and myself.

I was seated in between them now and stuck out my arm for Max to come and snuggle with me on the couch as Dylan finished his food.

"Who's our dad?" he asked very bluntly, but the question felt like my body had been struck with a lightning bolt. Making cold chills run down my back as my mind process what I was just asked by my son.

Well, I knew this would happen when they grew up, but I never thought it would happen this soon and besides, how do you explain to your kids that you're not sure who their dad was?

The last time they asked me that question was when they were still in kindergarten. They saw other kids with both their parents and wondered where theirs was.

I, however, told them at the time that things didn't work out with their dad, and he had to go away for work. Now they are old enough to realize parents don't stay away at work for this long and they probably formulated their own conclusions.

They never really had a care for a father because they had three father figures in their lives that filled that void. Now they realized that their uncles and grandpa can't be their dad.

The funny part of it all was that I'm kind of certain that man is their father. Everything is hitting me in the face all at once. How life gives you such unexpected surprises and challenges, I would never understand.

"Where is this coming from? Did something happen?" I question, trying to figure out what their reason is for asking.

"Well..." Dylan starts off, as he also places his plate on the tray "people have mothers and fathers. We know you are our mother, but who's our dad and where is he? Doesn't he like us?" he asked, with clear curiosity reflected in his eyes making my heart drop in my boots.

I never wanted them to think that they are not wanted, ever.

I closed my eyes for a brief few second because I never expected them to want to know anything about their dad, but who was a kidding. I should have known better, but what was I to tell them? That I was drugged and don't know who their dad was?

That's not something you tell your kids at this age.

Well, it's now or never... I thought to myself.

I cleared my throat, got up and sat in front of them on the coffee table facing them "Well boys, I got pregnant with you two when I was still very young and just done with high school. I didn't know your dad that well and by the time I found out about the pregnancy, I didn't know where to find your dad, because I had to start college and look after the two of you. Things were just too much at the time" I explained, hoping they would not remember what I told them when they were in kindergarten and accept my half-truth because some of it is a lie.

"I mean he should know of our existence. So, can we try to find him now?" Dylan asked again, hope and excitement clearly reflecting in his eyes. Such innocence, I thought to myself looking at their faces lighting up at the mention of the last part.

"Well, if that's what both of you want...mhmm, let me get someone to look into it" I said, as I rubbed both their heads as my mind went haywire while I pretended to be cool and calm in front of them.

"You have 30minutes left then you have to go to your rooms and read through your work for tomorrow's test, please" I begged, as they both groaned "and I'm going out with Uncle Chase, so Grandpa and Grandma will keep an eye on you" I said and they groaned even harder, because dad doesn't play when it comes to studies.

I gave them some smooches and left for my room, opening my laptop and waiting for the login screen to appear as I still had some time left before I had to get ready. While I waited, I decided to follow up on something that would cost me my license if it were to ever come out and the person, I took from decided to pursue the matter.

I picked up my phone and dialed our lab for the results I have been waiting for. The girl I normally contact there named Carmen picked up "Good afternoon, Dr, Harris, how may I help you today?" she asked in her usual chirpy voice.

"I'm calling to find out if you have the DNA results for one of my patients"

"Do you have the file number for me then I'll check if it's ready" she questioned"

"It's BK3169" I answered as the nervousness is about to consume me.

I could hear a lot of typing in the background and then she started to speak "Yes I do have the results ready for you; I will e-mail it shortly" she said.

"Thanks so much Carmen" I said, trying to sound just as enthusiastic as her.

If you're wondering what the heck I did. Yes, I took a sample of Mr. Giordano's DNA and my boys' DNA. I could lose my medical license because of this, but I just have to know. In order for me to eliminate their faces, I need to get behind the truth.

A few seconds later the mail came through, and I didn't second guess or wait and just opened it.

I headed straight to the important section after confirming it's the correct file number. My chest instantly became heavy.

I ran my hands through my still damp hair and started to lightly tug at it as my body was enveloped with chills. The results clearly show that he is their grandfather.

Matteo was the guy of that night, and he remembered me. He was their father, but he was on the brink of getting married. What if his fiancé decides to leave him because he has kids. I don't want to be the cause of there being issues between him and the love of his life and neither do I want my kids to be caught in a crossfire between them.

All of them deserve to know each other and if they don't want to be part of their lives then that's on them, but me and my family will always be here for the boys.

"Let me google this man and see what his deal is" I mutter under my breath.

I typed in his name and before I could look at the results, one of the maids came to tell me that the stylist and her team is waiting downstairs.

I'll come check what the internet says about him when I get back later tonight.

Chapter 16

Even though my thoughts were a warzone, I couldn't allow that to deter me. Disappointing my brother, who has always been there for me and the boys, is not an option. I will somehow find a solution for my personal matters. I know I will, but for now I must keep up appearances and get this night over and done with.

I decided to play it safe in an elegant off the shoulder, long black, tight-fitting dress that flared a little below the knee, with a pair of very high but beautiful strappy sandals.

I had the hair-lady cut a few inches off, but when she was done, I felt it was still so long. That's why I asked her to take a few more inches off, leaving my hair in the middle of my back. She did some wavy curls with light make-up and a smokey eye that made my eyes literally pop.

I can't look like a spaghetti mop next to my brother, regardless of me not wanting any attention. I will try to keep a low profile during this event that I still don't know anything about.

Regardless, I hope the food is nice.

It's been such a long time since I've dressed up like this. I used to love doing this and did it all the time for dad's business events. People would come in and style us and make us pretty. That was before life changed.

Checking my make-up for the last time, I grabbed my sparkly clutch and left heading downstairs where my handsome brother was waiting at the bottom of the stairway pulling and tucking his hair in the mirror.

He sure is one handsome man in his black tux with crisp white shirt underneath and expensive watch on his wrist.

His expression changed as soon as he looked up in my direction as I made my way down. The look I saw was pride. He held his hand out for me to take the last few steps.

He brought my hand to his lips, laying the softest kiss on it "You know" he said, making a thinking expression while rubbing his chin "I always knew there was a woman underneath that little boy façade you kept displaying" he chuckled, as I stood there with my mouth agape.

"How dare you?" I said, swatting his shoulder.

"Nah, I'm just playing with you. You are one gorgeous intelligent woman and my sister" he said, pointing his thumb to his chest and looking at me lovingly.

"Aah, thanks big bro. All is forgiven" I smiled and nudged his shoulder.

We were interrupted by footsteps coming our way as the rest of our family joined us "Vajza ime e bukur" (my beautiful girl) mom said in her native tongue, Albanian, as she gripped my hand and gave it a kiss.

"Thanks Ma" I said, giving her a hug as dad just gave a proud smirk, clearly too scared to ruin the master piece by touching my hair as he always does.

I've never realized how me having no social life impacted them. They just want me to be happy and not let what happened define my outlook on society by limiting myself when it comes to people.

Time...but how must time is enough. When is the start the start? Maybe I'm fine living like this. Why is that so unacceptable for them to grasp?

"You look pretty sis. You should be honored spending time with Mr. GQ" Daniel teased, giving me a wink. He is obviously taunting Chase. Chase has been on the cover of GQ for being one of New York city's most desirable men.

He never wanted to do the cover, because our family shy away from the limelight that other human species thrive on. Dad of all people convinced him because it would give exposure to the business he's currently expanding.

"You better look after my daughter and bring her back in one piece. She was never made for the vicious business world" dad said to Chase and gave him a firm look.

"As if I'm not your son and we'll be back in a few hours" he reassured dad.

"Wait where's the boys?" I asked, as i haven't seen them yet.

"Boys! Get down here! Your mom's about to leave!" dad shouted.

"Damn, pops still has a pair of lungs on him" Daniel taunted.

Max was the first one to rush down the stairs and reach us with Dylan a few meter's behind him "Here...Wow Ma! You look..."

"Pretty" Dylan ended off as both of them started to touch my hair. They also like to speak as one and finish each other's sentences off. There are so many similarities besides their look.

"Don't touch the hair. It has to stay like this for a few hours, at least" I said, as i ruffled their hair.

"The driver is here" Chase announced.

We bid everyone goodbye while I also reminded the boys to behave.

10 minutes into the ride Chase decided to break the silence "The event we're going to, there will be a lot of business people, but please don't leave my side. You will be my excuse to get out of the boring conversations I'm not interested in"

"Ok. How long will we have to stay there?" I asked, as Chase gave me a look. He's fully aware I don't want to be there for too long.

"A few hours. We can get some nice ice-cream on our way home for some brother and sister bonding time" Chase suggested.

"That sounds like a plan, big brother. You know i don't particularly like humans" I stated " thank you for making up for it".

He was quiet for a few seconds then cleared his throat. Giving me the indication he's about to talk about something not so comfortable "I know you don't want to hear this" he starts off. Making me sigh for what's about to come "the actual reason i wanted you to come with me, was so that you could get out of your usual cycle and live a little. You move between work and home as if it's normal. That's not what you call living" He said.

I turned my head to look at the scenery through the window "what is it with all of you being on my case about living my life the way I prefer to live it. That makes me comfortable and makes me feel safe? First Dan and now you. I don't see anything worth my time besides my family and work" I countered.

"And you call being comfortable and safe is living? Life is more than that, Danny. I feel sad that you think you don't deserve better" he scolds and continues his rant "It's not just us who think that way" he says, while turning his head in my direction as i do the same "mom and dad are too scared to discuss this with you. They understand why you close yourself off, but it's time sis. Go to a club and make friends, not all people are bad"

I just closed my eyes while shaking my head. I don't know what to think of all of this.

"Maybe you should go on a date or something" he suggested, making me role my eyes at his stupid suggestion.

"I'm damaged goods, remember. With two boys that just turned 9 a few months ago. I don't want a man and I don't need one. I'm good just like this" I reiterate, feeling beyond pissed at his rant the whole ride.

"Damaged my ass" he snorts "do you prefer to grow old alone? Mom and dad won't live forever and the boys will grow up, become men and have their own families one day".

"I think I've had enough of this conversation. I'm starting to develop a headache called Chase" I said, crossing my arms and turning my head looking out the window. Chase only gave a sigh, cause he's aware he won't win this one.

Yes, I heard him. I need time to process everything he just told me. I pretend not to get them, but I do. I can't process these heavy talks while I'm surrounded by people or moving objects. I have to center myself and think in a quiet calm environment. When I'm alone processing.

We reached a huge castle looking house after driving about 20 minutes. A long red carpet stretched from the door down a few steps, reaching the point where guests would be dropped off.

We did the pictures in front of the banner on the red carpet and than headed inside.

It was a humungous ballroom with huge sparkling chandeliers hanging from the ceiling. The color scheme is gold on gold. This person is a little too obsessed with gold, but it still looks stunning.

There were probably about 100 people just casually chatting and standing around. All their heads moved in our direction as we entered, making me tense like a statue. Chase picked up on this and took my arm and hooked his with mine.

It's so easy to disconnect from reality, but 100 stares prove to be a little daunting.

Servers were walking around with trays full of drinks and canapes. At least the food looks nice. Luckily, more people arrived, and now their gawking eyes settled on the new entrants.

We glanced around and saw Rafael making his way over in our direction. Rafael has been Chase's best friend since they were in 1st grade, and they are still inseparable.

Rafael now resides in Mexico and is busy with some shady business from what I remember. He's now part of their family business. I don't even want to know what business they are running, but I know it's shady and dangerous.

He loves to call me sis or sister and treats me as such because we basically grew up together, with his brother Carlos as well.

"Hey Sis, where have you been hiding?" he asked, as he gave me a hug and a peck on the cheek.

"Hey Raffa, nice seeing you after so long. I've been busy and you?" I answer, not liking the fact that all eyes are now on us again, even though we kept our voices low.

"No lucky lady yet?" I asked.

"Nah, there are many lucky ladies. Too many to count" he said, giving Chase a sly smirk.

"Eew, I thought you two grew up" I said, shaking my head, making both of them chuckle.

"Come on, let's head to the bar and get our drinks on" he suggested, leading me to the nearest one. I saw that they had a bar in each corner of this massive ballroom.

Even though I would love a whiskey neat, I asked for a coke because I'll be on duty for the next few months. This made Rafael frown.

"Why coke?" he asked, "You should let loose a little".

I chuckled and shook my head. I'm on stand-by dummy. When serious cases come in, I have to head in and can't be intoxicated and smell like a liquor store" I said.

"Oh, I totally forgot. You're a bigshot surgeon now. I saw the news articles about the famous Dr. Harris saving those kids" he reminded.

"You can stop it now. I don't like to associate fame with saving lives" I state, taking a sip of my coke.

"Our little butterfly did grow up" he said to Chase, who was standing there like an idiot smirking at something. When I glanced in the direction he was looking at, I saw he was looking at gorgeous brown skinned woman with a slender figure, nice booty and some Double-D cups to go with that.

"Mhm, seems I'm heading home alone, tonight" I said, making him look in my direction.

"No, sis. Believe me, I've tried" he stated, looking a little green around the gills. If I was not mistaken, I would say he's smitten.

After standing there talking and being introduced by my brother and Raffa to their acquaintances, I had to go to the bathroom. After asking one of the waiters for directions, I headed down a long corridor as she instructed. She mentioned that there's more bathrooms on the opposite side of the ballroom, but I obviously went to the nearest one.

Reaching the bathrooms after walking a century through the maze of corridors, I saw that there was only one lady heading into a door that had a lady painted on it. I followed her in and saw that there were 7 cubicles. All seemed to be empty, besides the one lady went in to, which was the furthest one from the entrance.

I chose the one nearest to the door. People tend to always go for the one furthest, but what they don't realize is that that's the one being used the most and hosts the most germs because of its frequent use.

I heard her flush as I did my business and when I came out, she was long gone.

I took my time washing my hands and holding it under the lukewarm tap. The longer I stay here the longer my ears can rest from the buzzing sound of the many people talking all at once.

I stood there dazed in my own world contemplating my next plan of action to get my kids and their father to meet and my biggest hope is that he won't reject them.

I was so deep in thought that I didn't realize someone had entered. I felt a presence behind me and as I looked up, I saw green eyes staring back at me in the mirror.

The very person who isn't even aware that he's the father of two of the most charming little boys. We both stood there staring at each other in silence.

Chapter 17

How will you treat my boys when I allow you to meet them, Mr. Giordano? I thought to myself. How knowing about them will impact his relationship with your wife-to-be and how will she treat my boys? Is she a good person and how much would you want to see them? Do you want them to be part of your life?

That's all the questions that have been flooding my mind as I stood there looking back at him without a word being spoken by either of us. Once thing I do know however, is that I will go to great lengths to assure the happiness of my own.

I don't know how long we were standing there, but both of us snapped out of our daze as we heard giggling woman approaching the bathroom.

I gazed in his direction to see what his next step would be, because it's totally normal for me to be in here, but him? Not so much.

He grabbed me by the arm and pulled me into one of the cubicles locking the door.

"Wha..." I uttered, as a hand was wrapped over my mouth.

"Shhh" he made an indication with his hands for me to keep quiet and he will take his hands off my mouth. I gave a nod as both of us listened to the voices on the outside of the door.

"When did you say is your wedding?" one of the ladies asked.

"In 5 and a half months and I can't wait to be part of the Giordano family. That's been a dream of mine since I was a little girl" the other lady said.

I looked up in his direction, meeting his stare. They are talking about him.

He just gave an eyeroll as he has been looking at me the whole time making my cheeks heat up. Damit! Rocks don't blush. Why is he looking at me like a creep.

I must admit though, this creep sure does smell like heaven. Menthol mixed with woodsy tint. At least the father of my children smells good.

The conversation was over on the outside with nothing interesting being discussed as both ladies as I assume relieved themselves and left. As soon as I heard the door close, I stepped out and saw that the coast was clear.

I didn't even bother to tell him to come out and walked straight out looking for a side door that would lead to a space outside that I could breathe. I eventually found one and was met with a gust of cool fresh air, hitting my lungs.

As I glanced around, and saw that people were busy smoking in the crisp evening air. I took a seat next to one of the flower boxes that had a little bench beside it.

Setling in I digest what just happened. I have way more questions circling my mind than anything else. Why did he follow me into the lady's bathroom? Why did he just stare at me and say nothing?

My thoughts were interrupted by the voice of the very same lady my brother has been staring at since we entered the door tonight.

"Taking a break?" she asked, giving me a genuine smile.

I gave a light chuckle "yes, too stuffy and all the voices floating around the room....is a little too much" I answered, looking at her trying to read her.

I first look at her features, looking at her from this angle, I must admit, she's one gorgeous black woman. My brother has taste, but I wonder why she rejected him?

"I take it, you're not a businessperson? I mean, I haven't seen you at any of these events before and to be honest, you look a little out of place, but not in a bad way. Damit, there I go a blabber again. I'm so sorry" she apologized, as she nipped her cigarette bud in the ashtray beside her. Clearly a little frustrated with herself.

"Your correct, not my scene. I'm in a different industry all together" I decide to put her out her misery and try to hold a conversation. I don't trust strangers, but I could tell she was harmless and hurt like a bird with a broken wing.

Who better to notice than someone who walked around with broken wings herself.

"Oh really? Which industry do you work in?" she asked.

"Medical, Doctor to be exact. So, this is nothing I'm used to" I said, making her look at me in surprise.

"Oh, that's so refreshing. Everyone I know is in business. It's nice talking to someone that's not in this minefield of a career" she said, giving me a genuine smile.

Damn brother, what a perfect choice. Why do I like her without knowing her?

"I take it you are businesswoman that don't take crap from the men in your industry?" I asked her.

"Well, being a female in the business industry is already a daunting task, but being female and black, is ten times harder if you don't show the business world your fearless and motivated you are. It's a vicious world"

"It's nice to see woman stand on their own feet and fight for what they in life" I said, assessing her from head to toe. It looked like she wanted to ask me something, so I put her out of her misery because I already knew what she wanted to ask.

"Ask" I said, making her lift her eyebrows in surprise "you want to ask me something, so go ahead" I said. All roads lead to my dearest brother. He will kiss my feet soon.

She cleared her throat and muttered something under her breath before glancing around than refocusing her attention on me again "Are you in a relationship with Chase?"

Aah! There it is. I chuckled and almost drooled on myself at the thought of her being under the impression that I'm in a relationship with my brother.

"What's so funny?" she asked, I could see her face dropping in sadness, so I decided to put her out of her misery.

"He's my brother" I said, as her face immediately changed to embarrassment.

"Oh, I'm so sorry. I thought the way you were standing and interacting, that you're in a relationship. I'm so sorry" she said, holding her hands up.

I decided to introduce myself and held my hand out to her "Daniella Harris"

She took my hand in hers "Vivian Gabriel"

After her calming down with relief written all over her face, I asked the million-dollar question "So, what's the deal between you and my brother?" I enquired, dying to know.

She looked at me with surprise, then started to explain "Well, it's actually kind of stupid and I can't believe I'm about to spill the beans with his sister of all people" she said before taking a breath and started to explain.

"We dated about a year ago, obviously meeting at one of these events when he accompanied your dad at the time. We just saw each other less and less, until no more. A few months ago, he tried to make things right and explained that he was now more than busy. His dad is now retired, and the workload is insane, which I know too well because I have a company of my own, but I was just too pissed and told him off. Obviously, regretting it immediately, but the proud fool I wouldn't stop him to hash things out" she shrugged, fiddling with her fingers

"Well, we were just seeing where things go and didn't make commitments to each other, but still. To be honest, I wanted more" she ended off looking me straight in the eyes.

Well, the relationship with Chase had a big impact on her, if she would go to the extent to approach me.

This girl is in love with my big brother without even knowing it. It's radiating through every action and expression. She's ruthless in the business world, but innocent when it comes to men. I am very, very good at reading people. That's the benefit of life lessons.

My phone started to buzz and as I took it out of my clutch, I saw it was Chase "Chase" I life my phone and before I could answer she gave me an expression not to tell him anything and I gave her a reassuring nod.

"Hello"

"Daniella, where are you? I've been looking all over for you" he asked, sounding a little panicked.

"I'm on my way inside. I sat outside catching a breather" I told him, making Vivian smirk.

I ended the call and we both swapped numbers and we promised to stay in touch. I have so much work to do in my personal life, but theirs will be a walk in the park.

As we made our way home, Chase asked if I was still up for ice-cream, but I declined and said we could do it at another time because he already looked a little sad and intoxicated.

Probably thought his girl left without talking to him, but he'll be happy soon.

Chapter 18

Matteo's POV

Vito and I are walking into a business event with some of the richest, respected people in the business world, but also some of the evilest. Some are trying to score new deals and make money.

It's more a Gala/networking type of event for all kinds of people. That includes the bad guys too, like me.

All rich people had to do something crooked at some point to get where they are today. Crooked doesn't sit right with all, that's why some stop in time and others are sucked into the world of greed.

You have to know when enough is enough. I'm a scumbag that's smuggling drugs and guns, but I know where to draw the line and not become too greedy for my own good.

We got here a little early, but this place was already packed to the brim and my mood dampened as soon as I saw my nightmare parading around with a smile etched across her face. How can she be this happy, while I'm on the brink of a bout of depression?

I still haven't found anything that would suggest that she's messing around, but she will fuck up, that I'm sure of, and when she does, I won't even embarrass her, I will thank her for her good deed of setting a man free. A man being me.

We decided to head to the bar and let the alcohol consume our senses instead of being cornered by the fiancé. As we stood there, my eyes went over the people moving around.

Some try to close the deals that would make or break their careers, some look for an olive branch to save their businesses from going under, others are looking at just the opportunity to swindle money out of the next person.

Vito discreetly nudged my side "five o' clock" he said, clearing his throat as he took a sip from his glass.

After a few seconds, I turned my head and saw the Doctor standing a little too close to a tall guy, with arms intertwined, as another guy approached them. The guy approaching them, I know all too well.

Rafael Garcia, leader of the Mexican cartel. Messy when it comes to murder and feared in Mafia world for his ruthlessness. He doesn't think twice when it comes to taking life. Psychopath for sure, but what is he doing with the doctor and the way they are chatting, seems as though they know each other...well"

I am unable to hear what they are talking about, because of the distance, but this woman has become more interesting as time progressed. A detached robot at work and a human with evil people. Cold...ice cold, but this piques my interest even more.

What makes my eyes linger isn't the fact that she's cozying up with Rafael Garcia, but her looks. She looks different from her normal hospital attire and attitude she displayed there, that's for sure. She looks like a super model, even better with the beauty she possesses. Who knew that body was hiding underneath those hospital scrubs.

Her face isn't overly pasted with make-up, just enough to bring out her natural beauty, that is untouched.

I watched them discreetly, but mostly her, as they made their way to the bar. It was still too far away for me to listen in on their conversation.

After a while, my nightmare decided to make her presence known "Good evening gentleman, fiancé" she announced, with two tails following behind. Standing like two statues beside her.

These are the times I could blow a lid, where she brings people along which puts me in an awkward position where I have to put up an act with her, because most people don't know that we're being arranged to be married.

"Good evening fiancé" I respond, keeping it short and sweet.

"Matteo, do you still remember my friends, Jessica and Keira?" I stretch my hand, shaking both their hands and mutter to myself to not lose my cool.

"Nice to meet you again, ladies" I said, trying to act as the best fiancé in the world. I'm so over this night and if it weren't for that dark haired woman standing a few meters away, I would've left a long time ago.

After standing like mutes and her so-called friends gawked at the both of us, they left with fresh drinks in hand, walking around and advertising their assets. That's the only reason these types of women roam around here, to find a rich husband, no matter the age.

After they left, I glanced in the direction of the doctor and saw her heading to the bathrooms "I'll be back" were the only words I uttered before I discreetly followed a safe distance behind her.

I saw a lady heading out of the bathroom into the corridor, I acted as if I was typing on my phone with my back against the wall in the corridor waiting for her to pass.

As soon as she left, I didn't waste any time because I didn't know how much time I had. What the fuck am I doing? I'm following a woman, but why? It's like my feet are operating on their own accord and I have no choice but to follow.

As I entered through the door, I saw her looking in the mirror, but not really looking, more like being in a daze. I approached her, but she didn't acknowledge my presence, while I stared at her like a creep.

It took a good minute for her to realize that someone was standing behind her, and I made sure to stand so close as to inhale her scent. My senses were assaulted with light fragrant lilies, mixed with a subtle hint of berries. Such a clean smell I would revel in.

After a few minutes went by, she realized that I was standing directly behind her. That's when it felt as if we were transported to another universe as our eyes met, frozen in time. She has the most beautiful, but hypnotizing gaze and I couldn't bring myself to start a conversation or ask her any questions because of the awkward situation I found myself in.

Here I'm standing in the woman's bathroom hypnotized by a married woman. I know I can't have her, but I can look.

I was snapped out of my daze as I heard woman giggling and talking making their way in this direction. There's no other way for ladies to go unless they want to head into the men's bathroom, which I don't think is the case.

In a moment of panic, I pulled her into one of the cubicles and as she was about to say something I placed my hand over her mouth and asked her to keep quiet. Both of us would be embarrassed should anyone find us in here.

It would only be my nightmare that would enter the lady's bathroom whilst I'm shacked up next to a married woman. I block out her squeaky pretentious voice as I glance down at the woman standing in front of me.

Her cheeks were flushed as she tried to remain quiet as possible. After a few minutes my nightmare and her crew were done and left with the door banking shut and their voices moving further and further away.

Without waiting or giving me the opportunity to apologize for my rash behavior, she left without scolding, or insulting me.

I felt so deflated as I made my way to my car. I took my phone out and messaged Vito, telling him I'm waiting so that we could leave, and he didn't take that long to reach me, and we headed home.

On our drive home, I told Vito everything that happened. I also instructed him to Romeo, our cousin, who is the head of the tech in our business to dig into the background of the doctor.

He didn't question because he is aware that I won't be able to rest until I know her inside out. He immediately gave Romeo the assignment.

At least I can rest knowing I will have information in a few days.

A few days later...........

My phone dinged with a message from Romeo "Need to talk about the doc"

My heart jumped in my chest, making me hold my hand over it as it was beating erratically. Fuck!!!!! She's a married woman, Matteo. I remind myself as I steer my car in the direction of the offices where Romeo resides.

Twenty minutes later, I strolled into the building, not acknowledging the greetings coming from the staff and heading straight into the elevator to the 26th floor.

I stepped in as he saw me, and once I reached him, we headed into his office. I took a seat and indicated for him to go ahead.

"Here's a copy of the file, if you feel like reading through it on your own" he said as he placed it in front of me on the desk.

"Fucking talk, cause I'm losing patience here" I muttered, sounding every bit as irritated.

He read from the file on his laptop "Daniella Harris, Neurosurgeon, not permanently contracted. She's the daughter of multi-billionaire John Harris. Nobody really knows anything more about their family. They keep out of the media and don't associate with the other wealthy folk. They keep to themselves and are rarely seen in the media" I interrupt him midway.

"You mean, she's rich-rich?"

"Yes, rich-rich, cousin" he says rolling his eyes at me before continuing "she works on a consultancy basis. She has two brothers, but it doesn't state who. I did a little digging, which was strangely very hard, but one of the brothers was featured on the cover of GQ magazine" he says flashing me his laptop screen with a picture of the brother and to my utter relief, he's her brother and not her husband.

Making me feel hopeful. Wait...why? I know I've felt heavy since the day I left that venue, but I'm surely not going to go against my parents for something that's non-existent.

"His name is Chase Harris, a businessman running multiple businesses and no detail about the other brother. That's it. Nothing interesting, just a normal doctor with a boring life" he finished the conversation.

"Something doesn't make sense though. If they were such prominent people, regardless of them not mingling with society, shouldn't there be more information about them? Does she have kids? It still doesn't rule out the fact that she could be married" I stated, and he just shook his head.

"Something's off. Get Gio to put a few guys on her for a week and they should report back on anything that is off or strange. I want to know everything. Tag all of them" I requested, getting on my feet then headed out. He didn't bother questioning me and gave the order through.

Chapter 19

It's 5 o' clock on a Friday afternoon and I'm busy updating my last file for the day, before heading home to get ready for the birthday dinner my family has planned for me. They have been insistent for the past two weeks on going out to eat at a fancy upscale restaurant that my parents still love to go to.

My rounds were done and dusted and hopefully I won't get any emergency cases over the weekend, because I really do need some proper sleep.

This week has exhausted the crap out of me, but I loved it because it kept me busy and being busy also occupied my busy mind from wandering to think about unnecessary things, that would cause me to overthink and then eventually become depressed.

We had injuries ranging from motor vehicle accidents, a few people being stabbed in the head, neck, back, accidents that happened at home and many more complicated cases that were already on the hospital waiting list. Some nights I would only get 4 hours sleep at most.

The positive part is that I've cut the number of scheduled cases by half in such a short time, making the Director of the hospital very happy as the ratings of the hospital will count greatly in his favor.

I wasn't able to tuck the boys in at night, but at least I made sure to fetch them after school every day and dropped them off at home, then heading straight back to work. I want to remain present in their lives regardless of how busy I am. I would rather suffer, than to let them feel like they're not worth my time.

I have a few months to go with this hospital contract but to be honest, I cannot wait for it to be over and done with. My boys will be sick of me over mothering them because I will smother them with all the love I have.

That man has been on my mind even more since the night of the event we attended. I can't seem to understand why he would go to the extent to follow me into the woman's bathroom and then stare at me.

I also don't want to know what went through his mind because I don't need his fiancé on my ass, and I also don't want his fiancé or anyone for that matter to get the impression that there's something going on between us.

Trouble is the last thing I want in my life now.

Right now, I just need to get home, take a quick shower, then meet my family at the restaurant. They insisted on leaving a little earlier.

A hard knock could be heard on my office door as I pressed submit on the last file and closed my laptop. Who the heck would knock so hard? That's just plain rude. I thought to myself.

"It's unlocked" I said, waiting for the person to make his or her appearance.

The door swung open and once the person came into view, I'm met with the stoic face, of the father of my children. Without missing a beat, he made his way over to my desk without greeting or making an attempt to state his reason for being here. His eyes remained focused on mine.

He's dressed in a black suit without a tie and a white dress shirt with the first two buttons unbuttoned. Hair sleeked back with clean shaven face. He looks...very forbidden.

I Internally scold myself for these inappropriate thoughts. The well might be dry but I'm not ignorant to these pretty and oh so dangerous men.

I did my own little research on him and found out a lot of, let's just say, most were not so nice things. With the help of my family's head of security, I found out that he's the Capo of the Mafia and that he's rich and ruthless, but many in the industry respect him.

His whole family are somehow connected to the mob and that they are 'family above all else' type of people.

I never thought that I would have kids from someone that's in this industry, but it's something I didn't have a choice in. Men would stick their sausages anything, and I was probably just a lay for him that night. Meanwhile, he wasn't even aware that I was drugged and didn't have a decision in who I slept with or how my body reacted.

That choice was taken from me, by people that played me like a puppet.

I really do hope when he finds out that he will be a decent father regardless of his status, but what I hope for the most part is that he keeps them safe when he's with them.

My intention is to be the best mother and I hope he will accept them and be the best father to them. He will luckily be married soon, and I hope his fiancé treats my boys right. If she doesn't, at least my boys know how to defend themselves and they know who raised them.

I have thought of contacting him after the event, but I couldn't bring myself to do so. This is so freaking hard. I thought it would be best to do it in a few months when my contract is over, and I could focus better on figuring out how to tell him.

I shiver at the thought of what this man is capable of, even though he looks like someone that was cut from a magazine, you can see the evil clearly visible in his eyes. He's not someone to be trifled with but I'm not scared of him.

I sat there blatantly staring at him, watching his every move, as he sat back with his back against the chair resting his left ankle on his right knee. Elbows resting on the armrests of the chair, sitting there taking his good old time to start the conversation.

Why would he come here? His father should be fine and there should be no issues.

If he doesn't start, then I probably have to start the conversation because I have to leave this place if I want to make it in time for my own birthday dinner.

"Is everything fine with your father, Mr. Giordano?" I asked, making him cringe.

"Mattheo" he said, clearing his throat as he continued staring at me. Watching my every move and expression trying to read me.

I ignored what he said and continued talking "Can I help you with anything? "I need to leave in five minutes, and you don't have an appointment scheduled with me" I announced, lifting my wrist to check the time on my wristwatch to see it's 5:18, before looking back at him.

"Is there anything you need to inform me of, Daniella?" he asked, with his deep husky voice sending chills down my spine as my name left his mouth.

"Excuse me?" I asked, flabbergasted at the question he's throwing my way. Could it be? Nah, it couldn't.

"Let me rephrase that" he said now bending forward with his elbows resting on my desk "is there something you are withholding from me?" he questioned, not taking his eyes off mine.

He knows. I know he does.

I sat up straight and decide to take the bull by its horns "Don't waste both of our time. State your reason for coming here because I don't have time to play whatever games you intend on playing" I said, bending down to pick up my backpack from the open drawer on my side.

As I straightened my back and glanced up, he threw a stack of printed pictures on my desk.

He nudged his head in the direction of the pictures, and I didn't hesitate to pick them up because I knew there could only be one possibility.

As I glanced through the pictures, I could see that they are all from when I picked the boys up after school or dropped them off at practice on certain days. After placing the pictures back on the table, I glanced back at him with a blank expression clearly displayed on my face.

I've been having this gut feeling that this would happen sooner or later even though I wasn't mentally ready to face the music.

"What do you want?" I asked, dropping all formalities and niceties, which could clearly be heard in my tone. These are my kids that he's probably going to talk about, and I don't play when it comes to them.

He cut straight to the point "Are they mine?" he asked, not dropping his gaze.

"Look here, I won't beat around the bush because I don't have the time or energy. They clearly are an identical copy of you and your father, so there's a big possibility, but a DNA test will have to be done to put the facts to paper"

"Daniella, I asked you about that night, but you blatantly lied and denied it. You kept this away from me for years. Why?" he asked, leaving me in utter silence for a few seconds.

Once I gathered my thoughts "what makes you believe that I would be so selfish to keep something of this magnitude from you? What makes you believe that I would keep my children's father whom they want to know away from them?" I questioned.

"You knew you slept with me, but you didn't notify me that you were pregnant or that I became a father. How many years have I been missing out on?" he asked with an elevated tone, which I don't have the pleasure of listening to. I was and will never be a slut.

"First off, you don't ever speak to me using that tone, ever" I said, pointing my finger in his direction and straightening my back "two, I was drugged that night by people I considered or thought of as friends, so the chances of me wanting to remember my first time or to look at the face I left that morning in that bed, was the last thing on my mind. Maybe I didn't have any control of my body the night before, making me feel embarrassed with the whole situation and sick to my stomach for allowing those people to befriend me. Believe me, every woman would want her first time, to be her choice" I stated, making his face drop even further.

"Three, you have no clue what I went through after that night mentally and physically being pregnant at the age of 16, so how dare you come in here and accuse me of hiding such an important thing from someone I didn't even know or knew what the person looked like?" I stated.

I didn't even notice my cheeks were wet until a teardrop fell on my hand that was placed on my lap. My pent-up emotions took over and busted at their seams.

Years and years of beating myself up for the mistakes of my past. Stressing about the day my kids became old enough to realize that their dad wasn't in the picture and would ask me about their father. I wouldn't know what to answer them because how do you explain the situation to such innocent minds without polluting it.

Luckily, the events that transpired since setting foot back in the country, led me to their father. Now, I must figure out the introduction part of the equation.

"I need to know everything that happened, starting from that night" he said, as I looked up into his stare. As I wiped the remnants from my cheeks with the back of my hand.

"I am willing to tell you everything, but it will have to be another day, because I have to be somewhere in an hour and I'm already running late" I said, writing my number on a piece of paper and handing it to him.

"Send me a message then I'll have your number. You can give a DNA sample to the lab on the 8th floor, and I will make sure the DNA of the boys also gets delivered tomorrow. The results should be available by Monday. We can arrange to meet after then. Could we also keep this between us for now, please? Until the test results come out, please?" I asked, getting up from my seat and he just gave me a nod. Making me sigh in relief.

"What are their names?" he asked, looking down at the floor. Was it that hard to ask me that?.

"Dylan and Max" I said, as I heard him repeat their names under his breath.

My phone started to buzz, I saw Vivian's name popping up and as I picked it up from my desk.

"Hey, I know I'm running late. I'll be there in 40 minutes. I'm leaving the hospital now" I said, before she said anything. She just said 'Ok, no problem' and we ended the call.

"Who was that?" he asked, making me scrunch up my face in confusion at his straightforward, unapologetic rudeness.

"Why is that any of your business?" I asked.

"I need to know who's around my kids, Daniella" he said, making me give him an eyeroll as I grabbed my bag as I walked past him.

"No tests were done confirming this and I don't have time to argue with you now. Close my door behind you" I said, leaving him to his own devices.

PS, Will be posting tomorrow as well. A little action to come.....

Chapter 20

The talk with Matteo went better than I expected, and I internally feel that some weight that I've been carrying around with me for all these years has been lifted, in a sense.

The self-inflicted guilt and shame associated with not knowing who their father was, was way worse than the effects it had when my father's family berated and shamed me for becoming a teenage mother.

I thought he was going to go off on me or try to fight me for custody, well he might still, but he's not aware who he would be messing with.

The conversation did, however, give me a sense of relief to know that I would be able to fulfill the wishes of my boys and not just that, but the most important part is that they won't have to grow up without a father.

Matteo also seems very eager to accept them into his life, but seeing is believing. I could be wrong, but I also know I'm very good at reading behavior and from what I've picked up is that he would have liked to be in their lives sooner.

Next time we meet, I will tell him everything. He has to know so that he doesn't continue to resent me for not knowing his kids or blame me without knowing the full story. I knew the DNA results, but I couldn't just announce that I used his dad's DNA, it's unethical.

I have to sit down and inform my family before the weekend is over. I've been keeping everything from them. I will only inform the boys after I speak to Matteo.

I know they will be happy because it's not about them, it's about my sons knowing they have a real father and their happiness. They even asked me a few years back if they could help me search for him, but I wasn't mentally ready for any big changes yet.

I drove home in less than 15 minutes. I will most probably get a few speeding tickets, but that's tomorrow's worry.

Mom made sure to leave me a thousand messages reminding me to get dressed in the dress she bought and left in my room.

The dress was a white, one shoulder, long sleeved dress, that had an extra piece of removable material clipped to the side. I must say, my mother has very good taste. The only issue I do have with the dress is that it's not what I normally wear.

This dress is an attention seeker, much to my displeasure, but to please my mother, I will wear it. Once done getting dressed and styling my hair, I rushed out the door and headed to Vivian's apartment, to pick her up.

She lived two blocks away from the place where we were having dinner. Even though I'm a little awkward with unknown people, I mustered up the confidence to message her and start a conversation to try and make my brother happy.

I can't wait to see his face when he sees me walking in with her.

I have never seen my brother like that over any woman and I could see she must have made a huge impression on him, for him to be sulking the whole ride home.

Even though she's a ruthless businesswoman, she clearly showed me her vulnerable side that night when she approached me. A woman that would go to that extent to start a conversation, just to find out if Chase has anything to do with me, is a woman worth fighting for.

She's clearly that ride or die type of woman.

As soon as I stopped in front of her apartment complex, I saw her exiting her building. I gave her a wave and she made her way over in my direction.

She was dressed in a little black sparkly bodycon dress with a side slit on the thigh. Hot Damn!

"Thank you so much for inviting me and happy birthday. This is for you" she said handing me a small box after giving me a hug.

"Thank you, you shouldn't have" I said.

"Please, it's your birthday girl. It only comes once per year" she said, giving me a genuine smile.

This girl is just so real. We've been chatting for the past few days, and I love her straight forwardness and the fact that she doesn't sugarcoat things to make people feel better about themselves.

We headed in the direction of the restaurant and reached the building in less than 10 minutes. The valet opened our doors and took my car away. The hostess smiled instantly recognizing me "good evening, mam. Your family are waiting upstairs. Enjoy your evening"

Our family is so well known here, you would think we own the place. Well, it could be, but I don't really keep track of the businesses my family owns or invests in.

"Thank you" I said as we headed to the elevator in the lobby next to the hostess's desk. We headed to the 19th floor, where everyone with money likes to enjoy their meals, while the common folk used the floor where the entrance is situated.

"Chase will be happy to see you" I said to her as we waited for the elevator door to open.

"I hope so" she said, while smiling and winking back at me.

Once we headed inside, a host, who also recognized me, gave both of us warm greetings as he led us to the table where my family sat. I instantly recognized faces that I hadn't seen in more than a year due to my travels.

"What are you doing here" I said, sporting a shocked expression when I saw my mother's brother and his family, standing up from their seats with huge smiles when they saw me.

It made me tear up a little, because the people that have been supporting me and have given me the most love was my mother's side, who doesn't even reside in this country. They were a huge motivation through mu studies and always came to visit the boys while I was away at college. Unlike my dad's side.

"Vajza ime e shtrenjtë" (My precious girl) Uncle Besim, said as he took me into his arms, giving me one of his smothering hugs.

"It's so good to see you. I've missed all of you" I said, giving everyone hugs in a row. My uncle Besim, his wife Drita, sons Bujar, Fatmir and Erving, their daughters Elira and Flamur.

"Kushëriri i mallkuar, kush do të mendonte se rosa e shëmtuar e familjes do të kthehej në një mjellmë" (Damn cousin, who would have thought the ugly duckling of the family would turn into a swan) Ervin, my cousing said as he also came in for a hug.

He always called me ugly when we were growing up because my eyes looked so strange to him.

"Ha ha ha" I said, while rolling my eyes at his dig at me.

"Kush është kjo zonjë e shkëlqyer që qëndron pranë jush?" (Who's this fine lady standing beside you?) Bujar asked, as he gave me a hug.

"Everyone, this is my friend Vivian, and Vivian that is my mother and the queen of my heart Sarah, my dad John, my brother Daniel, my other brother Chase" i said, squinting my eyes at Chase as he stood there just staring at Vivian, making me smirk "this is my mother's brother Besim, his wife Drita, my other mother" i said, giving her a tight hug "their children Ervin, Bujar, Fatmir, Elira and Flamur"

"Good evening everyone" she said, as she gave sly glances in my brother's direction.

"Mom, where's the boys?" I asked.

"Rafael walked with them to the bathroom, they should be back any minute now" she said, glancing in the direction of the bathroom.

Soon enough the boys arrived "Happy birthday Ma!" both of them said as they engulfed me in hugs. Max played with my hair "Ma, you look pretty" Dylan said as he gave me a kiss on the cheek.

Happy birthday's were heard around the table "thank you my babies and thank you my lovely family, who i wouldn't trade for anything" i said, while hugging my boys.

"Boys, I would like you to meet my friend. This is Aunty Vivian, Aunty Vivian, this is my boys Dylan and Max"

She sat there looking from me to them.

"You mean to tell me, these beautifully, charming young men, are yours? Do you accept any applications for daughter in-laws" she asked making the whole table burst out in laughter while the boys cringed.

The funny part about all of this is that my mother was born into the Albanian Mafia, which my Uncle Besim took over when my grandparents were killed. Ervin took over from his dad a few years back.

Mom came to the America to study, where she met my dad. She had to change her name to make sure that she's doesn't get targeted by any of their rivals. Dad took some time getting used to the Mafia, but are one of Uncle Besim's best friend's.

My Uncle Besim, is also my godfather and they also made sure that we kept that family bond with the Albanian side. Mom made sure everyone, including the boys know Albanian to keep a part of her heritage alive.

That's probably why finding out about the Giordano's didn't have that much of an impact on me. Even though mom doesn't live there, we still remain under the protection of the Albanian Mafia. My dad's whole security team is Albanian.

That's also another reason why my mom insisted that dad build us a huge house, so that when family visited they could stay with us in order to spend more time together instead of staying at a hotel.

My uncle has a lot of business ties in America, and when he leave his country to come here, it's always more then just visiting his sister.

Rafael gave my a kiss on the head, but i could see from his facial expression that something is bothering him. He took the seat on my other side and whispered in my ear "we need to talk" making me glance in his direction with him already looking at me.

I gave him a nod and all proceeded to catch up. The conversation was flowing, with Flamur and Elira catching me up on their love lives and things in Albania. It seemed though all of them were in relationships, but their dad didn't allow their other halves to come with them.

We were interrupted by a familiar voice "excuse me, apologies for inter-rupting Dr. Harris" I glanced up and there stood Mr. Giordano senior looking at me and then to my boys. The whole table went silent while my heart was beating a million miles per second.

Is this a joke? Why can't life wait until i decide to resolve things myself? My brain decided to answer itself. It's because you are too slow Daniella, too freaking slow when it comes to your own life.

I was about to get up when Uncle Besim held up his hand "uluni" (sit down). "What is your business with our daughter, Mr Giordano?" Uncle Besim asked as the Hyseni men including my two brothers, Rafael and my father of all people got up from their seats as if this was rehearsed by by them.

Wait, obviously my uncle would know the ex don of the Italian Mafia.

"Xhaxhai, zoti Giodano është një pacient i imi. I shpëtova jetën disa javë më parë" (Uncle, Mr. Giodano is a patient of mine. I saved his life a few weeks ago) i said, making all their heads snap in my direction. I was trying to stop a war from breaking out.

"Ky është pacienti që keni ndihmuar në aeroport?" (This is the patient you helped at the airport?) Chase asked and i gave a nod while looking down at the plate in front of me.

I know they know after seeing his face that he as a connection to the boys. Daniel is somewhat aware it's his family being connected with the boys, but i didn't inform him of the DNA test.

"If I'm not mistaken Mr. Giordano. Your not my daughter's patient anymore, so you may state your reasons for wanting to talk to her" dad stated.

"Isaac, what's going on here" I heard a female voice ask, belonging to Mrs. Giordano, as she's glancing at the men standing around the table, but her stare stopped at Dylan and Max, making her gasp as she held her hand in front of her mouth.

"Fratello, cosa sta succedendo? (brother, what's going on?" The rude woman that I met at the hospital asked.

"I hoped the doctor would answer us" he said, as i glanced between myself and the boys. Dylan and Max watching this whole interaction got up from their seats and stood in front of me, blocking their view of me, who was still seated.

"Mom, Dad, What's going..." my head snapped in the direction of Matteo, who now also joined us with his whole family standing behind him.

It seems though they just arrived and saw us sitting here. We were too happy to catch up with each other to notice anything happening around us.

"We are waiting for Dr. Harris for that answer, son" his dad said.

"Dad, I am the one you should be asking for answers" he said, not taking his eyes off the boys making my heart melt as i saw his eyes starting to look glossy. I know my boys knew from that moment that they were standing a few meter's away from their father because they were very intelligent.

"You kept this away from us?" his dad asked, but before he could answer, my boys decided to ask a question, silencing everyone.

"Mami, është ai?" (Ma, Is it him?) Dylan, the expressive naughty one of the two asked. Assuring all attention was now focused on the boys. Matteo's mom stood there wiping her eyes.

"Po, por a mund të flasim në shtëpi, ju lutem?" (Yes, but can we talk at home, please?) i said, while glancing at my family and they all gave me a reassuring nod. I know my family would protect me regardless, but they knew my mental health would take a heavy blow if they made a scene here.

"What is going on here? Oh, here's those two brats we saw earlier in the hallway that looks just like Matteo" a pretty girl with long black hair said as she gave the boys a ugly stare.

"What did you just say?" Matteo asked, while I followed up "excuse me?" while getting up from my seat.

I glanced in the direction of Rafael to confirm if this was the reason why he wanted to talk to me. He gave me a nod, confirming things for me.

The girl's face instantly went pale when the realization kicked in as she glanced between Matteo and the boys.

Matteo's fiancé then ended the silence "Matteo, who are they?"

"They are my sons" he said, while looking at them as they stood there looking back at him, face to face.

We were met with silence and then gunshots rung through the room, followed by creams.

Life said, no deciding when I expose your truths because I will decide it for you.

Chapter 21

N ot all are made for this life, regardless of being born into it, on the other hand you get some who live for it and thrive off the adrenaline rush or level of authority that's associated with this life.

Then you get some who have no choice but to adapt to the life they were thrown in and tonight you could clearly see the difference. People from the Mafia ducked taking cover as if this was a movie scene they were rehearsing, while others were screaming and running around frantically not knowing what to do.

Before I was able to react, Dylan and Max turned around and shoved me to the ground. Both fell on top of me, with Matteo falling next to them with his arm stretched over us.

Though I felt flattered at his reaction, I knew his family and his fiancé were also there and it didn't make any sense for him to run past them to protect us. Matteo held his gun in one hand while glancing around trying to establish where the threat was.

"Ma, are you ok?" Max asked, looking at me with a bewildered look in his eyes, making Matteo look down at the two of them with pride displayed in his eyes.

"Yes, I'm good and you two?" I asked looking both of them over.

"Yeah, we're good Ma" they vigorously nodded, assuring me they were fine.

I tried to glance around to look for signs that my family was ok, but the long tablecloth was blocking that side of my view. I saw Vivian facing me with sheer panic portrayed in her eyes as she was lying there a few inches away from my head.

I felt so bad for her, so I touched her arm to give her a sense of reassurance that I'm here with her. She gave me a faint smile back, but panic was clearly evident in her expressions.

A few minutes later someone was shouting "shooter down" and then the screams followed indicating some people were injured.

Matteo helped the boys up and then the boys helped pull me up. They didn't look too pleased with him. I glanced around and saw at least five people, whom I didn't recognize, bleeding on the floor with family members or friends huddled around them trying to help.

Matteo left our side and went to go check out the person that attacked us.

I first checked that my family were all fine and walked to where my parents were sitting and saw mom being held by dad that was rubbing her back. She's obviously a little shaken up "mom, dad, are you ok?" I asked.

"Honey, go and help the people, none of us are hurt, but it seems some of the Giordano's are hurt" mom said, making me wonder if she knew them. Probably because they were blocked by the Giordano family while sitting more to the corner of the floor.

Chase was busy comforting Vivian, making my heart flutter with pride looking at my handywork. Seems my plan worked, but there's no time to celebrate, I have to make sure these people are not critically injured.

Matteo was busy shouting instructions to his men and my cousin Ervin did the same. The Albanian guards caught the guy and handed him over to the Italians as this is their territory.

Matteo's fiancé was looking at me with pure hate radiating from her stare, but that was the least of my concern because I don't owe her anything, nor do my kids. How could people still have time to hate in situations like these, anyway?

The boys were following me around this whole time "Boys, stay here with grandma and grandpa. I'm going to check the injured people out, ok?" I knew they wouldn't go against me. "Daniel, can you come and help me, please?" I asked, and he got up after helping Aunt Drita get situated on a chair with a hard look on her face.

Aunt Drita is one woman that was truly made for the Mafia. Soft exterior but wouldn't think twice to blow someone's head off.

I was getting annoyed with all the screams because it causes more confusion and panic than anything else.

I placed my two fingers at the sides of my tongue and gave the loudest whistle I was able to muster up, gaining everyone's attention and immediate silence.

"Now, everyone listen and listen well! If you want your family or friends to get through this and make it out alive, stop screaming and focus on helping because panicking won't solve anything!" I spoke.

There were probably 50 people on this floor with the Giordano's and mine making up the bulk of it.

"Get away from your loved ones if you don't have any medical experience" I said, as most will cause more harm than good when moving an injured person, not knowing the impact that movement might have.

I took off these silly heels that were preventing me from moving fast enough and chucked them to the side.

I glanced around at the waiters staring in shock "all your first aid equipment or anything that would help patch up these wounds, please bring it my way" I instructed a blonde waiter who looked a little less shocked. He gave a nod and left pulling one of the other waiters with him.

"Daniel, I need my satchel in the trunk of my car" I said, instructing him to get my car keys on the table. Everyone was now a little quieter but still panicked following my every action, much to my dismay. I hate attention, but I just have to suck it up and do what I'm good at.

I went to the first person who was the nearest to me. A man in his late 40's or early 50's with the rude woman from the hospital sitting on her knees with his head in her lap semi-conscious. A look of distraught clearly visible on her face.

"Can I have a look" I asked her out of respect, not wanting to offend her by just touching the man who was clearly her husband. She looked with tear-stained eyes in my direction and gave a nod and answered with a pleading look in her eyes "please".

The waiter brought the first aid equipment and Daniel brought my satchel with some medical equipment that the first aid bags won't have.

"Put some gloves on and help me, please" I asked Daniel, who was the calmest of all the people here. He's also the only person I'm aware of here with advanced first aid training.

Once both of us were gloved up, I assessed the man's body and after listening to his organs and breathing, I established that the bullet pierced his left lung which penetrated the side of his chest.

'Daniel, give me those scissors in the first aid kit. After handing it to me, I cut through his shirt to assess the bullet wound and listened as his lung was being filled with blood with each strained breath he took.

There were a few people standing around him watching me work on him, probably his family and the rude woman is probably his wife. I should stop calling her rude woman in my head. The hard look she gave me in the hospital is long gone and her sole focus is the man Infront of her.

"Anthony, wake up Anthony! Stay with me" she said, trying to shake him. It seems he lost consciousness.

"Mam, please calm down. I'm going to help him. He's experiencing pneumothorax" I said.

"What is that?" she questioned with tear stained facing making my heart shudder at the love and hopelessness in her eyes.

"The lung that took the bullet collapsed, but I'll help him" I assured her before she panicked and not going into detail of his condition.

"Mam, can you please get on your knees and lay your husband's head down on the floor. Daniel, lift his head in the right position and bag him" I instructed my brother.

"He's bagged" Daniel said, after he was done. I sealed the bullet wound so no air could escape or enter. Now I have to alleviate the pressure.

"Daniel, pass me that large-bore needle, a 14 gauge please and can someone take over with the bag, please" I instruct one of the guys kneeled next to the man.

The woman gasp and the other younger guy standing around them scratching the back of their head in panic.

The paramedics arrived just in time" mam, can you stand back, please" the guys said.

"I'm a Surgeon" i said, not waiting for his response and instructed him to give the man something for the pain and something to keep his heartbeat elevated. He didn't go against me and helped as soon as he was able to.

"Don't worry mam, he will feel better after this, and he gave him something for the pain through the IV I inserted" I said. Then I focused on the task at hand. Inserting the needle in between the rib cage, I could clearly hear the air escape.

"You can transport him to the hospital, I'll go check on the other people" I said, and he gave a nod as he and another medic moved the patient on a gurney.

"Dr. Harris, over here?" the same medic that helped at the airport waived me over"

When I got to him, I saw Matteo's brother unconscious with a chest wound.

"Chest wound, slow pulse, his breathing was strained so I gave some oxygen, but it doesn't look good" he said.

I took my statoscope and listened to his organs "I think I've found the issue" I said as I put on a fresh pair of gloves. "He's bleeding out, he won't make it to the hospital, I have to stop the bleeding here" I said, making Matteo's mother cry louder into her husband's chest. I didn't even notice them and saw Mr. Giordano give me a pleading look to save his son. I gave him a nod and proceeded to do my business.

I made a small incision on the gunshot wound and it didn't take me too long to find the source of the bleeding, which was an artery. After removing the bullet, I clamped it. I packed the wound to suck up the blood and re-packed the wound to keep it sterile.

"I'm done with him" I said, followed with the gas of his mother "give him some blood and take him to the hospital" I said getting up and removing my asked gloves, looking around for more people that required help.

The medics already attended to two women, one was shot in the arm and the other the leg which was bandaged up.

I heard a scream and glanced to my right and saw that Matteo's fiancé and a woman who I presume to be her mother hunched over a middle-aged man.

I made my way over and didn't see him bloodied or anything "Vincent, wake up!" The wife sounded panicked as the husband fell unconscious to the ground.

I went down on my knees next to him and listened to his heartbeat which was non- existent. One of the medic's came over to help "cardiac arrest" I said.

I opened his shirt and started to do chest compressions as the medical gave him some oxygen. We did that for 10 minutes, but nothing. I decided to continue as I heard the people around him start to curse and cry.

"If my dad dies, you die" Matteo's fiancé threatened and that's when my uncle whom I thought was gone already responded "then that will be the end of your whole bloodline my dear"

I shocked her dad with a defibrillator and continued massaging his heart. 30 minutes went by, and the place was so quiet, you could hear a pin drop.

The small heart machine monitoring his heart went flat as soon as I stopped compressions. I sat back to breathe in some air and took a quick glance around to see where the boys were. While doing so and saw my mom and the others left. My uncle, brothers and cousins were the only people in my family that stayed. The Giordano's were mostly gone, probably to go check on Matteo's brother and other family members.

I used a piece of gauze to wipe my face and threw it to the side. The silence remained. The medic looked at me waiting for instruction.

I balled my fist and lifted it high up in the air and gave his chest a hard slam making the wife and daughter scream. The beeping on the machine could be heard and the medic gave me a faint smile followed up with a nod.

After going over him one last time, I instructed the medic to take him to the hospital.

I got up off the floor and made my way over to my family that was standing to the side waiting for me. My uncle took his coat and wrapped it around me as we walked out of the restaurant to hide my bloodied dress.

When we got home the boys had already gone to bed, but the ladies were sitting at the fireplace with their mugs of coffee. Mom was stretching her arms out to hug me but stopped in time "go take a shower in the guest bathroom, I'll bring you some clothes" mom said.

By the time I was done with my shower, mom held a nice cup of hot chocolate out for me. I wrapped one of mom's throw blankets over my shoulders and joined them next to the fireplace.

"Danny, you are a real freaking, Doctor. I felt so proud to see you in action" Elira said.

"That's my daily life, thanks sis" I said, taking a sip from my drink. I love all the family on my mother's side because they truly treat family like family.

"Daniella, so now we know who their daddy is. Why didn't you let us know sooner?" Aunt Drita asked.

I sighed, exhaling a deep breath "I wanted to be sure before saying anything" I said, making mom snort.

"You knew from the moment you saw that man's face at the airport that he is either the father or related to the boys" mom said. I gave her a nod.

"When will you learn my dear? We are here and will always be here for you and the boys. If you succeed in life, we will cheer you on and if you fail, we will pick you up and dust you off, but we will never forsake you" mom said.

"Thanks Mom" I said, wiping my eyes.

"Where are the men?" I asked.

"They went to the hospital to check up on Giordano's and also to find out who that guy was after" Elira said.

"I am so tired" I said, glancing at my cellphone light flashing. I groan as I wipe rub my eyes in frustration when I see it's the hospital.

Picking up the phone, one of the nurses informed me of two MVA's that just came in and 3 people with head and spine injuries.

"I'm on my way" I said, ending the call.

"Looks like I'm heading to the hospital" I said.

"Just a few months then you're free, then we can go on a nice long holiday" mom said, trying to reassure me.

Ps. New Chapter will be posted in a few hours......

Chapter 22

Matteo's POV

Growing up, my parents were my biggest inspiration in life. People I admired and looked up to. The fact that they always gave their best to us as children and made sure we were always happy, is still engrained in me as a man today. My father would kill to see us happy and assured we are protected.

That's why I was never able to go against them when they informed me that I would be marrying Gina in a few months, even though it made me the most miserable person I've ever been. I respected my parents' decision.

I have been drinking way more than I should. I've reached the point where I cannot go to bed without being intoxicated and sleep doesn't come easy regardless of how drunk I am. I just want to be numb to this world, but when I wake up the next day, I realize that I'm only human.

I have no other way of coping with the realization that I would be marrying a person that I don't love or feel attracted to. It sounds more like a death sentence.

Once I say 'I do' I will be locked in for life. My mother is of no help because she's just too sweet for this world and won't go against dad. I sometimes tend to think she holds a deep fear of him, but at the same time loves him too much.

Earlier yesterday, when the guy working for me gave me the pictures of her picking the boys up from school, I first felt betrayed, but then I realized there might be something more to this.

Seeing their faces, I wanted to faint because my mind couldn't grasp how, out there in this world there were two human beings that would look so identical to me. No DNA test would convince me otherwise, I knew they were mine by just looking at them.

Then the emotions started, I was beyond pissed that she would keep something so important from me. Then my mind went to all the enemies we have. What if they put two and two together and figure out that they are my kids and decide to harm them to get back at me?

I went to the hospital to confront Daniella and when I got to her office, I had so many questions on my mind and wanted to berate her for keeping the kids away from me. Surely, she knew me, or so I thought. I wanted to let her know that I would be taking the kids from her, but when I heard part of her explanation, I couldn't bring myself to do so.

I felt horrible when I heard of her being drugged and the fact that I was the one that took her first time away from her. If it's one thing I don't do, then that's non-consensual sex. So, I felt horrible knowing I was the one that caused her so much pain. I already felt bad the day I saw that bed when she left and the expression of the pain clearly visible on her face.

I would never go against any woman that said no, but that night, I was drugged too, and I feel so bad for her and my kids that had to grow up without their dad. I feel there's more to her story, though and I'm ready to hear it all.

After I left her office, I went to my parent's place, and they informed me that the whole family, with extended family would be going out to celebrate dad's recovery and that includes Gina and her parents. I don't understand why they always had to be in attendance.

We hadn't even made it to the table yet when my dad saw them. He saw their interaction with Daniella and heard how they called her 'mom' and he knew they were mine from our previous awkward interaction.

I walked behind everyone and when I stepped on the restaurant floor, I heard dad and saw him with a pissed expression on his face and I knew something was wrong. When I got nearer, I saw that it was Daniella. When I heard him confront her in front of everyone, I was beyond pissed, but then I saw them, and my heart crumbled. I loved them instantly. I couldn't believe they were mine.

I started to get pissed at dad for the tone he used when he spoke to Daniella and the fact that he didn't wait for me before talking to her and in front of her family, also doesn't sit well with me. The boys didn't have to be witness to his disrespectful behavior. That's why I had to jump in.

What type of man and fatherly figure am I for those boys if I allow him to talk to her in that manner? Will they ever accept me after the stunt my father pulled, or would they look at me the same? Don't even get me started on that bitch of a cousin, Emma and the soon to be ex-fiancé Gina. I will deal with both of them soon.

If only I knew about them sooner, this would never have been an issue. Dad looked more pissed that they exist than the fact that he wasn't aware that they existed and that doesn't sit well with me. It seemed that this would be a stain on the family name if people were to find out, like being in the Mafia isn't a stain already.

I was disgusted with his behavior. Those boys are my blood regardless of how they were conceived.

I respect and love them, but where do you draw the line? Do you continue on the path they carved on your behalf and self-destruct, or do you go against your family for your own and carve your own path.

I hoped that my family finding out that I have kids would stop this whole fiasco, but on the way to the hospital last night, dad made it clear that this doesn't change anything and that he made a promise to his friend.

He didn't mention meeting them or wanting them in his life, nothing. That felt like a punch to the gut.

The family business has never fully been under my control as I look at it. Dad always has to have the last say and approve everything I do.

Dad always said that he would take away the family business and hand it over to Julian, should I decide not to marry Gina. That was the main reason I caved and agreed to marry her. If he's unwilling to accept, would I be able to leave and go against him. I'm willing to lose everything and what's more dangerous than someone who has nothing to lose.

My kids grew up without a father for nine years and I won't share my time between them and a fake wife. Now it is time for me to take responsibility for all the years lost. So, I don't give a damn. I have made up my mind and this was the push I needed to not get married to Gina. Now I have a reason to go against anyone that stands in the way of what I want in life.

I want her, I want them, I want Daniella and my kids, but most of all, I want them to experience having a dad. There's no question about that. I don't know if she will give me a chance, but I am sure as hell I will try my best and fight for us. I hope she's let me.

I know meeting someone for the first time wouldn't have that much of an impact on someone, but we have history. Ten years of her face haunting me my every being. Ten years of guilt following me. I guess what they say about soul ties is true.

I felt a connection to her since the first time I laid eyes on her and when I saw her again, I knew I was done for, but didn't realize it at the time. I want to properly meet the boys with no other family besides Daniella and me around. I need to show them that they do have a father and that's my first priority now.

What still bothered me about Daniella was the fact that there's so little information about her family until I saw her last night with the Mexican cartel and Albanian Mafia. I need to find out what her connection is with them.

The Mexicans are dangerous, but the Albanians are something totally different. They run the biggest cocaine and marijuana trade in the whole of Europe and they protect what's theirs by all means. What is their connection with her family?

Another surprise was the boys speaking just as good Albanian as the rest of them, which means they have deep ties. Why does that make my chest feel uncomfortably heavy?

Damn, she did good with them regardless. My heart wanted to bounce out of my chest with pride. The way they stood up for their mother, knocked my socks off. The fact that me as their father didn't have to teach them to protect their mother indicated that their uncle's and grandfather did a good job instilling good values in them.

They even tried to protect her when shots were fired, which also made me believe that they had some form of training, but what I want to know is, who is shielding them from the public eye and how?

I know damn well; we have some of the best guys when it comes to surveillance, and this was the first time they struggled to get information on someone.

The fact that Daniella is connected with the Mexican cartel and the Albanian Mafia, doesn't sit well with me, but I need to talk to her and find out what their relationship is with those two groups of people.

Vito and I are currently on our way back to the hospital after torturing the shooter that attacked us. The fucker didn't give anything away, even after I cut a few of his fingers off. I then burnt both to stop the bleeding and saved the others for tonight. I will be patient until he has no choice but to say who sent him and who he was after.

"Why didn't you tell me about them?" Vito asked, taking my mind off my jumbled thoughts".

"I had no time" I shrug "as soon as I got the pictures from surveillance, I went straight to the hospital to confront her. After that I went home, only to discover everyone will be at the family dinner to celebrate dad's recovery"

"And?" he asked, waiting in anticipation "did she say why she didn't contact you?"

"We didn't go into much detail, but she said she will tell me everything I want to know in a few days" I told him.

"Damn, but she is good at what she does. Did you see how she brought Vincent back from the dead. If only his saliva went down his windpipe at the same time his heart decided to stop" he said, making me smirk and shake my head at the nonsense coming from his mouth.

"What? Just mentioning his name gives a bitter taste in my mouth. He's just too close to your dad. They are either fucking or he has some dirt on your dad. There's no way in hell your dad would still want you to marry that plastic ornament after finding out you have a kid, or kids for that matter with such a stunning woman, that has made a name for herself with a career only some can dream of"

"I know, maybe my dad would change his mind after meeting the boys, but that must happen after I get acquainted with them first. I want a solid foundation with them before they become part of their lives" I said.

"I still have to find out what her connection is with the Mexicans and Albanians"

"Maybe Rafael is fucking her?" Vito question, making me smack him behind his head.

"That's the mother of my kids, dude"

"It doesn't mean she's not fuckable or are you planning to reconcile?" he asked, making me look at him for a few seconds before answering.

"I wouldn't mind, but time will tell" I said, smirking "I heard the Albanians came to the hospital to check stuff out last night after the shooting?".

"Yeah, even the doc's brothers and father came, which was strange. Do you think they might be connected the scum that shot at us last night?" he asked.

"Nah impossible. We were blocking them from getting shot and I don't think they would have put their lives in danger by getting people to shoot us because they were in the line of fire as well."

"True, let's see what our dogs bring us" he says, referring to our hunters in the mafia.

"We're here" I told Vito, who was nose deep in his phone as we entered the gates of the hospital.

We headed upstairs to my family who are all situated on one floor. The floor was a little livelier today. With nurses and doctors moving around.

I first visited my brother and when I entered, I could see mom sitting and holding his hand, while he was chewing ice chips from a small white plastic cup. Dad and Alessia were nowhere in sight.

"What's up, brother? How are you holding up?" I asked, making everyone look in our direction.

"I'm good thanks to your baby mamma" Julian said, placing the empty cup on the bedside table.

I walked over to my mother and gave her a peck on the cheek "Ma"

Mom gave me a smile "when do we get to formally meet them?" she asked, referring to the boys.

"I'm not yet sure mom, I want to get to know them first before I introduce them to anyone else" I said.

"I understand, but you have to keep in mind that your will be getting married in a very short time" she said.

"Mom, don't you think the wedding should be cancelled? I mean, the reason you wanted me to get married in the first place was to produce an heir. Now, there are two options" I said, sounding confident.

"You have no clue who those people are, have you?" mom asked, making me frown at her comment.

"What are you trying to say, mom?" I asked, as Julian sat there munching on his ice while watching us.

"Your so-called sons have Albanian blood in them and are under the protection of the Albanian Mafia and the Mexican cartel" Dad announced, as he stood in the doorway.

"Where does this come from? I know the Albanians were there with them last night, but how are they family?"

"The doctor's mother's birth name is Ilir Hyseni, born in the Albanian Mafia. She came to America and changed her name to Sarah. She married Johan Harris, and he had no choice but to become part of the Albanian Mafia. All of them are part of it, if he wanted to stay with his wife and remain alive. The Harris's part is to launder money for the Albanians, but besides that they focus more on the legal side of things. Rafael Garcia, best friend of the Doctor's brother and basically grew up in their house"

I have to say, hearing those detail did come as a shock "so, you are saying that I should stay away from my own children?" I asked dad.

"I'm saying that you will get married and produce a heir and that no-one with Albanian blood in them will run the Italian Mafia" dad said, finality clear in his voice.

His words felt like a knife being shoved in my chest and I knew not to continue this conversation any further.

Chapter 23

Matteo's POV

I didn't even bother to answer my father and left the hospital after checking up on Uncle Antonio as the rest of the family were already discharged. Uncle Toni was still in the ICU, but doing much better than last night, thanks to the doctor.

I left after seeing him and didn't bother to go check on Gina's dad. I saw no reason to argue with him over spilled milk or have a discussion about anything concerning marriage.

Knowing my dad, I knew exactly what he meant by his words. It's times like these that I question if he really is my father. How does he expect me to reject my own flesh and blood, just because they are related to the Albanians? How can he even reject his own grandchildren who have part of him inside them?

Then he might as well ...reject me.

Since the marriage proposal was brought up, all the demands were made by him, followed by disrespect and decisions made on my behalf.

One thing I do know is that I already love them without even truly knowing them and as I said, my mind is made up and I will never deny my own flesh and blood. They are part of me as I am part of them, and no-one will be able to stop me from what I want in life, from this point onward.

There was no time to sit and sulk about my dad's choices when I had an enemy to catch and besides, I won't allow his decisions to impact or dictate my life anymore. This is where I draw the line because I might just miss my future if I allow him to continue making decisions for me.

Instead of waiting for my men to bring me the culprits, I decided to blow off some steam and go on the hunt for them myself. It's time to turn the city on its head.

We visited many gangs that we had civil relationships with, to try and get information about the shooting and went as far as beating a few up that didn't pay me on time, to relieve some stress and it was also killing two birds.

Vito hasn't left my side this whole time and it has been like this since we were in diapers. He knew remaining quiet by my side was the best for both of us. I always have his back while he has mine and he's aware of the inner turmoil I'm experiencing, that's why he doesn't even attempt to question me.

Our last stop was at Frankie's Casino at 1:00 in the morning and we were met with all kinds of woman in sparkly underwear as uniforms.

Woman are seen as objects of pleasure in this place. A sad world indeed, that the giver of life is objectified like that. Regardless of being in the Mafia, I never had any desire to start or go into trafficking and I have my mother to thank for that.

She made me understand the importance of the role and purpose of woman in society, that's why I will never even lift a hand to a woman. Me choking Gina was the result of everything that happened and her constant nagging, but it still doesn't excuse or justify my reaction.

I still feel bad for allowing her or life to influence my emotions and decisions that brought me to that point.

Two women made their way over in our direction as we approached the main floor. Even though I could do with a good fuck by now and it has been a few months without getting any, I still wouldn't go that far just to get a release. My hand is doing just fine for now, so I waved them off and made my way to the main floor.

Reaching the main floor, I stood there waiting for the person I came here for or his men to notice me.

"Big boss, what are you doing here" I heard someone say and when I glanced in the direction where the voice was coming from. I saw, Marlon one of Frankie's guards making their way to me.

I gave him a nod in greeting "Marlon, ask your boss to meet me at the back" I said, as Vito and I made our way to Frankie's office at the back. This is a place we know all too well. Many underworld meetings take place here on a daily basis, so we know our way around.

Frankie is a 60-year-old underground businessman who is also known as Fox. He dabbles in a little bit of everything and has been my go-to guy for information since I started working with my dad. My dad doesn't like him much, because he is someone that has dirt on everyone, but why fear if you have nothing to hide?

Once we reached Frankie's office Vito started to talk while we sat there waiting for Frankie to get here. One of the servers came in and gave us some whiskey and left.

"Are you good?" Vito asked, under his breath as he sipped from his whiskey tumbler, making me glance in his direction.

"Better than I'll ever be" I said, tapping frustratingly on the desk with my fingers. He knew that I was being sarcastic and meant the opposite.

"We need to get this whole Gina book closed, but what if your dad decides to take away the Mafia?" he asked.

"You already heard countless times how he threatened me with that title and that pisses me off more than anything. He never fully signed the Mafia over, even though I've been making way more profit than him or the old man ever made combined since taking over. Luckily, I made sure to keep my own businesses separate and if he decides to take the Mafia, he will shoot himself in the foot. I'll tell them tomorrow after they pick Julian up from the hospital that I won't marry her"

Vito sat in his seat staring at me in a daze that turned into a smirk before eventually answering "I'm with you 100%"

I got up and gave him a hug "Thanks" I said, before getting situated in my seat again just as the doors opened.

"Teo! To what do I owe this pleasure?" Frankie asked in excitement, sporting a huge grin while shaking our hands.

"Old man, you already know why I'm here" I tell him, making him chuckle.

Once he got positioned in his seat he started to speak "how can I help you, son?"

"You probably heard about last night's shooting?" I confirm and he gave a curt nod, which gave me the indication that I may continue "I need to find out who and why"

"Were you able to get anything out of the shooter?" he asked, fishing for clues to take to his men to start the hunt.

"Nothing, not a word and he doesn't look like he belongs to any mafia, but he's affiliated with someone or an organization".

He reached for his cellphone and dialed a number "come to my office when Teo is gone" he said to one of his men and dropped the phone, then focused on me again. That's probably the guy that will be starting the search "I'll get your information, but I need something from you" he said.

"Name your price" I stated.

"I need to transport my product through your shipping company" he said, to which I gave him a look to elaborate.

"Son, you know in this business no-one can be trusted and I need that shipment of coke to hit the shores on your next run from Europe. You are my only hope to make bank on that deal".

Everyone in the business world, including the Mafia, is aware that I own a shipping company that has nothing to do with the family business because it belongs to me solely. This was one of the means I used to boost my personal revenue, instead of paying another company to ship for me. Now people pay me to ship anything for them to any shore worldwide. The family business also makes use of my services at a discounted rate, obviously.

"Ok, but by when will I be able to get my information?" I question.

"Give me a few days, a week at most" he said, with confidence and I know he will get me what I need. He always does.

I stood up and shook his hand "then your powder will be on the next ship"

"Thanks, my boy, I appreciate it" he said.

"No, thank you"

There was no need to give Frankie any more detail because he already heard about the shooting. He has people everywhere so that counts in our favor.

After leaving Frankie's we went to one of my clubs. The club was packed to capacity with drunk bodies dancing and swaying, having the time of their lives while my mind is pre-occupied with everything that happened the last few days.

Now, I only need alcohol to numb my mind.

Vito and I got situated in the VIP area with some whiskey to soak in everything that happened in the last few hours.

A few minutes into us trying to relax, we were joined by Gio and Marco making their way in our direction.

"Hey guys, what's up?" Marco was the first to break the ice and you could feel the tension in the air. Gio looked stressed and raked his hands through his hair continuously after giving us nods in greeting. He's probably feeling guilty for the shit his sister spewed last night, but why would he? He should know by now that his sister is a grown adult, unless he's scared of what I will do to her.

I sat there silently listening to the banter between Marco and Vito for about 30 minutes, when Gio started to speak "Hey Teo" he said, making me look in his direction.

"I'm sorry about Emma's behavior towards the boys. I have been trying to talk sense in her head but it's a struggle sometimes. I told her to change her attitude, or her allowance would be cut" he stated.

"You know she has been meddling in my business for some time now and I've been constantly warning her, but the boys and their mother is where I draw the line" I stated. He could only nod in agreement.

Everyone in our family gets an allowance from the day they are born, but if the Mafia is taken from me then I don't have a say if Her's will be taken or not.

"When do we get to meet the boys, Teo?" Marco asked.

"Soon" I said, continuing to take a sip from my drink.

"I can't believe you had kids with the same doc that operated on your dad and both of you acted as if you weren't aware of each other. And they look just like you, so there's no denying who the pappa is" Marco chuckled at his own shit.

I spent another hour, then decided to head home because I was clearly drunk and needed my bed.

The next day......

I luckily put my phone on silent before I hit my bed last night, otherwise the buzzing would have interrupted my sleep by now. Not that I have the liberty of sleeping in, I just feel like taking a 'fuck the world' day.

I woke up around 10:00 dehydrated as fuck. I don't get a stomach hang-over, but it's always the headache and thirst that follow me around like a bitch for a few hours into the day and the next day the same issue for the last two months now.

I took a long hot ice-cold shower, then got dressed in a pair of black jeans with a white T-shirt, still not bothering to check my phone.

By the time I was done hydrating, ate something and was fully dressed It was 12:00 already and just in time for me to head to my parent's house. It's times like these that I'm happy I don't live with them.

I checked my phone and saw that I had a few messages relating to the Mafia, so I responded accordingly, and I saw that my mom was also looking for me. Seeing that I'm on my way there, I decide to not call back as I will be seeing them.

As I took the drive up the driveway of my parents' secluded home, I saw lots of cars here. This indicated that the whole family was here, but why though? Probably to see Julian, I thought to myself.

I was greeted by my aunts and uncles and some cousins "Morning Teo" my aunt Theresa greeted giving me a hug. She's my dad's brother's wife.

As I'm greeting everyone, I also see Gina sitting next to my mother as I made my way to her "hey mom" I said, as I give her a kiss on the cheek, ignoring Gina's presence.

"Hallo, son. We were just waiting for you" mom said, making me scrunch up my eyebrows in confusion.

As if on que all my family left leaving just my mom, Gina and myself in the room "where is Julian and dad?" I asked.

"Your dad will be here shortly" mom said as she got up and said farewell to my family who was on their way to visit Uncle Antonio.

A few minutes later dad made his appearance, and I just gave him a nod because I was too pissed to start any conversation with him. I first want to see what he has to say before I tell him the wedding is cancelled.

I also see Gina still sitting very cozy in anticipation. She won't be happy after I burst her bubble.

Dad cleared his throat "Son, Gina will be staying with you from now on" he announced without even bothering to ask me.

"Excuse me dad?"

"I don't have time for you to be difficult. The driver will drop her at your place" he said, pointing to the suitcases that I didn't even notice in the corner "and I don't want to hear any complaints from you nor do I want to hear Gina complain about your behavior towards her and that is final" he said, with finality clear in his voice.

Why have I never noticed this side of dad? Or was I just too blinded by my respect for him?

Chapter 24

Daniella's POV

The hospital was in a constant buzz this whole weekend. There were just too many emergencies to attend to. I have been working 20 hour shifts and wasn't able to fully sit down with my family to enjoy their company.

I only saw my boys asleep cause of how late I reached home. After that, I could only grab a quick shower because I had to head straight back. I did make sure to kiss them and breathe in their scent while they were sleeping to satisfy my heart a little.

My uncle and his wife will be staying with us for the next month and my cousins will be leaving at the end of the week to keep the family business running that side in Albania. I really need to clear up as many surgeries as possible so that I can spend some quality time with them because my cousins will be leaving this coming Sunday night.

The boys also have a Judo competition on Saturday that the whole family will be attending and that includes Rafael too. I'm still contemplating if

I should invite Matteo, but I'll have to ask the boys first, to see how they would feel about it.

My mind has been constantly occupied with Matteo. Not because I am attracted to him or anything like that, but because I don't know how things will play out with him and the boys. I also don't know how involved he will be in their lives, if I would lose them to him or if they reject him because of the events of last week.

Like, will he demand the boys to live with him certain times? How would parenting with him work? I just hope and pray he's reasonable, otherwise I have no choice but to make his life miserable.

I shudder at the thought of them wanting to live with him instead of me.

I did not have time to sit and talk with the boys to see how they felt about their dad, because I went back to hospital in the early hours of Saturday morning and came home the next day when they were already in bed, but I will make time to talk to them tonight.

Matteo messaged me earlier to say that he's on his way to the hospital for the DNA test. I just came out of a consultation and finished my lunch, so I am busy getting a few files out of the way before he gets here. I have at least two hours to spare before I have to go back in for a three-hour long surgery.

I still can't get over what happened on Friday. My family had an idea of what's going on, but I didn't get time to sit and talk with them, yet.

I never thought that being occupied with work would piss me off this much. I used to love the fact that work filled the times that would be wasted otherwise, but now I can't wait for it to be over.

A knock could be heard on my door "It's open" I said, expecting Matteo to be the person entering my door because he knew where my office was, but I'm met with the cold hard glare of the woman I'm still trying to figure out.

I have an idea why she would be here but let's see what her story Is, I thought to myself.

"Hi there?" I acknowledge her presence, giving her a questioning look because she has no business with me.

"Russo, Gina Russo, soon to be Mrs. Giordano" she stated, as she made her way over to my desk like a slithering snake with her expensive eight-inch heels clicking on the tiled floor.

She made herself comfortable in the chair in front of my desk without even asking if she could take a seat. Says a lot about her manners and respect for others if you ask me. Why is this lady rubbing me the wrong way from the get-go?

She's beautiful, I must give her that, but she resembles a statue that is frozen in time and if she attempted to smile, her face might just crack. Too many fillers and Botox I presume.

What a shame for someone that's still so young and she doesn't sound like a pleasant person to be around. I just hope she keeps the sassy attitude to herself and does not project it on my boys.

"Aah yes, Matteo's fiancé" I acknowledge, acting surprised without introducing myself. She already knew who I was "nice to meet you again, Miss Russo" I said, stretching my hand towards her out of courtesy and trying to be nice, not bothering to stand up.

She shook my hand and subtly raked her eyes over my appearance from head to toe. I noticed it, but I ignored her wandering eyes.

"How can I help you, Miss Russo?" I asked, leaning back in my seat, my blank facial expression on full display. This should give her an indication to her that I'm not intimidated by her at all. On the other hand, I love drawing clear lines in the sand with regards to people trying to intimidate me. I'm not in high school anymore and won't let anyone take advantage of me, intimidate or influence me to do anything I don't agree with.

She cleared her throat and crossed one leg over the other looking like a spoiled little girl "I came here today to try and get to know you a little better, seeing that we will be co-parenting. I don't want us to misunderstand each other or cross any boundaries that shouldn't be crossed" she said, giving me a calculating stare and the last part was a clear warning directed at me.

"Why would any boundaries be crossed? And if any boundaries were to be discussed, I think you should be taking that up with your fiancé" I said, instantly silencing her attempts of taking over my life or the lives of my kids. Does she think I want her man? Ridiculous! I don't have time for her silly games.

You could see that she wasn't happy with my choice of words, but she tried her best to compose her emotions, but it didn't work because her visit went downhill fast.

"You listen here and listen well" she said while pointing her finger at me "I know you have a history with Matteo, so I want to make sure that we are on the same page regarding him and your children. I won't allow you to use your children to get back with him. I will do everything in my power to make sure you and your kids stay in your lane" she stated, clenching her jaw.

But I'm having none of it. I'm already sleep deprived, tired and I miss my kids. I really don't have time for bullshit like this when I'm on my last nerve already.

"I don't want to come across as rude or inconsiderate even though you are being disrespectful towards me, but I am their mother and will go to great lengths to protect my own. Matteo is the one that has to inform or discuss things that impact your life with you. I don't see why you had to come to my office and place of work to discuss my children because I do not have any business with you. I am not interested in Matteo. Let me repeat that for you, I am not interested in Matteo Giordano! Lastly, you threatening to hurt me in order to get what you want, is a clear reflection of the weak, insecure individual you are" I said. I got up from my seat and walked to the door and held it open for her to leave.

She got up with a red face while trying to hold her composure. Making her way towards the door "With you making the kids public, I wouldn't want Matteo to get distracted along the way and besides, you are not teenagers anymore. People change and move on and the sooner you understand that the better"

I internally role my eyes at the insecure person standing in front of me "What gives you the impression that I'm interested in him? Matteo is the least of my worries. I do have a life and besides, I think you should get the fuck out of my office before I make you. How dare you come into my workplace and disrespect me?".

"I'll say it again, you shouldn't hold any hope for a relationship with Matteo. Having children with him doesn't mean you have the liberty to intrude on our life. I would just like to make that clear, so you are on the same page as us and that you respect our privacy" she finished, as she abruptly walked out.

I closed the door closed "bitch" I mutter under my breath.

What the fuck was that. She's a fucking delusional person to disrespect me like that. I'm so pissed right now that my hands are shaking.

I need to let Matteo know that he should keep his barbie in their barbie world because I am not the one.

My phone chimed at that exact moment indicating a message came through as I tried to compose my emotions.

Glancing at the screen. I see its Matteo. Just the person I must speak to.

Matteo: Hi, I'm Here

I typed a quick response back.

Me: Meet me on the 3rd floor at the elevator.

I made my way there and took the stairs down. It's strange how I love to do everything to avoid the human race, but my job consists of interacting with them.

When I arrived there, he stood with his back facing me busy talking on his phone. So, I stood there waiting for him to finish his call with my shoulder resting against the wall.

My kids clearly got the looks from him, I thought to myself as he stood there dressed in black jeans with a white dress shirt and black coat with black ankle boots. Though, after the visit from his girlfriend I wish that he weren't.

As he turned around, he noticed me and immediately ended the call. I was still pissed with what just happened so my face remained stoic. Even though I wanted to address his fiancé's behavior, I couldn't do it here. There were too many people walking around.

Peering into his gaze, pain, sadness, defeat was clearly visible in them, and he looks like someone that hadn't had a wink of rest in the last few days. Even though he's clean shaven and neatly dressed, I could still see those emotions deep in the pits of his orbs.

Who better notice someone else's pain than someone who's experienced in life's pain. The person that created a new identity to mask the fragile one because of pain.

"Hi, where to?" he asked, as he tucked his phone back into his pocket.

I cleared my throat after realizing how stupid I looked trying to read him "this way" I said, leading him to the lab.

"Hey Dr. Harris" I heard someone say. When I glanced in the direction, I saw Dr. Mitchel making his way past me.

"Hi Dr. Mitchell. Oh, before I forget" I said, stopping him halfway "Can you make sure the rest of the team are here tomorrow morning at 8:00 to go over the Murphey case, please?" I asked.

"Yes, no problem, Doc Harris" he answered sporting a smirk as his eyes roam around my body immediately evoking an uncomfortable feeling inside me. He's just too friendly that it seemed off.

Matteo moved behind me until I felt the heat of his body against my back. I turned my head and glanced in his direction, and I could see him clearly glaring at Dr. Mitchell.

Dr. Mitchell's eyes widened at the sight of Matteo, probably realizing who he is. Everyone's aware of the Giordano family.

"Thanks, Dr. Mitchell" I said as I turned walking in the direction of the lab. Matteo followed behind me like a lost puppy.

After doing all the necessary things and providing the relevant samples, we left heading to the elevator still in silence. The results should be ready in a day as I asked the technician for a rush of the results.

"Can we talk to you somewhere?" he asked, as we stood there waiting for the elevator to arrive.

"Yeah, I need to talk to you too. The cafeteria or my office?" I questioned, while he scratched his head.

"Office would be best. We don't want people to hear our business, now, would we?" he said, making me internally role my eyes.

"Agreed" I answered, as I made my way to my office again, taking the stairs. He just followed and said nothing.

We got situated and I waited for him to start talking first.

"How will this work with the boys? Do I visit them at your house first so that they can get used to me or do we meet in a public space?" he asked.

"I think we should first wait for the results, and I will also have to talk to the boys before you can get to meet them because I didn't get any time to discuss this whole situation yet"

"What's holding you from talking to them? I know they are mine, Daniella!" He raised his voice making me flinch.

"They look damn identical to me, so there's no denying or having to wait for results. I have already missed out on so many years of their lives" he said, rubbing his face in frustration. Which pisses me off even more.

In my calmest voice I answered him "You have missed out on so many years?" I sat there putting my bravest façade on display.

"I just turned 16 a month before my high school graduation. I never had any real friends in school because of my age difference with the kids in my grade. So, everyone was two years older than me. Me, obviously envying them for the awesome life they had. They were partying and having the times of their lives while I was a homebody and constantly in my books because no one wanted to be friends with the clever nerdy kid that always outperformed them in every test. What they didn't know was that I didn't even have to try to get those good marks" I sighed.

"Their life looked alluring, if only I knew" I said, looking up at him then refocusing my stare on the door.

"Three of the most popular girls made friends with me, so I became part of their friend group. Little did I know they were gaining my trust in order for me to attend the graduation after party, so that they could drug me, and a few footballers could take my first time from me. I always heard of them attending parties praying on virgins, but never thought that I would be their next target"

"Did they?" Matteo asked.

I shook my head "no, a few minutes after the girls left me there, you made your way into the room. The years that followed weren't the best for me. More mentally then physically"

"Did you tell your parents what happened?" he asked.

"Well, I kept it to myself and became like a hermit. I never went out with my family and always stayed in my room. Until I got severely ill, and mom took me to the doctor. He confirmed I was pregnant and then I had to come clean with my family"

"Did they help you...I mean, with the boys" he asked.

"Oh, if it weren't for them who stood by me and helped me even after I thought abortion was the only solution, I don't think I would have been here today"

"Abortion?"

"Yes, luckily, I was born into the best family anyone could ask for. They helped me raise them while I went to medical school. They followed me all over the world to places I had to work. When the boys started school, I wanted them to have a more stable life. So, I my parents came every school holiday to wherever I was"

"I was also drugged that night" he said, making my eyes bulge out of its sockets "I took a drink from a tray without asking who's it was and that's how I ended up in the room with you"

"You're kidding me?" I asked flabbergasted.

"No word of a lie, I promise you, but to be honest your face has never left me. I always felt a sense of guilt because I knew that was your first time from the bedsheets, but your face when you left that morning told me that something wasn't right and that you regret what happened. I'm sorry for my part in this, but I won't apologize for impregnating you"

I looked up at him shocked.

"I don't know the boys yet, but I think I understand why your face constantly came up in my mind. It's because of you being the connection between them and myself. Who would have thought that I would become a dad?" he said, as if tasting the word 'dad' coming out of his mouth "I would love to be a father to them and i will protect them with everything in me.

"There's something else we have to clear up" I said, making him instantly look in my direction.

"Your fiancé came to see me earlier"

Chapter 25

AN: Hi Everyone

Hope you all are doing well in this crazy world.

I would like to apologize for only posting once per week. Life has been lifing and work has been hectic. I will however be posting more during the week.

To all my new followers, THANK YOU FOR GIVING ME A CHANCE!!!!!!

To the oldies that stuck by me since day one, i can only give you love

----

"She what?" Matteo asked, as he tried his very best to hold his composure.

The windows to his soul clearly displayed his anger away, though. Betrayal was also clearly visible in them.

"I take it from your reaction that you weren't aware of her visit" I stated, before continuing "She left a few minutes before you arrived, but I had to kick her out. I just want to make one thing clear" I say, as I sat forward with my elbows resting on my desk "I will not apologize for my reaction toward her. I won't allow her or anyone for that matter to threaten me or my kids" I said, with finality in my voice.

His eyes snapped towards mine as I mentioned the last part.

He shook his head with a frown on his face "I Honestly had no clue she was here. I hope you believe me when I say, I was not aware of her coming here. I'm so sorry" he apologized, looking down at the floor.

"Did she mention what her reason was for visiting?" he asked, leaning back in his seat while running his hand through his hair.

What should I tell this man? Should I be honest or keep the truth from him? I was a little pissed earlier, but I must admit that my anger has subsided.

The truth is the only way to get through life itself. I'm starting to develop a headache and I still have surgery to prepare for once Matteo leave.

I didn't feel like going into too much detail, so I just relayed the main points "she started off saying that she wants to get to know me better as we will be co-parenting. Then she warned me to stay away from you"

His eyes went wide at my revelation, but he continued to listen "she obviously threatened me, and I had no choice but to kick her out"

He cleared his throat "Look, as I said, I had no clue she came to visit you. I think it would be best if I'm honest with you" he said, as his gaze peered into mine.

"I am not marrying her because I want to. It's an arranged marriage" he announced, making me look at him in pure horror. Me not being able to decide wouldn't sit right with me.

"In this day and age?" I question.

"Yup, in this day and age. Believe me when I say, there's no feelings from my side towards her and this is for business purposes. Nothing else" he said looking down at the floor again, making me feel bad for him.

"I need my kids to be safe when I'm not around to protect them and obviously when they're near your fiancé. I just don't trust her after the stunt, she pulled she pulled today. I know they can physically defend themselves, to a certain extent, but they are still kids and will need to be protected still" I told him.

"I understand and I'll make sure she understands" he all of a sudden snapped his head up "did they get any formal training?" he asked.

I gave a nod "yes, they still attend regular Judo training, two to three times per week. I mean, they have to" I say, making him instantly frown.

"What do you mean, they have to?"

"My family is part of the Albanian Mafia and as long as none of my cousins have kids, they will be next in line to take over. I know my cousins will have kids eventually though, but just as a precaution" I say, making him flinch.

I smirked at his reaction when my phone started to ring. Glancing at it, I saw Rafael's name flashing on the screen "sorry, I need to take this" I say, pointing to my phone.

"Hey Raf. What's up?"

"Hey Sis, I'm picking the boys up and taking them to take them to practice. Chase is stuck in meetings the whole day. I'll take them out for a late lunch after they are done. Just letting you know" he rambled, making me roll my eyes.

"Ok Raff, see you at home later" I said, ending the phone call.

Matteo sat there with a visible frown on his face, to which I gave him a questioning look.

"Was that your boyfriend or husband?" Matteo asked.

"No" I answered honestly "that was Rafael. He called to inform me that he will be taking the boys to practice and after that he will take them for a late lunch" I said, which made him frown even more.

"Is there something wrong?" I asked him.

"What is your family's relationship with him?"

"Rafael basically grew up in our house. He's my brother Chase's best friend and more like another brother to me"

He gave a nod, but I could see that he wasn't happy with what he heard. It also seems though he wanted to ask more questions relating to Raff but held back.

"Tell me about them" he asked, making me give him a questioning look "the boys" he stated.

"Well, both of them look exactly like you for one, but you already knew that" I said, making him smirk with pride.

"Dylan is very outspoken and loves to speak his mind. He is like the spokesperson for both of them. Max is the quiet one. He is his brother's protector and has a heart of gold. Both of them are respectable, well-mannered boys, but will go to great lengths to protect each other and the family. They are just very good boys, and they will love to meet you. I mean, they were the ones asking who their dad was".

"I can't wait to be part of their lives" he said, as he sat with a dazed look on his face.

"I will speak to the boys later tonight and keep you posted on meeting them" I said.

We discussed the boys for a little bit more and then we ended the conversation there as I had to go into surgery. The sad look on his face gave me an unsettling feeling.

What a shocker it was to hear that they were arranged to be married. I understand that some mafia's still believe in doing it that way, but that's just cruel. I still have hope in my heart that his life with his bride won't have a negative impact on my boys.

***

As I made my way to my car in the hospital basement, I saw that two of my car tires were flat. On closer inspection, I saw that there were slashes made in it and the paint was scratched with a sharp object.

My mind immediately went to Matteo's fiancé. She's the only one I have beef with or that I believe would go to such an extent.

I took out my phone and decided to call my brother. He would know what to do.

After the second ring he picked up "Hey Sis"

"Chase, where are you now?" I asked, immediately alerting him that something was out of place.

"I'm busy driving. What's wrong?"

"All my tires were slashed and my car's paintjob..." before I could complete my sentence, he interrupted me.

"Are you hurt? Where are you now?"

"I'm fine, I'll take an uber home. I just came down to the basement and saw my car in this condition"

"Wait for me at security I'm 5 minutes away from the hospital. Don't wait in the basement. I'll be there shortly" he said, then cut the call.

This car has been the first thing i bought when i started to earn serious money. I'm not someone who has any attachments to early possession or that likes to dress up or wear pounds of make-up, but I loved this master piece i customized to my liking.

It's sad to see it go, but maybe it is time for some change, like so many things in life.

I took my last step to the security office, which is situated in the basement, Chase's car came screeching around the corner and through the basement.

He was dressed in his normal office attire, which was an expensive black suit with a white shirt and black tie.

"Are you ok?" he asked, as he gave me a hug then scanned my body to see if I' injured.

I role my eyes at this "I told you I'm fine. When I got off work and got to my car, I was in this condition"

"Do you have an idea who this might be?" he asked.

I gave him a nod "I think it might be Matteo's fiancé" I said, making Chase give me a questioning look. He made a gesture with his hand for me to continue.

"She came to visit me today and threatened me" I said, looking down at the tarred floor.

"Bitch!" he exclaimed "come, let's head home. I'll get one of the guys to get your car" he said, leading me to his car.

On our way home we discussed the whole Giordano situation from the day I stepped foot on American soil, until today. Chase was a little pissed at me for keeping everything to myself once again.

He's scared that I would fall into depression or get panic attacks again. He feels that I've come a long way with my mental struggle and situations like these would only set me back.

I obviously didn't divulge the fact that I already had a panic attack at the hospital on the day I saw Matteo.

We got home just in time for dinner.

"Good evening my lovely family" Chase announced as we made our entrance.

"Oh Danny, my baby. You must be tired. I didn't see you properly since we got here" Aunt Drita said, as she gave me a hug.

"I'm so sorry, it was emergency after emergency, but I hope the cases don't increase during the week" I say.

I gave everyone hugs as we were in a happy hugging mood.

"Ma, she's a big shot at the hospital. My own cousin is the famous Dr. Harris" Flamur said.

"I'm definitely not famous" I said, in response while I threw my arm over her shoulder.

"Mommy!" Dylan came running in my direction as Uncle Besim came in after them.

"Hey, my baby, how was your day?" I asked, smothering him with kisses.

"He's on his way downstairs"

"Ma!" Max said while running in my direction.

"Hey baby, don't run" I said, which was no use.

"Come on guys, food is done" my mom said as she made her way to the dining room. We were too many people to sit on the kitchen island.

My other cousins trickled in, and we ate and had a lovely time chatting and catching up. Chase didn't bring up the car situation, but I knew it was just because the boys were still at the table.

After we ate, I ordered the boys to take a shower as we headed to the lounge to eat some bakllava with our mountain tea that my family brought with them for us to enjoy.

I will go and discuss Matteo with the boys once I head up in a bit.

As we got settled, my uncle cleared his voice and started to speak and the whole room fell into silence.

"Did you hear about the Italian's trucks that was hijacked?" he asked, waiting for me to answer.

I shook my head "no, this is the first time I'm hearing about hijacked trucks" I respond.

"They suspect us" Ervin, my cousin said.

I scrunch my forehead in a frown "Why would they think it's you?"

"Because of the shooting that happened at the restaurant. They also bombed Giordano's yacht and two warehouses" he said.

"Well, that's bad" I said, not really taking in the severity of the situation.

"They almost killed the boy's father. He was outside one of the warehouses when the bomb detonated" dad who has been quiet this whole time, said.

Now I understand why he's so stressed. He looked off from the last time I saw him. I mean, he is the father of my kids, and I wouldn't want any harm to happen to him.

"Do you know who it is?" I asked.

My uncle gave a nod "it is people from the underworld. They are not part of the mafia, but love doing dirty deeds. I just don't want word to get out about the boys and their lives being in any danger.

"I understand" I said, as I got up "I need to tuck the boys in. I'll be back" I said, pushing the thought of their lives being in danger to the back of my mind.

When I entered Dylan's bedroom, I saw both of them cuddled next to each other watching some cartoons. Both of them have their own bedroom, but they enjoy sharing a bed more than anything else.

"I need to take these Tv's out of your bedrooms" I said, making them groan in response.

"I need to tell you something" I announce to both of them.

"Your dad came to see me today"

Both of them snapped their heads looking at each other, then back at me.

"Yes Ma. What did he say?"

"He wants to meet you both, if you'll let him. I thought we could maybe do dinner with him tomorrow night?" I question.

Both of them responded in unison "Yes"

"How do you feel about meeting your dad?"

"Excited, I mean, we want to get to know him, but will you be like a couple now?" Max asked, making me laugh.

"No, he's engaged to one of the ladies that we met last week at the restaurant"

Both of them stopped smiling.

"What is wrong?" I asked.

"Will we have to see her if we see him?" Dylan now threw a question.

"Guys, your dad's a nice guy, and he will never allow anyone to lay a finger on you. Don't stress about her, ok? You have both of us, grandma, grandpa and your uncles. Oh, and don't forget about Uncle Besim and his whole family" I said, making them give naughty smirks.

"Will he like us?" Max asked, making my heart skip a beat.

"Aah, I think that man is already smitten with the both of you. I only saw stars in his eyes when I spoke with him today"

"You really think so?" Dylan asked.

"Yup, I believe so. I know you two wouldn't want to meet him for the first time without me, so can I send him a message to let him know that we will see him for dinner?"

Both gave a curt nod, making me smile at their hopeful innocence. I'd be damned if anyone broke their hearts.

I gave them some wet kisses and I tucked them in refraining from separating the two for the night. They always find their way into each other's room in the middle of the night, anyways.

I sent Matteo a quick text to get the meeting over and done with.

Me: Hi there, will you be available for dinner tomorrow night with the boys?

Matteo: ANYTIME!

Me: 19:00 at Tasha's?

Matteo:

Chapter 26

C hase and Julian decided to give the boys and I a lift to school and work this morning. They both decided to work half days for the whole week in order to spend more time with our cousins before they leave on Sunday.

I don't have the liberty to do so, but I have scheduled my surgeries so that I could be at home by 16:00 every day.

I need to get myself a new vehicle because I don't like taking Ubers or depending on people, even though I know my parents have vehicles I can borrow. I don't have any interest in keeping Range Rover after its fixed because I don't want to be reminded of what that bitch's guts.

I just hope Matteo can put her in her place.

As I walked into the hospital the corridors were quiet today, which is always a good thing because it means fewer sick people.

As I made my way towards the elevator, my thoughts went to Matteo and the conversation we had yesterday.

He doesn't come off as a bad human being. Well, I didn't mean that he doesn't kill people for a living, but I feel like he's a caring person underneath that cold façade that he's forced to display.

His eyes though, held a look of pain and helplessness in them. I hope getting to know the boys will brighten his life a little because they are just the purest.

My family told me that the trucks transporting the goods for the Italian Mafia are being highjacked by someone, but they don't know who yet. Their business has been losing a vast amount of revenue, setting their Mafia back financially.

Matteo built a name for himself in the legal business world according to my cousin and can hold his own. He will probably use his own funds to make up for their loss.

Even though my brothers and parents aren't directly involved in running the Mafia. We still use the family businesses to launder money for the Albanian Mafia as my family has to do their part. The thing is, we were born into it due to my mother being born into it and there's no way not to be part of it.

The mafia funded dad's businesses when he finished college, and he took the opportunity at the time to make a name for himself in the business world.

The mafia money cannot be traced back to my family due to my brother Chase that worked out a system to conceal the origins of it. Thus, to the world it seems though we aren't part of it, even though we are.

I try to shut my ears at the mention of the mafia business, but I can't help but to take in the information when I do spend time with family while they are discussing these things. My goal in life is to save lives and not take them, my family is aware of how I feel about that.

My mom and Uncle are the only two children that my grandparents had, and we don't have any other choice but to carry the legacy of the mafia shqiptare (Albanian Mafia) forward, in our own way.

Chase received the video footage from the hospital, but the guy that damaged my car had a mask on his face and wore a hoodie. So, it's hard to confirm who the culprit was.

As I know them, they won't give up until they find the culprit.

Matteo didn't respond to my last message last night confirming that he would meet us for dinner tonight. There's probably too much on his plate and I do understand, but a response would have been in order.

Now the boys are looking forward to meeting their dad. I just hope he responds before my workday is over.

I made a cup of coffee and got settled at my desk contemplating if I should send Matteo a message as I'm finishing my cup of goodness. I don't want to sound desperate or be a nuisance, but I'll go to any lengths to make sure my boys are happy.

I decided to place my pride in my back pocket and sent him a message.

Me: Hey, please confirm if dinner tonight is fine with you, if not then I will explain to the boys. Or let me know when you'll be available.

Let's hope he responds before tonight.

I was about to leave my office when my desk phone started to ring. The voice that spoke on the other side was the hospital director.

"Good morning, Dr. Harris"

"Morning Dr. Williams, how can I help you?"

"Could you come and see me after your surgeries at the end of the day before you leave, please?" he asked, sounding a little nervous.

"Is there a problem?" I asked, cutting straight to the point.

He starts to giggle before answering me "I don't want to take your focus off your work, but could you come and see me later today?" he insists, without answering my question.

"Ok" I said, thanked him and dropped than dropped the phone.

I then went ahead and had a meeting with my team that's assisting me with a high-risk surgery we're performing today.

Before I knew it, the day was over and done with. The last thing I had to do was go see why Dr. Williams wanted to see me.

Upon reaching his office I gave a brief knock, and he gave permission for me to enter.

He was sitting behind his desk with a document in front of him, looking utterly uncomfortable and red in the face. He's probably about to tell me something bad, so let's see.

"Good afternoon, Dr. Williams" I said in greeting, as I made my way over to his desk.

"Aah Dr. Harris, come take a seat, please" he said while directing me to the chair in front of his desk.

As I got situated, he started to clear his throat while fidgeting with the papers and stationery on his desk. Nervous much? But why?

I sat there waiting for him to compose himself while watching his every move like a hawk. I didn't say anything because I wanted my stare to reflect my un-botheredness with whatever he's about to throw my way.

I fear no man and what he's capable of. Life has taught me too much over the years.

"Dr. Harris, thank you for coming to see me. I won't keep you long, so I will cut right to the chase. You have been one of the best additions to my staff I've had in a very long time" he said, then paused to rummage through his drawer pulling out a piece of paper before continuing,

He slid the paper in my direction across the table. Upon glancing at it, I saw that it was a cheque with many zeros on it.

I remained silent and gave him a questioning look.

"You are one of the best at what you do in the world, but unfortunately the hospital has no choice but to let you go. Today has been your last day with us. The cheque is the amount we promised to pay you for the 6 months with us and I've added a little more" he announced as if I'm stupid as to what's happening here.

To tell you the truth, it came as no shock. I knew I was going to get heat.

"How much?" I asked him.

"That is 3 mill..."

"Not how much you are paying me. How much were you paid to get rid of me?" I asked, in a calm voice while cutting straight to the chase.

His face started to portray a panicked, shocked look, which told me I was correct.

"N...no" he said, while rubbing his face in annoyed panic. Probably contemplating if he should tell the truth or continue to lie. I remained calm even though I wanted to give him the middle finger and walk out.

"Well, you had a scuffle with the daughter of one of our biggest investors and if we were to keep you as part of the staff, then we would be losing a substantial amount that is required to keep the hospital operational"

"Good to know" I said as I got to my feet and picked up the cheque that read 3 million dollars. I started to laugh like a maniac while looking at the piece of paper in my hand.

After a good minute, I stopped and looked him straight in the eyes now with a blank expression on full display. I tore the cheque to pieces and made a little heap on his desk. I slid it over and straightened my back.

"It was nice knowing you and I wish the hospital success" I said, then exited his office without fighting or arguing because I feel there's no need for being petty.

Those that do unjust things toward others eventually meet their own downfall because of their own dirty deeds.

Luckily, I never brought anything personal to the hospital like pictures or files, so there was no need for me to get a box. There was also no reason for me to say goodbye to anyone because I did not make any friends while being here. Not that I would've.

I took my bag and my jacket and left the premises. I hailed a cab home and thought of the fact that I was just let go. The fact that, that bitch is clearly under the impression that she would be able to get me down.

But I have to thank her next time I see her because she did me a favor by getting out of this work contract with the hospital. Now I'm able to fully focus on my babies and family.

I have future plans for my career, but for now I want to enjoy life a little before I jump into anything new.

I totally forgot to check my phone, so upon opening my messages, I saw Matteo had responded a few hours earlier.

Matteo: "Hi there, I'm so sorry for not responding. I will be happy to join you for dinner. Can I pick you up?"

Me: "Yeah Sure"

Matteo: "Address?" he responds immediately.

Soon I reached home and my whole family were busy lounging around with drinks and some had hot chocolate. The weather has been chilly the last couple of days and the winter cold and snow will be hitting us very soon.

"Hey Danny" my brother Daniel said as he engulfed me in a hug.

"Hey bro, how was your day?" I asked as we made our way to the rest of our family.

"The day was awesome and yours?" he asked, but before I could answer he continued "I need to talk to you about something, but how was your day?" he asked as we headed into the lounge where the rest of the family were.

"Yeah, we can chat later" I told him, then faced the rest of the family "hej familje" (hey family) I announced as I made my way to my mom giving her a hug and holding her tight.

Everyone gave their greetings. Chase and the boys are probably on their way home from the boy's practice.

I breathed in mom's smell which calmed my soul. Sometimes all you need is your mother to remind you that all will be well and that bad situations does not last forever.

Mom tensed after a minute, probably realizing that something was wrong. She rubbed my head and back "what's wrong Daniella?" she asked in the softest motherly voice.

I pulled away from her and saw that all eyes were on me when my eyes scanned the room, which made me smile. We don't keep secrets from each other and regardless of how bad it is, it's better to share the good and bad times. That's why i love them so much.

"I was let go from my job. Today was my last job" I said, making mom gasp and the rest asked in unison "WHY!" making me chuckle.

"Matteo's fiancé" i said "she came to visit me at work yesterday and wanted to discuss co-parenting with me, seeing that she will be in the boy's lives. She then proceeded to make a scene in my office. She asked that i stay away from her man and when she talked about me using he boys to get to him i flipped and asked her to leave my office".

My family stood there with open mouths.

"What did Matteo say or didn't you ask him to keep his kurvë (bitch) on a leesh?" Aunt Drita asked, making me laugh.

"It's an arranged marriage and Matteo doesn't look to happy about marrying her from the interaction I saw between them" I answered.

"One would assume his family would come and ask for your hand in marriage seeing you two already have kids together" my cousin Fatmir taunt.

I role my eyes before answering him "No thank you. I just want the boys to have the presence of their dad in their life. They have missed out on each other for too long. That it, nothing more, nothing less"

"That boy if forced to marry the child of his best friend. He doesn't have a choice in the matter, unless he gives up being in control of the Mafia" Uncle Besem said.

"Uncle, how do you know all these things about their mafia, when you are living in Albania?" I asked.

"Femija im" (My child) there are some secrets that bastard Isaac must come clean with. He is putting pressure on that boy of his and trying to control him like a puppet, but we'll see who the real puppet is, eventually"

"What do you mean Uncle?" I asked because it sounded like there's much more that I'm not aware of.

"Don't worry your pretty little head sweetheart. The truth will turn the Giordano family on their heads, but that's a worry for another day" he said in his mysterious tone. Which indicated that he was done with the conversation.

This made me even more nosey now.

"Oh, before i forget. The boys and I will be having dinner with Matteo tonight. He's coming to pick us up" I informed my family and everyone looked at me like i was a ghost.

"Sarah, you better go help your child or she will walk out of this house in a potato sack" dad said, making me gasp in disbelief.

"Dad!" I whined.

"What?" he asked in his nonchalant attitude. I shook my head as i heard the garage door open and a few footsteps making their way in our direction.

"Ma!" they said before running in my direction and giving me hugs.

"Hey boys, how was your day?" i asked.

"Good mom. Why are you home so early?" Max asked.

"Well, today was my last day at work. I finished all my contract period and now I'm all yours. Morning noon and night" i said, as both of them stood there with grins on their faces.

"Your dad is picking us up at 18:30. We are going out for dinner" i said, making them stare up at me with shocked expressions.

"What's wrong?" Chase asked.

"Really Mom?" Dylan asked, with hope clearly visible in his eyes. Making my heart melt at the innocence in them.

"Yup" I said with a smile. As i glanced in the direction of my mom, seeing her wipe her eyes.

Chapter 27

I jumped into a quick, but oh so deserving hot shower and watched as the remnants of the crazy stressful day went down the drain. I didn't grasp the extent of the impact it had on me earlier, but I'm glad the day is over and I'm more than happy to be done with the hospital.

After finding the father of my kids, it feels like I can finally be the new best version of myself. Like a weight had finally been lifted after holding me back for so many years mentally and emotionally.

I never really understood the impact of not knowing who their dad was, actually had on me. In the back of my head, it always boiled down to, 'what if they asked me about him'. Luckily that's stress is over now.

After drying off, I wrapped my body in a fluffy towel and exited my on-suite bathroom into my bedroom.

I decided to get dressed in a little black dress with long sleeves, pantyhose underneath to keep warm and ending it off with a pair of black knee-high boots with a long beige coat to break the all black colored outfit. The coat must wait till I dry my hair though.

A knock could be heard as I was putting on my gold jewelry

"Come in" I said.

"Danny, do you have a minute before you leave?" my mother asked from the doorway with sadness and worry visible in her eyes.

Mom is a tough woman but will kill for her family. So, I wonder what's bothering her.

"Hey mom, sure" I said, as I made my way over to my bed and patted the spot next to me as I rubbed my hair dry with the towel it was wrapped in. "You know we love you right?" she asked.

"Yeah, mom and I love you too. What's wrong?" I asked.

"I feel so sad knowing you lost your job and I just wanted to make sure you are not beating yourself up over it. I mean, you worked so hard to be respected in the medical industry and helped so many over the years. I just hope this doesn't affect you...hmm... like..."

I knew what my mom meant. She was scared that what happened today, or these last few days would impact my mental health and that I would become the person I was for years. I have to assure her that I'm fine.

Before my mother could finish her sentence, I put my hand on hers and looked her straight in the eyes to give her some assurance "Mother, oh my beautiful Mother, I am doing well, actually she did me a favor by ending the contract for me with the hospital" I said, making mom scrunch her face up in confusion.

"You know, I thought that I had to have a job in order to prove to others that I made it in life regardless of my past of being a teen mom. You are aware that the reason for my traveling was because I wanted to build my knowledge and expertise in the shortest timeframe to become what and who I am today, but most of all to also to provide for the boys so that they don't lack in anything?" I question and she nods.

"Well, the more I spent away from the boys and my family, I started to develop a deep regret for taking on so much even though it was only for 6 months. I was beating myself up internally for missing out on important things or every time Chase, Daniel or Rafael took them to practice, or you and dad took them places after school. I missed out on so much and they won't stay small forever. One day I will open my eyes and they will be all grown up with their own lives and they will resent me for not being there when they needed me the most" I said, as I smiled looking at my mother's wet cheeks.

I wiped the tears from underneath her eyes. This is the strongest woman I know, but she's a softy when it comes to her loved one's. She loves all of us so much that she would give her all to make sure we were happy.

"If that means we will see more of you, then I am very happy" she smiled "you know you don't have to work at all. We could go on shopping sprees even though I know you are not a material person, but now we can spend more time with you since your back and it seems for good"

I shook my head in agreement "Thanks mom, and I think I should get away from my normal routine, live a little and enjoy life as all of you have been nagging me about"

Mom lifted her eyebrows in surprise "what a pity he's about to marry that girl" mom muttered under her breath as she got up from my bed.

"Mom, I heard that" I reprimanded, giving her a questioning look.

"What? I mean, it would've been nice to see the boys grow up having both parents that are together under one roof in their lives. Even though he doesn't come from the best family in the world, his blood still flows in my grandbaby's veins. What is so awful about wanting that for my babies? " she rolled her eyes.

I sat there with my mouth agape and in shock at what my own mother was uttering. I guess the Mafia does flow in her veins.

"I must give it to you though, he's one attractive young man and it's a great shame that he's with the daughter of that scum and the apple sure didn't fall far there. Oh, and don't think about forgiving that bitch. You have to make an example out of her, so that the rest of those backstabbing cowards can see that the Mafia shqiptare (Albanian Mafia) is not to be trifled with. We don't rule over Europe's underworld because of niceties" she stated, as if she was tasting something disgusting on her tongue.

"I know she's not the nicest person in the world, but what do you mean mom? Do you know her family?" I asked, ignoring her request for revenge, now even more curious than ever.

"The mafia world is a small world regardless of where you are based in the world. Everyone is somehow connected with everyone and knows about everyone. He isn't part of the Mafia but he's the best friend of Matteo's father, he gets exposed to the world and does business in our world. He is a serial cheater in his personal life and the same in the business world. He built that wealth by screwing so many people over, but he gets protection from Matteo's Mafia, so he does whatever he wants. They are no good, but I can see Matteo is something different" Mom said, deep in thought.

"He's being forced to marry her and from my conversation with him, he doesn't seem too happy about it" I said.

"What a shame" mom said, shaking her head "and that mother of his is like a puppet that kisses the ground that man walks on. No brains in that empty head of hers only air and definitely no backbone"

"Why do you say that?" I asked, knowing my mom is on a spilling tea mission.

"She came from a very poor background. So, the day she met her husband she started living for him instead of herself. I sometimes think that she loved him and his money more than her self-respect. Poor puppet" mom sigh, deep in thought.

"In the beginning of their marriage that man cheated so much and on occasion he would disappear with woman at events from what I saw with my own two eyes. She would always look so sad and dejected when she saw what was going on, but still tried her best to look past it and held up a brave face" mom said and started to giggle.

"He also tried his luck with me at some stage, but I wasn't interested and at the time I was already dating your dad and so madly in love that my parents couldn't stop me from remaining in this country after my studies"

"Really Ma?" I asked, shocked.

"Yes, but the Giordano's were also forced to get married very early like they wan, that's probably why. Maybe he didn't love her in the beginning, but he changed his ways for her when they started having children because later in their marriage the seemed like a real couple as time went by"

We were interrupted by a knock on the door before I could ask my mom more questions about Matteo's family. The door opened slowly. I smiled at my two cousins and my aunt making their way into my bedroom "What's up cuz?" Elira said as she sat down in my chair Infront of my vanity.

"Oh, about to do my hair" I said.

"Nah, I'm here to do that" Flamur said as she made her way in my direction. She pulled me up to my vanity as Elira got up and took my place on the bed.

"So, dear. Will we have a wedding soon?" Aunt Drita asked, almost making me choke on my spit.

"What!?" I asked in horror at the thought "No, he's engaged to be married and I don't have the desire to be with anyone, much less an engaged man" I said.

"Is the woman he's engaged to a mountain?" Aunt Drita asked, making me frown.

"What do you mean, Aunt Drita" My mom and cousins started to laugh. I just sat there looking at them waiting for an answer.

"What mom is trying to say is, if she's not a mountain then she can be moved right out of his life" Flamur said.

I sat there shocked at the unadulterated nonchalance of these woman. The fact that they want to see us together is laughable.

"Well, I'm not interested in him in that way. I just want him to be a good father to my boys, that's all" I stated.

The conversation was over as quickly as it started, when another knock could be heard on the door. When mom opened the door, my brother Daniel said that Matteo was waiting downstairs.

"Where are the boys?" I asked Daniel.

"They are already dressed, waiting downstairs while staring at the man that is the reason for their existence" Dan said.

I took my purse and left my room with the ladies following behind me. When I reached the front door, I saw Matteo standing there dressed in a black suit with a white shirt, no tie and the first two buttons undone.

The boys were standing and shamelessly looking at him from head to toe and he did the same, but you could see the playful smirk Matteo had on his face.

All their eyes snapped in our direction as we descended the stairs. Matteo could be seen taking huge gulps. Oh no, please don't look at me with those eyes like you want to do sinful things to me. I don't feel like having more drama in my life, please.

"Good evening" I said, and he sent a greeted back as I caught his eyes raking over my body. I introduced him to my mother who gave him a good intimidating look from head to toe before shaking his hand.

I introduced the boys to their dad, and they only said, 'good evening' and continued staring at him.

"Where's the other's" I asked, glancing around. My aunt and cousins were also nowhere to be seen.

"The men left before I came up. They went to a cigar bar" mom said.

"It was nice meeting you, Mrs. Harris" Matteo said to my mom and then focused his attention on me "shall we leave?" Matteo asked.

I gave him a nod and we made our way outside with the boys after bidding mom and Daniel a good night.

Matteo held the back door open as well as opening the passenger door on the driver's side. I wanted to get in at the backseat of the car, but Matteo stood in front of the doorway and only allowed the boys who's still silent to get in at the back

"Really?" He questioned, and I just rolled my eyes ignoring his question as I climbed in and sat in the front seat next to him in his sleek black car with heavily tinted windows.

We arrived at the restaurant or steakhouse to be exact in less than 20 minutes and drove there in total silence. The boys would have bombarded him with questions by now, but I think they are just as nervous as Matteo seemed.

When we made our way inside the eatery all eyes were on us. It's probably because of Matteo's status as a businessman. I heard he was quite the famous one in the business world.

We took our seats in and gave our drinks orders and as the waiter left, I decided to break the silence because this was becoming ridiculous, but before I could Matteo started to talk to the boys.

"So what grade are you boys in?" he asked, but they remained quiet, so I decided to help them.

"Max, Dylan" I said, gaining their attention "remember the day you mentioned you wanted to meet your dad?" I asked and both of them nodded to my relief "he's here now and he wants to be part of your life. He wants to make up for all the years that he did not know about the both of you, so please don't blame him or treat him any less than you do me" I asked, as I glanced in Matteo's direction, I could see his eyes soften.

"Are you a bad guy, like the people last week at the restaurant and was that man who confronted our mom at our table also your family?" Dylan asked.

"I am really sorry for the way that man, my dad have spoken to your mother and I'm also really sorry for the way the rest of my family behaved that night, but I can assure you that I will never allow anyone to disrespect you or your mother ever again" he said, glancing at all of us.

"You know, I was surprised to find out that I had two handsome boys, but I felt bad knowing you had to grow up all these years without a dad" he said, when Max, the quiet one of the two interrupted him.

"Why didn't he know about us mom?" Max, my quiet child, asked me, but before I was able to answer Matteo saved me.

"Your mother was looking for me, but she couldn't get hold of me because I was out of the country for training" he said, saving my behind on that one.

"I and truly sorry for missing out on your lives, but I just want to be part of your life from now onward and be there for you, if you'll let me" he said.

"OK, but you have to come to every competition we have" Dylan demanded, while Max sat there with a smirk.

"I will. So, when is your next competition?" Matteo enquired.

"We have one this Saturday. Will you be able to make it?" Max asked.

"I won't miss it for the world" their dad said.

"Matteo, how does it feel to look at two exact copies of yourself?" I asked, breaking the ice between them.

"Freaky, but in a very good way" he said, giving the both of them a huge grin.

As the night progressed the boys started to loosen up more and they talked about all the things they love to do when they are not practicing Judo. Matteo listened to them intently and tried to ask as many questions in order to learn more about them.

We left the eatery at 22:30 and the boys were busy yawning on the ride home. As we drove down the secluded road towards our estate, Matteo took me out of my stupor.

"When you gave me your address earlier today, I never knew it would be in such a secluded part of New York. Actually, I never thought that there were such huge estates just outside the city" he said.

"Yeah, we love and value our privacy a lot"

"That makes sense why there's not much information about your family on the internet" he stated.

"You searched us on the internet?" I asked in shock.

"Yeah, I'm not going to beat around the bush and lie. I was intrigued by you since the day I met you" he said, without shame.

I didn't answer him because I didn't want to entertain whatever It is he's trying. Luckily, we arrived home, but the boys were fast asleep and lightly snoring.

"Can you please help me carry the one and I will carry the other one please?" I asked.

Matteo got out and scooped Max in his one arm as I was about to pick Dylan up, he asked me to put Dylan in his other arm.

"Won't they be too heavy for you to carry up the stairs" I asked.

He just gave me a blank stare. I directed him to our upstairs quarters of the house.

"You can put them both in Dylan's room. They like to share a bed" I said.

He stood there as I undressed the boys and dressed them in their PJ's, then tucked them in.

"Would you like to drink a cup of coffee before you head out?"

Chapter 28

Matteo's POV

I stood in the middle of the bedroom with my arms stuck to my sides, watching Daniella undress the boys who were half asleep and dress them in their Pj's.

Like she had done so many times before and she did so probably alone. She raised them and I respect her for raising such respectable, good-mannered kids who would clearly jump a bullet for this woman they call 'Ma' as I've seen with my own eyes.

If that isn't a reflection of them being raised with true family values, then I sure don't know anything about what real family is.

They could have hated or resented me for not being in their lives, but they didn't.

I've missed out on her pregnancy, on them being born, becoming toddlers, the nighttime nappy runs, the feeds and 9 years of their existence.

I want to catch up on the time we've lost and make the most of what we have now and not a damn person will stop me.

Watching their mannerisms and little interactions with each other gave me a glimpse of how close they are with each other. I know they are twins and would be close, but for heaven's sake, it's like the one already knows what the other don't like or what the other's reaction would be.

Can you believe they are mine? Because I sure can't.

Knowing about them and meeting them gave me a better perspective on the life I'm living and the direction I want my life to go with them in it. I had a plan since seeing their innocent eyes and I plan to follow through.

"Would you like to drink a cup of coffee before you head out?" Daniella asked, taking me out of my thoughts.

"Sure" I answered her as we made our way out of their room.

This estate is massive, well hidden, and this house is so huge, but very Beautifull. It appears they have their own part or wing of the house for privacy probably.

I follow behind Daniella to the open plan kitchen lounge area on this side and take a seat on the couch. She was busy preparing the coffee machine as I sat there watching her.

"This house is huge" I said, gaining her attention.

She looked up "Yeah, my parents made sure to build each child a wing and attached it to the main house with the hope that we never move out. It also assures everyone's privacy should any of my siblings decide to get married and start a family"

"Are you not interested in marriage?" I asked to see where she's at on that topic.

She shook her head, which made my heart drop a little "I have my boys and that's enough for me" she said, as she walked over in my directions and placed my cup in front of me on the coffee table.

"Well, that's sad. I mean, you are one beautiful, smart woman and deserve someone that will appreciate you for who you are" I said.

"Nah, that ship has sailed. I used to have these types of hopes and aspirations when I was a teenager, but life sometimes throw curveballs which change the trajectory and perspective on one's life"

She seemed very uncomfortable talking about the topic and changed the discussion to the boys.

"The boys have a competition on Saturday. Would you be able to attend?" she asked.

"I wouldn't miss it for the world"

"Good, good, they will be happy to know you will be attending" she said.

"Really?" I asked, making her look up from her cup.

"Oh yeah, they are just shy because I mean, it's your first-time meeting each other, but I can assure you they will warm up to you once you spend more time with them"

"That's good to know. You should also send me some of their expenses and things you want me to cover, and I'll settle it. I don't want you to take anything on yourself financially, but I know you won't allow me to cover all their expenses" I said, smirking at her.

"Then I have to admit, you know me well. My dad and brothers have been the best with them and always go over and above for them, but they are not their dad. I just want you to be the best dad to them and be there for them as a father figure. That is the most important and if you're unable to meet commitments, just communicate and we can work together to make sure the boy's needs are met. I also have more time now, let's start there"

"You have more time?" I asked, making her eyes go wide as if she did not want me to know.

"Oh yeah, that" she said while rubbing her face and sitting back in her seat "I was fired today"

"What?" I asked shocked because she is a freaking good Doctor and since knowing her this short time, she has saved so many people in my family already.

"Yes, the day you came to visit me and just before you came, your fianc..."

"Don't call her that" I said while holding my hand up for her to stop, making her frown "I'm sorry, continue"

"Well, the woman in your life put in a complaint about the day she came to my office, and I already told you what happened that day. She threatened the hospital obviously and they had no choice but to give me the boot"

I got up and paced as my heart started to beat erratically out of anger, but I know anger won't solve this problem that is spilling into her life, just because she's the mother of my kids.

"I need you to promise me, that what I'm about to tell you will remain between us?"

"Yes" she said, nodding vigorously.

Two days later....

I left Daniella's house with more confidence than I ever had in the last few days as I made my way to my hotel. Yeah, I moved out the first night that bitch moved in.

My family isn't the happiest with me moving out and Gina's dad has been blowing my phone up saying his daughter is distraught, but I don't give a damn. Who still runs after dick in this day and age?

Thank heavens he's still in the hospital.

It's Aunt Paola's birthday today and she decided to host a dinner for the whole family. They can't go big because of all the injuries everyone sustained that night at the restaurant. She also requested that I bring the boys.

I asked Daniella if she would allow the boys to attend the dinner with me and she agreed as long as they remain safe. I also got a warning that she will send the whole Albanian mafia to eliminate us.

Aunt Paola has always been a little more of a motherly figure to me when my mom stood by dad against me at times. Aunt Paola is the one with the backbone.

That's why I couldn't refuse her request even though I felt it was a little too soon for me to introduce them to the family.

I was getting ahead of myself, by asking Daniella to accompany us, but she is one clever woman explaining why it would be a bad idea. After our talk last night, it made sense.

FUCK!!! I want her so bad. She's perfect!!!!

I just stopped in front of her house after driving through the main gate with guards that always seem to pop out of nowhere. I have to admit they have one awesome setup that seems to be away from the city but still part of New York and only people with their amount of wealth would be able to afford something like this.

I mean, they are most probably wealthier than our Mafia, but you would never know that if you saw any of them because they look like your normal everyday people.

I reached their front door and wanted to knock, but the door was opened by her mother, and she held a huge smile on her face.

I stuck my hand out for her to shake "Good afternoon, Mam"

"It's Sarah, dear and here we don't like shaking the hands of people we know. We give hugs" she said, stretching out her arms, then whispered in my ears "hurt my babies and I'll cut off your scrotum and shove it in your mouth. Then I'll deliver your lifeless body to your family's doorstep" she said, while holding that smile tapping me on the back.

"I understand" I said while gulping, not wanting to start any argument with her. I thought the woman in my family were tough, but this woman is something else.

"Boys! Your dad is here" she gave a shout down the hallway. I heard a voice being cleared behind me and when I turned around, I saw Daniella's dad and uncle standing in the hallway.

I walked in their direction and shook both their hands "Mr. Harris and Mr. Hyseni, nice to meet you" I said.

"Good to meet you son" Mr. Harris said, while Daniella's uncle just assessed me with his scrutinizing gaze.

"We need to talk sometime next week if you have time" Daniella's Uncle said.

"No, problem. Just let me know and I'll be there" I said, and he just gave me a nod as the boys came running down the hallway.

"Boys don't run" Mr. Harris grumbled, making me smile.

"Sorry Gran..." the one twin said. I think It's Dylan because he has a little scar on his chin. Other than that, I don't think I would have been able to distinguish between the two.

"Hey boys" I said, as I looked at them with a smile.

"Hi...mhmmm...dad" Max said, making Mr. Harris and Mr. Hyseni smirk. You can clearly see the love in both of their eyes for the boys.

"Hi dad" Dylan said without any qualms.

They were both dressed in Navy blue chinos and white three button t-shirts.

Daniella came walking down the same hallway that everyone came out of "Hi Matteo" she said, giving me a smile.

"Hi Daniella" I said, sounding like a schoolboy. My eyes lingered on her a little too long and her mom cleared her throat.

"Boys it's cold outside. Scarves and coats please" she said, taking me out of the spell this gorgeous woman has put on me.

We said our goodbye and I headed out with both the boys in tow. They got in the back seat, and we drove off to my aunt's house.

I decided to break the ice "how was your day boys?"

Dylan was the first to talk, like always "It was good, we had school and practice and then we came home in time to get ready to go with you"

"And you Max?" I asked.

"The same as him" he said.

He has a totally different personality then Dylan.

"Ok boys, here's the deal. We are going into a house where my whole family will be"

"Is it the same people of that night at the restaurant?" Max asked.

"Unfortunately, yes, but I want you to inform me if they say or do anything that you don't like. Remember that I am on your side always, but don't be disrespectful towards them first"

"Will we see you regularly now that we have found you?" Dylan asked, making my heartbeat erratically in my chest that I even start hearing it in my ears.

I smiled, while looking into the rearview mirror "I'm not going anywhere, and I will always have your back for as long as there's air in these lungs of mine" I assured them. I could see them looking at each other smiling.

We stopped in front of my aunt's house "ready boys?" I asked looking back at them.

Both of them gave me nods, then we headed inside.

Chapter 29

Matteo's POV

I walked past the guards with my boys, one on each side, and headed inside like the proud father I am. I have been going through shit with my dad since he found out about them, but nothing makes my chest swell more with pride than seeing the two exact copies of myself exist.

I could see both of their demeanors instantly change into an expressionless façade as soon as we stepped inside.

I must thank the person who trained my boys. They are way ahead for their age. I was still playing around being a kid at their age, way more than I trained. Daniella and her family did good, and, in the world, we reside it's required.

Their Mom did good.

When we entered the huge dining room, everyone was busy standing around, chatting and drinking some beverages, probably waiting for the rest of the family to arrive before dinner started.

They didn't even notice that we entered until I cleared my throat "good evening family" I said as we stood there, each holding the gifts I bought earlier.

"Aah! Teo! Welcome, welcome. Oh, look at these two handsome boys, Teo" Aunt Paola said while making her way towards us.

All attention was now on us as Dad stood there talking with his brothers and brother's in-laws, who were sitting in the corner loungers. They turned and looked at us as soon as Aunt Paola greeted us.

Dad didn't look happy, but I didn't give a damn.

"Happy birthday Aunt Paola, these are for you" I said, ignoring the daggers my dad was throwing my way. I gave Aunt Paola a hug then handed her the gift.

"Thank you Teo and thank you for bringing the boys" she said the boy's part subtly under her breath so the rest couldn't hear the last part.

She turned her full attention to the boys "hi boys, my name is Aunt Paola. Thank you for attending my birthday dinner" she said while hugging them. I wanted to burst out laughter at their facial expressions, reflecting just how uncomfortable they were.

"Hey Fratello (brother) and hallo my nipotti (nephews), I am your dad's brother, Julian and it's nice to meet you" Julian said as he offered his hand to the boys.

"Nice to meet you" both of them said simultaneously. Julian continued to chat with them while glancing around looking for my sister so that I could introduce her to them.

All the cousins, aunts, nieces and nephews introduced themselves to them and I could see their awkward expressions.

Alessia came walking through the door with my arch nemesis, Emma, and made her way in my direction with a huge smile.

When she reached me, I wrapped her in my arms and gave her a hug "hey, little sis. How have you been?" I asked ruffling her hair. I haven't seen her in a few days due to my falling out with dad and we used to see each other daily.

"Oh, brother bear, I've been good but I'm not here for you" she said while focusing her attention on the boys "hallo nephews" she said while approaching them with her arms out, pushing everyone away from the boys.

"Alessia, you're scaring the boys" Julian said, making the boys chuckle. Julian introduced the boys to Alessia who couldn't get enough of them while my dad stood there staring.

My mom entered and I could hear her dramatic gasp from the doorway "Matteo, oh Matteo" mom said, as she teared up while looking at them.

I knew what that meant. She wanted to be a grandma so bad but she's scared of dad.

"Boys, come meet your grandma" I said.

They walked over in her direction and stood in front of her "hi Grandma" both said.

Mom placed her hands on the boys' shoulders "hello my babies. You are so handsome and look just like your daddy did when he was your age" she said.

Vito was the last to arrive as he came walking in, giving me a nod, then his eyes focused on his target, the boys.

"Hey guys, my name is Vito. Please don't call me uncle, I'm too young for that sh..." he said, then stopped himself as he realized that they were still kids.

"Everyone, please take your seats in dinner is about to be served" one of my aunts announced.

I sat next to Dylan and Max decided to sit on his other side, then the bitch Emma decided to place her behind next to Max. She has been awfully chatty and bubbly tonight and look like she had a few before she came here from the red tint of her nose. That has always been her giveaway.

The dinner table was lively as everyone was talking and trying to keep the boys entertained.

As dessert was served, I glanced to my side and could see dad approaching me. I first thought he was on his way to the bathroom, but he stopped while I faced Vito who was sitting opposite me.

Dad is currently not talking to me. He has made my life a living hell. He took back all the properties he gave me and started running parts of the Mafia again.

I feel so disappointed in him for not recognizing my contributions to the family business that I've made since running it. Making money means so much to him, that he's unaware who catapulted the revenue to where it is today.

He cleared his throat making me look in his direction "dad" I said, not bothering to introduce the boys whom he doesn't like to him.

He nudged his head in the direction of the doorway, which means that I must follow him. I gave a signal to Vito to keep an eye on the boys and then I turned my attention to my boys to let them know.

"Dylan, Max, I am quickly going in there to talk to your grandpa. I'll be back" I said and left the table after both of them gave me a nod in agreement.

I went into Uncle Antonio's office and saw dad sitting on the long leather couch with a cigar in his hand smoking. He indicated to the leather chair opposite him, and I sat as indicated.

I didn't start the conversation because just as mad as he is for me, I am mad at him as well.

"What are they doing here?" he asked, as he inhaled the cigar smoke.

"With all due respect dad, those kids are my flesh and blood. Do you expect me to deny being their father? Do you realize what you are asking of me?"

"I don't care" he stated, elevating his tone a little.

And for the first time in my 26 years of life I could see the pure unadulterated evil in my dad's eyes. The eyes that looked at me with so much pride and love throughout the years and now I am seated in front of an unknown monster.

I am aware that Mafia's consist of monsters, but to deny your own grandkids is a step too far. I have never been so hurt and disappointed as I am today because the foundation of our Mafia has always been our family.

"What do you mean you don't care, dad? They are your flesh and blood as well. I know you haven't formally met them, but they are my kids, and it would be wrong of me to turn my back on them. That goes against everything you ingrained in me since birth. Family above all else, or did you forget that dad?"

"So, I see you made your decision. Good, good" he said, as he nipped the cigar in the ashtray, while nodding his head "from today onwards, you will no longer be the Capo. I am taking back the business and will run everything on my own. I don't care if you visit your family, but you are not welcome at my house anymore" he said, with finality in his voice.

I was preparing myself to end things with him and now he did me a huge favor.

"Pops, did you forget?" I asked, then continued "the business was never mine to begin with. You never fully signed the business over to me. So, I'm not losing anything"

"It's a good thing I didn't then" he stated.

"NO!" I shouted as I slammed my hand on the oak coffee table "You never trusted or respected me enough, even after I turned the business from a million dollar to a billion-dollar operation. After I increased our clientele. Why do you hate Daniella and the kids so much? Why do you hate her family?" I asked looking into his eyes, not giving him a choice but to answer me, but my attempts were futile after he said the last part.

"Take them and leave before I make you leave this house" he said, with finality in his voice without even bothering to answer me on the Daniella question.

I got up without giving it a second thought and reached the table where everyone was still sitting but was arguing amongst each other as the boys stood there with angry expressions on their faces.

Before I could react, I saw Alessia slap Emma across the face.

"What is going on!" I asked, in a loud voice gaining everyone's attention "boys, what's wrong?" I asked as I made my way to them.

They gave glances to each other, but Alessia was quick to answer.

"Our dear cousin over there was busy bullying Max and Dylan defended his brother"

I was already pissed at my dad, and I didn't want to deal with this bitch today, but I've had enough.

When I glanced across the room everyone was quiet while Emma stood there with an evil smirk on her face.

How dare you? You did it at the restaurant and now again"

"She what?!" Aunt Theresa, her mother Asked, in shock.

"Emma has been bullying the boys at the restaurant the night of the shooting" Julian said, with and equal pissed expression on his face.

"I'm sorry, Matteo. I will sort this out with Emma, and I can assure you that this will never happen again" Aunt Theresa said, then she turned her attention to the boys "boys, I am so sorry for you aunt's behavior. I am her mother, and I will make sure that she does not lay a hand on you again"

Emma sat there at the table with her smirk still evident not giving a damn. She is the fruit of her parents' labor. She has been spoilt rotten since birth.

"Aunt Paola" I said gaining her attention "thank you for having us, but I have to get the boy's home. They still have school tomorrow"

"No problem, Teo. Thank you for attending tonight and please bring the boys again"

"Boys, come get your coats, we're leaving" I said as I held it out to them.

We said our goodbye and left.

I checked the time on my watch and saw that it was 20:30, so I decided to spoil them, and I could also get to know them a little better "boys, would you like some ice-cream?"

"Yes, please" the both of them said in unison. I chuckled at their response.

We spend another hour walking around in Central Park with a few of my men following behind. The boys have loosened up so much around me that they started to crack jokes in between our conversation.

They were interested in my childhood and life before I met them. I told them as much as I could, but I also assured them that I would never turn my back on them, ever and that I loved them from the moment I heard of their existence.

Seeing their faces light up at my confession of love for them, told me that my life is moving in the right direction.

It also made me think of my dad whom I also looked up to. Regardless of how much I love my family, I will never allow them to cause a rift between my kids and me.

My father's behavior has changed my perception of what a true family is and I won't allow any of them to harm what's truly mine.

My boys deserve my world.

Chapter 30

Daniella's POV

I was taken out of my daze when I heard my mother mention my name to gain my attention.

"Daniella"

"Yeah, Mom?"

"Please, take the salads to the table for me" Mom ordered, giving me the side eye accompanied with a frown.

"On It, Mom" I said, as I took two bowls out into the dining room to escape her stare.

It is late Friday afternoon and we're busy setting up for our traditional Albanian feast, as my dad call it. We were busy the whole day slaving away at all the ethnic dishes prepared by all the ladies.

I only helped to chop and slice where I had to cause I clueless when it comes to cooking, but ask me to cut open a body, then I'll filet....what the freak am I thinking. I need to do something to get back into a surgery or two before

I lose my mind. Maybe as a hobby while the boys are in school during the day because I think I'm busy losing my good mind.

We made berek, fasule, tavie kosi, dolma, different salads, lots and lots of lamb because we love our meat and my cousins made sure to bring us some raki from Albania, which is an alcoholic beverage with high alcohol content.

My mind isn't really fully focused on our family night. It's more focused on Matteo and the troubles he is going through currently with his family.

I mean, he is the father of my babies. How can I not be concerned? If anything happens to him, it will affect the boys.

He took it upon himself to pick the boys up for school and drop them off at home after school, and they are totally smitten with their dad, which I'm thrilled about too. I can see he's trying to make up for lost time and having him be part of their lives was the best decision I've made since giving birth to them.

They have missed out on each other for too long and it seems though the boys were all Matteo needed, to give his life some purpose.

He told me so much and I didn't share any of it with my family, even though I know I can trust my family, but I promised him that I would keep it between us.

My family is the best at keeping secrets, though, and they do not judge people. That's why I love them so much.

I forgot to inform him how I'm an overthinker and will be stressed on his behalf.

One of the points he mentioned was that he was looking for a way not to marry his fiancé and then the next night he came here dropping the boys off after his aunt's party, to tell me that he told his dad he wouldn't marry her.

But then he told me about his dad not being happy about the boys' existence and that he's not the head of the Mafia anymore for that reason. That made my heart drop. How could that man not like his own grandkids?

I shake my head trying to get my thoughts on the night because my mother is on my ass and watching me like a hawk.

I made sure to contact Vivian as I hadn't heard from her in a while because she was out of the country for a long time on business and returned earlier today.

Apparently, they ironed out their issues and Chase agreed that he would make time for her, going forward. He also realized that he's not getting any younger and that she is the perfect one for him. I couldn't agree more.

My parents adore Vivian and think she is a kind and beautiful woman. I, however, think I just made my first friend.

We have been keeping each other updated on life, and she's an easy person to talk to. I like her because she's not pretentious and lets money get to her head.

Everyone was busy in the lounge, playing board games, cozying up next to the fireplace as we were waiting for Vivian to arrive.

I saw the wine tray was full of raki and other alcoholic beverages, which gave me the indication that it would be a very long night. It also indicates that my family intends to fully let loose tonight.

Aunt Drita and my cousins were busy setting the table while I was busy loading the table with food.

Just as my mind went to her again, the guards called to let us know she was on her way onto the property. I couldn't wait any longer, so I rushed to the door to meet her there, with Chase following directly behind me.

Vivian had to be informed of our family connection with the Mafia after the restaurant shooting, mostly because Chase wanted to be an open book from the start, and it seems she is 'it' for him.

I opened the door as the gust of chilly air entered through the front door.

Chase stood next to me with his arm around my shoulder with a huge grin on his face.

"Oh, what a sight to behold, my brother is in love" I said as he looked down at me, who was way shorter than him.

"Damn right I am, Sis" he said as her car stopped in front of us. Chase went and opened the door.

"Hey Babe. I missed you" he said as he wrapped his arms around her and crashed his lips on hers.

"Hey, I missed you too" she responded by reciprocating his kiss and included a few giggles as his hands went to her butt.

"Guys, can we keep it PG13, please. My heart won't be able to handle all of this" I said as I drew circles in the air with my hands, making the both of them laugh.

"Danny! Oh, I missed you too!" she said as she stretched her arms in my direction and rushed to hug me. Making me giggle and I did the same meeting her halfway.

"Maybe It's time I arrange a date for you. There's nothing that a good lay won't fix" Chase said as he gave me a taunting smirk.

I just gave him one of my best 'throwing up' faces.

He ignored me and grabbed Vivian's overnight bag from the back seat. I just smirked in surprise at my big brother having a sleepover with a girl. I proceeded to walk into the house with Vivian as Chace eventually followed behind.

Vivian caught me up on her time away as we walked, and I swear I thought her head was going to break off as she looked around in awe of our house.

"Hallo sweetheart, it's so nice to see you again" My mother said, coming from the corner and giving her a hug.

"Ah the beautiful girl of the other night" Aunt Drita said, also giving her a hug.

"It's so nice to see all of you again and thank you for having me" she said "this house! I'm at a loss for words. It's so beautiful" Vivian said, making everyone laugh at her facial expressions.

"Maybe you should move in with us then the house will be a little fuller" Daniel proposed and proceeded to hug her as well.

"I might just take you up on that offer" Vivian said, then laughed it off. She probably thinks Daniel was lying.

My mother would also be very happy if more people could live here. She has been trying to fill this house up since they started having kids. I swear, if she could've had more kids, she would probably have ten. Unfortunately, her womb had to be removed after Daniel was born, due to complications.

"Dinner is ready. We can head to the dining room" Flamur announced.

"Boys don't run" Dad said as Dylan and Max left the board games and ran towards the dining room.

"Mom, will dad also come tonight?" Dylan asked, looking at me with a hopeful expression clearly visible on his face.

"No baby, why do you ask that?"

"I just thought that he might come because the whole family is here" he answered.

Mom jumped in before I could answer "bebet e mia te vogla (my little babies), your daddy is probably with his family tonight, but we will make sure to invite him next time, ok?"

"Ok" was the only response he gave in satisfaction. Mom just gave me a slight glance. I don't know what she's trying to tell me. She will probably corner me another time or did she want me to invite him? Nah.

"Good evening, lovely people" we heard someone announcing their entrance from the doorway and saw Rafael and his brother Carlos making their way to the table.

"Hey, how have you two been? I haven't seen you in some time" I asked as Rafel came to sit in the seat next to me and Carlos joined on the other side of the table.

He whispered into my ear "good, but I need to talk to you later" he said.

I looked in his direction and gave him a questioning look, but he ignored my stare and continued to talk to the rest of the people at the table.

"Hey Danny, nice to have you back home" Carlos said.

"Nice to be back" I said "but, where have you been hiding?" I asked, as I haven't seen him in some time.

"He has a girlfriend now" Chase pipe's up, making Carlos blush.

"Ah, the baby is no baby no more" I say, making everyone laugh and Carlos go red from embarrassment.

"You better bring her home, so we can meet her" Dad said.

They are part of our household and my parents made sure they had their own rooms in our house when they were in the country, and they are here every other week.

Carlos is in college, so he sometimes comes home to eat a proper meal and get the maid to do his laundry. The funny thing is, they call my mother and father mom and dad, which has always been the cutest thing to hear. Actually, my crazy mother insisted they call her that.

We prayed and then stuffed then started to stuff our faces as the conversation and laughter flowed through the room.

Once the boys were done it seemed as though they had had enough of the day. I walked with them to make sure they got settled and dressed in proper sleep attire.

They still had a competition to compete in tomorrow, but luckily it starts at 11:00 and not 8:00 in the morning like other times. They had no choice but to hit the sack early.

"Hey boys, are you exited for your competition tomorrow?" I asked, as they snuggled next to each other. I turned the heat up in the room because it was freezing cold in here.

"Yeah, kinda. Will dad still come tomorrow?" Max asked.

"He said he would, but why are you constantly talking about him. Are you too throwing me to the dogs now?" I joked, tickling them and smothering the both of them with kisses.

"No, we would never do such a thing. You are our first love, Ma" Dylan piped up through the giggles.

"I better be" I said giving them the playful side eye "I'm just kidding. I love the fact that you have a good relationship with your dad" I said giving them both some kisses.

"How is your arm and thigh, Max?" I asked.

"Better, but the bruises are still there" he said, with a sad look in his eyes.

Max isn't a confrontational person, and it takes him a long time before losing his cool, but he will protect the ones he loves with all he has.

I didn't forget about that ex-fiancé and now I have Matteo's cousin also on my hitlist. All chickens eventually come home to roost, and I will make sure that both of them see their day.

You can fuck with me all you want, but my kids are a no-go zone.

After tucking the boys in I went back downstairs and saw everyone moved to the entertainment area. Daniel was dancing with my mother as the rest were chatting and laughing.

As soon as I entered, I saw Raff make his way in my direction as I settled my behind on the couch.

"What's wrong? You wanted to talk to me?" I asked him.

"What is wrong with Matteo?" he asked, which made me frown.

"What do you mean? What's wrong with him?" I asked, scrunching up my eyebrows.

He wrapped his arm around my shoulder "word on the street is that he is unhinged and that he had a falling out with his family, he is not the big boss anymore"

"I know about the title but where does 'unhinged' fit in?"

"Apparently, he shot his cousin in the shoulder for fucking with Max" he said.

"He what?!" I asked, gaining the attention of the rest of the busy bodies, I call family.

"Danny, Raff, who got shot?" Flamur piped up.

"Matteo shot his cousin for bullying Maxy" Rafael repeated.

"Good, very good, or I would have been the one to pull the trigger myself" Mom said, making us gasp.

"Uncle Besim, your sister is just as evil as the day you dropped her off in this country" Daniel said, making everyone burst out in laughter, while mom just gave him a side-eye.

"I heard he also cancelled the engagement and evicted Barbie from his penthouse" Rafael, the true epitome of a gossip girl, said.

"I wonder why" Ervin said while nodding his head in my direction.

I just rolled my eyes "guys, can you stop talking about Matteo now please?" I asked.

"Why, do you want to go rescue your baby daddy?" Chase asked.

"Guys, stop it now, it's not funny" I said, while getting up to pore me a drink. I decided on the raki to start the night off on a good note.

Everyone was busy talking about other things, while I decided to be a drunken master. After a while the old people went to bed and that's when we started the real party.

We sang karaoke and danced the night away and we eventually went back to bed around 3:00. Everyone was so intoxicated, the last I remember were me and the girls heading to my side of the house and Chase and Vivian undressing halfway down his corridor.

I'll worry about the hangover later....

I swear I was about to put my head down, when my phone that I left in my room started to buzz. Glancing at the screen, I saw it was Matteo, so I answered.

"Hello"

"Hey, are you still in bed?" he asked and in my intoxicated state, I could hear his drunkenness,

"I just got into bed"

"Are you drunk, Daniella?" Matteo asked, making me giggle.

"No"

"Well actually my family decided to party at home tonight, or last night, or until now. Sorry, I'm rambling nonsense".

"Can I sleep here for a few hours" he asked, making me sit up straight.

"What do you mean?" I asked, half sober now.

"I'm outside your front door. Can I sleep here for a few hours. I don't feel like going to the hotel now. I just need..."

"I'm coming"

Chapter 31

My behind left the bed as fast as my drunken ass would allow, while almost bumping my head against the bedroom door from stumbling over my feet.

When I made my way downstairs and opened the front door, Matteo stood there in all his manly glory my drunken eyes were able to absorb. I stood there watching him lean against his car door while giving me one of those funny looks he gave that particular night of that event where he cornered me in the bathroom.

He was dressed in an all-black bad boy outfit, looking innocently dangerous. Sporting a pair of jeans, sweater, jacket and ankle boots, but something looked off. I could sense that something was wrong with him.

I could clearly see he hadn't had a wink of sleep in a few days, with the dark circles under his eyes and the stubble evident on his face. Sad, sad eyes but why would he need a place to sleep when he has the means to make other arrangements? Let's see where this goes.

I held the door open for him "hi, you are coming? Or do you plan on freezing outside?".

He gave a nod and proceeded to remove a duffle bag from the car's trunk and made his way through the door inside. As we headed upstairs, I got the smell of something I'm all too familiar with, blood.

I didn't mention anything and directed him towards Max's bedroom, that's vacant because the boys chose Dyl's bedroom tonight.

If he's able to walk, then he'll survive whatever is wrong with him, hopefully.

I switched on the light and as I turned to observe his body, I could see the bloodied stain on his black sweater. He stood in the middle of the room and just watched as I walked to the bedside table and sat on it.

"Where's the boys?" he asked, but I decided to ignore him on that and rather confront him about his bloodied clothes.

"Spill" I demanded while pointing my finger at his sweater, making him scrunch his face up in confusion, so I reminded him of my profession.

"I'm a doctor or did you forget? Is it yours?" I asked. He didn't even bother to glance to where my finger was pointing.

He ignored me "are you drunk?" he asked, giving me one of those panty dropping smirks.

"How dare you ignore me, Matteo?" I countered, now losing my patience with his nonsense.

"It's mine" he said, and all the playfulness was instantly gone, and it didn't sit right with me, but my million questions had to wait.

I left the room without saying anything and fetched my satchel with all the medical supplies I would require.

When I got back to the bedroom, I saw him standing in the same spot busy typing on his phone. He glanced up and placed it on the desk.

"Bathroom" I said pointing to one of the doors in the bedroom. He walked towards it "you have to strip so I can assess all your wounds"

I took the basket in the corner and placed it in front of him. He removed piece by piece of clothing and placed it in the basket. When he stood in front of me in his white Calvin Klein boxer briefs, that was also stained with blood as it dripped down his body.

I could see four stab wounds and it's not surface scratches. One on his shoulder, one on the side of his torso luckily missing all vital organs, one in his arm and the last one in his thigh barely missing his main artery.

I could feel his stare on me, but I ignored it. After assessing the wounds, I could see that the blade was probably not that long, but it sure did cause some damage.

I gave him a few stitches on each wound and patched him up. I covered the stitches with waterproof patches, then ordered him to take a shower. I left the bedroom and headed downstairs to the kitchen to fix him a plate of the leftover food.

After heating it up, I went back upstairs with the food and water.

I stepped back into the bedroom, just as he came out of the bathroom with a towel wrapped around his lower half. I could feel my neither area starting to moisten seeing him like that.

Well, I'm not dead. I have these random thoughts and desires sometimes, but the past constantly made sure to quickly suppress those feelings when it came to men.

"Here, eat up and take these two tablets. It will help to prevent infection and with the pain and swelling" I said, placing everything on the desk "did you drink any alcohol tonight?" I asked and he nodded his head in agreement.

"How long ago?"

"3 Hours ago, maybe" he said.

"It's fine, you can still drink it" I assured him "but you have to eat something first".

He took a seat at the desk and started to gobble the food down "who made this?" he asked.

"We had family night, so mom, Aunt Drita and my cousins made all the food. It's Albanian cuisine"

"He nodded as he stabbed the food with his fork "It's good, It's really good"

"Thank you" I said, "what happened tonight, Matteo?" I asked, as I sat at the foot-end of the bed.

"I had some trouble tonight, but I've resolved it.

"Do you think I'm a softy? That I can't handle the truth? Did you forget my life and how hard I had to fight to get to where I am today or the fact that I am vastly familiar with the mafia lifestyle, even though I'm not actively involved in it, I do, however, live in it. If anything happens to you, what will I tell your kids, or did you forget that it's not just about you anymore?"

His eyes softened and he nodded in agreement "You already know about the fiancé story that's over now and my cousin Emma, who insulted the boys that night at the restaurant, then my dad took the title that was never mine to begin with and is now running the Mafia again. The night of my aunt's birthday dinner, I went back and shot Emma out of rage for disrespecting my son and constantly picking on them whenever she see's them"

"How is she?" I asked.

"Why do you care about her? She hurt our kid"

"I know and I would have choked her if I were to see her, but don't you think shooting her was a little extreme? And what about the Mafia now? Will you still be involved?"

He shrugged "I don't care about that bitch and the mafia; it was never mine to begin with. He never fully signed the business over in my name. That's why I never stopped doing my own business on the side, which was all legal before I started helping the Mafia out, but that funding I gave to the Mafia has also ceased now. I refuse to fund something that feeds ego's and will cause my demise. I don't plan on being involved and working for the Mafia because my business will keep me busy. I have a few plans up my sleeve to expand"

"All this happened because he found out about the boys. What if you tell him, you cut them off, but still see them in secret?"

"Are you listening to yourself Daniella? How could you expect me to deny my own flesh and blood. Why should I keep them a secret and what kind of man would I be if I hide them because my dad doesn't like your family? I would choose you and the kids over anyone and anything without thinking about it" he stated.

I was shocked at his confession about choosing me too. I don't know how to feel about that, though. I just want him to be a present father.

"Matteo, It's not about me, but about your kids. You just have to be there for them"

He just looked at me and didn't bother to correct me. Almost like he does not want to get into it now.

"So, what happened tonight?" I asked, trying to steer the conversation away.

"I killed the people that have been high jacking the trucks, but someone got to me with a fruit knife, a fucking fruit knife and I killed him. I think there's something bigger going on, though. I can't put my finger on it, but I think someone is trying to erase me from this earth"

My eyes snapped to his as soon as he mentioned the last part "what do you mean?"

"I've been followed for a while now, but I pretend to not notice it. I don't think I can trust my family anymore. I basically have no-one. I'm on my own now. That's why I asked you to ramp up the security for the boys or I will. I've asked the guys in the mafia to look into the people following me, but they constantly hit dead ends. I don't believe them. I think they are hiding shit from me".

"And your family?"

"All of them know what my dad did, but none of them said anything, because, as long as their cozy lifestyles are funded, they remain quiet. My aunt and cousin are both pissed because I shot Emma, but I've passed the stage of giving a fuck"

"Danny" I heard someone say from the bedroom door. Matteo's eyes started to bulge out of its sockets. I internally cracked myself up at his expression.

"Yeah, in here Raff!"

The door creaked open with Rafael standing in the doorway rubbing his eyes, with only a pair of boxers on. To Matteo this would look very strange, but all the men in this house has this habit of walking around in their underwear.

He probably didn't notice Matteo sitting at the desk because he was looking straight into the bedroom at me "I need one of those magic tablets, please, this Albanian Raki fucked me up. My head feels like it's about explode. Wait, why are you sitting there like a ghost? Is something wrong? You know you can speak to ..." he stopped his babbling then glanced towards the desk.

"Oh, Sis, so, you were dicked tonight?" he questioned, obviously still very drunk because all of us headed to bed at the same time.

"Stop it right there" I said, as I got up and scratched in my bag then handed him the tablets. I shoved him out the door and was about to close it when he stopped me.

"Wait Danny, wait" he said in all urgency, and I paused to listen to what he had to say.

"Remind me to buy you one of those caramel chocolate cakes you like so much. I mean, it's not every day my sister gets some" he said, bursting out in laughter, then stops midway to look in the direction of Matteo "you better dust that shelves off really good. She has been sitting there for 10 whole years" he said, then continued to laugh his but off.

I gave him one last push and closed the door, taking my seat on the bed again. I could feel the heat on my face that was caused by him embarrassing me.

"Why is he in his underwear walking around in your house and why Is he here?" Matteo asked, not looking very happy. I thought he would continue making fun of the 10 years, but he's more concerned about the underwear.

"He is basically my brother, who has lived here since the age of eight and has a bedroom that belongs to him in this house, and his brother also lives here when he's not in college. Why do you ask that?" I questioned.

"It's just strange that my kids and their mother would live in a house with a mass murderer, who walks around in his underwear in the middle of the night" he said with a frown.

"Let's continue this conversation tomorrow. I'm tired and I need my bed now" I said, while holding my hand in front of my mouth to cover my yawn as I got up from the bed. I also don't have the energy to have a fight this time of the morning.

As I made my way to the door, I felt a hand pull me back and I landed against a hard chest. The man was still dressed in just a towel, making me blush.

"What are you doing?" I asked and realized that my face was now mere inches away from his as I felt his minty breath on my face.

"Stay with me tonight?" he asked, with a vulnerable look clearly visible on his face.

I feel so bad for him because all he wants is comfort and I'm not the one to give it in the way it seems he wants it.

"I can't. Can you let go of my hand please" I said, gaining my self-control back.

"Why not, Daniella?"

"Why should I and besides I don't go to bed with random people, and I told you I don't want a relationship or relations with anyone" I said, elevating my tone. Which I could see, hurt him, but he's a big boy and he should know better.

"I don't want to have sex with you, Daniella" he said, making my face heat up again "I just want you near me, to cuddle with me. I promise I won't touch you inappropriately. I just need someone, now" he begged. He sounded very needy, but I am not the one to fuel that flame for him. I don't want that type of attachment. I can't

"I'm sorry" I said, then grabbed the dirty clothes basket and left the room. As I walked out of the bedroom, I bid him a good night's rest, turned my back and left him standing in the middle of the room.

Was I being childish? Him wanting me near him goes against everything I've ingrained in me to protect myself from people.

I'm too tired to stress about this now so I just went to bed and fell asleep as soon as my head hit the pillow.

I was woken by two little bodies joining me in bed as they always do. I still felt so tired, only to realize that it's 9:00 already.

"Morning Mom" Dylan said with Max's greeting following behind.

"Morning my babies" I said kissing them on their heads. A soft knock could be heard and a few seconds after the door creaked open, as Matteo's head popped into view.

"Morning guys" he said, with his beautiful smile on display as he entered the room upon seeing the boys.

"Good morning" I said, while looking at the shocked expressions of the boys.

"Dad?" the both of them say simultaneously as they sat up straight while rubbing their eyes.

He made his way over to the bed and Dylan got up jumping on him for a hug with Max following behind. He was dressed in fresh clothes that were probably in that duffle he brought in.

Max has always been the quiet one who always depends on his brother to protect him or to give direction, but he has a heart of gold when it comes to family and will protect everyone but himself. That's where his brother comes in and helps out.

"Dad, when did you get here? Did you come to pick us up for the competition?" Max asked.

"I told you; I wouldn't miss it for the world. I'll meet you guys and your mom there. I just need to sort out a few things" he assured them.

"It starts at 11:00" I reminded, and he gave me a nod, still not looking too pleased with me. Probably still a little sour about earlier.

"Boys, go clean up and get dressed and ready for breakfast. father of my children" I said, gaining Matteo's attention "can you assist them, please. I need to take a quick shower, then I'll see you out"

The boys didn't wait and scurried out of the room. Matteo looked at me from head to toe, but his gaze remained on my chest. Upon glancing down, I saw that my boob was halfway exposed but luckily my nipple was covered.

I keep on embarrassing myself in front of this man. When will I become a civilized person?

It took me 15 minutes to shower and get dressed. I decided on a pair of light blue high-waisted jeans and a white knitted polo-neck.

The boys came flooding back into my bedroom as I grabbed my bag and coat. Daddy dressed them in decent clothes, so 10 points for him.

"Mom, where's our bags with our clothes for the competition" Dyl asked.

"It's packed and downstairs. We need to head downstairs so you can eat something" I said.

"Are you staying for breakfast?" I asked Matteo.

He glanced at his watch "I can't, I need to go check on something" he said, but I had my suspicion that he's avoiding my family.

We headed downstairs and we were about to head to the front door to see Matteo off, but my mother decided to make her presence known.

"Are we sneaking out after spending the night?" she questioned in her authoritative voice.

"Morning Mrs. Harris" Matteo greeted and looked at me for help.

"Morning mom, we're quickly seeing Matteo off. He has to be somewhere. We'll come join you shortly" I said, trying to save him, but I could already see the naughty glint in my mother's eyes.

"No, you won't. Come and have breakfast with the family, Matteo. We have been waiting for you to get up and explain this sleepover dynamic to us and don't you dare call me Mrs. Harris again. It's Sarah" Mom said and made her way towards the dining room.

Matteo stood there with eyes as wide as saucers. I knew he didn't want to see the whole family and made up the excuse that he had to leave, but I digress.

Once we headed into the dining room, everyone was quiet and sat there open mouthed.

"Sarah, I never expected my daughter of all people to sneak a man into our house in the middle of the night" my dad said. I knew he was trying to stress Matteo out.

"I have to agree brother in-law, never expected my niece to become a buddy call or what do these kids call it" Uncle Besim asked, making everyone burst out in laughter. He knew very well It's called 'booty call'.

"Hey Danny, are you tired?" Rafael asked, as he entered the dining room, now fully dressed "I hope you knocked at least eight years off last night, Giordano" he said, making everyone laugh again.

Matteo didn't look so happy, so I decided to jump in "Common guys, you guys know nothing happened, so stop the jokes"

"Sit son, we're just pulling your leg" Aunt Drita said, and you could see the relief on his face. Poor guy.

"Are you good?" mom asked.

"As good as can be, mam" he said, looking down at his plate as I dished him some eggs, sausage, toast, a few small pieces of steak and some onion relish. He looked at the plate then at me.

"We don't always do the American sugar breakfasts in this house" I told him.

"Yeah, here we eat meat" Chase piped up.

The conversation flowed around the table with laughter and taunting in between. My cousin Ervin, Chase, Daniel and Matteo went into a deep conversation about business, but my attention was focused on the state of happiness my family was currently in.

By the time we had to leave Matteo and the guys were laughing about something.

All of us left to go watch the boys compete and, in a sense, my heart was full, like every piece of the puzzle his place and that the picture was complete.

But the question we have to ask is, how long with it remain in place.......

....

Chapter 32

The place was already packed by the time we reached the venue, and the items were about to start.

I rushed the boys into the changing rooms with their dad who had been attached to my hip since this morning, following right behind me. The rest of my family went to find seats.

I still don't really know how to feel about him constantly being in my vicinity.

When the boys were ready, we headed to the stands, but there were no seats available near my family, so we had to settle for seats in the opposite block.

All the hungry eyes of the female spectators were fully focused on Matteo as we walked to a few seats that was available in the corner.

Why are these stares not sitting well with me? Why am I having these possessive thoughts about this man, as if he belongs to me? I need to get him out of my head.

It seems the interaction we had in the early hours of the morning is playing with my head. I shook the feeling off as we took our seats in.

This competition was a welcome challenge for the boys because they were competing against students from another state, instead of competing with the same kids from this region.

"Is it always this packed?" he asked.

"Yeah, sometimes, but today there are kids from other regions also competing"

"Thank you" he said out of the blue, making me turn my head to give him a questioning look.

"For?" I asked.

"For taking this stray in for a few hours" he said, while pointing at his chest.

"No problem, but why are you living in a hotel?" I questioned.

"I've been staying there since Gina moved into my apartment" he said, making me frown.

"I thought you always lived together"

"No, after the whole boy's saga, dad demanded that she be moved in, but I moved out into a hotel the same night. I was done with the whole setup"

"What about your family or other properties you own that you could have stayed at, not that you're not welcome at my house, I'm just curious. I assume you're a rich man without the wealth of the family business" I stated, referring to the mafia.

"Yeah, I know. My family will be cut off by my dad financially if they take me in and I am busy renovating a property that will only be ready in two weeks for move in. All my other properties are rented out and that's basically why I decided to stay at one of my hotels. I just needed somewhere to go after what happened last night and where no-one is trying to kill me.

The hotel just didn't feel like I wanted to be there at that time. You and the boys came to mind" he said as he placed his hand on my thigh. Causing chills to run through my body.

"I just wanted to be near you guys. It's like the only part of my life that's making sense now" he said, and the sadness could be heard in his tone as he took my hand and interlaced our fingers.

I looked down at our hands and then looked up at him entranced. He was already looking at me with an unknown expression reflected in his shiny eyes. I sat there in a trance as he lifted his other hand to take a stray piece of hair that dangled in my face and placed it behind my ear.

"What are you doing to me?" I asked without realizing what I'm asking.

"What do you want me to do to you?" he asked. I just shook my head and removed my hand from his as the announcer spoke, advising us that the competition had begun.

There were 10 different spots on the floor where kids performed in different categories, the boys had Matteo on the edge of his seat the whole time.

Matteo jumped up a few times in excitement, making me chuckle under my breath. It was his first time seeing them compete and he looked like a proud dad because they are really good at this.

I hope him being part of the boy's lives will impact their growth in life positively.

Max really needs some guidance to not just protect and stand up for others but for himself as well. He is currently heavily dependent on Dylan when we are not near, but people won't always be around to protect him. He can sometimes be a little too quiet as well, while Dylan does the talking for both. Dylan does it without realizing it because he loves his brother.

Matteo got up almost at the end of their last performance and was now standing courtside and a blonde woman decided to join him. Their conversation seemed interesting from the way she was throwing her head backwards in laughter and touching his arm.

I ignored their interactions and stuck to watching my boys. Both of them won in all their categories and after the medals were handed out, I left the stands to go get the boys on the floor so we can get them dressed again to head out.

I was just about to walk past Matteo and his blonde acquaintance when he grabbed my arm.

"Babe, I want you to meet someone" he said, making me peer up into his desperate eyes that was pleading for me to bail him out of the situation.

'Babe? Wtf', I thought to myself.

I glanced between him, and the girl and she was a gorgeous blonde lady but was clearly glaring at me. Luckily, I am very good at keeping up appearances, so I ignored her childish expressions.

"This is Santina, I did a few business deals with her dad a few years back"

"Hi, Santina, my name is Daniella" I said, while giving her a smile. Something I rarely display to people I don't know.

"Hi, nice to meet you" she said with a smile that's not meeting her eyes.

"Do you have a child that's competing today?" I asked, trying to make conversation as the vibe I was picking up was not sitting well with me. This woman want's the man standing here next to me.

"No" she said then gave a fake laugh "I don't have any kids. I'm not ready to ruin my body for kids just yet. I came with my sister to support my nephew and you?" she asked just as Max and Dylan made their way over to us with their medals dangling around their necks.

"Mom, dad, look!" Dylan shouted enthusiastically as he made his way in our direction.

"They are yours?" she asked referring to my boys, looking at Matteo, clearly unhappy about their existence. No sporting a sour look on her face.

"Yes, they are ours" Matteo said as he took both the boys into his arms for a hug "hey well done guys. That was awesome. You did so well," he said, kissing them on their heads.

My family also made their way over to us and everyone gushed over the boys winning their categories.

"Daniella, we are heading to the restaurant to eat something, are you guys joining us?" dad asked.

"Yeah, I just need to get the boys out of their clothes, then I'll be there" I said.

"You can go ahead; we will meet you there" Matteo said. Before I could protest, I remembered this girl standing here.

"It was nice meeting you, Santina, but I have to get go my boys sorted" I said, giving her a smile and left pulling the boys with me. I didn't care if Matteo followed or not.

"Boys, take a quick shower in there. I will wait outside the door. Here are your clothes and shout if you need anything" I said, then as soon as I turned around, I bumped into Matteo's hard chest.

"Ouch! Are you trying to unalive me?" I asked rubbing my nose.

"I'm so sorry I didn't mean to. Are the boys in there?"

"Yeah, they are busy taking a quick shower. So, what's with the 'babe' situation outside?"

He rolled his eyes "you know why I did that" he said, as he stood with his shoulder against the wall typing on his phone.

"You can just drop us off if you have to be somewhere" I said.

"Why?"

"I mean, you have been with us since early this morning. Don't you have stuff to do?" I asked, without even realizing how rude that might have come across.

"Is it wrong for me to want to spend time with you and my kids?" he asked, clearly not happy with my comment and question.

"I'm sorry, I didn't mean it that way. You are a businessman and normally businessmen are busy. I didn't mean for it to come across in that way" I said, trying to correct my statement, but he still didn't look happy.

The boys came out and we made our way to the restaurant with Matteo still silent. I never feel bad about what I say or my actions because I try not to offend anyone, but I feel like a piece of crap right now.

He was already going through shit with his family. The boys were his only happy place and now I'm also adding onto his load by being nasty to him.

We stopped in front of the restaurant where my mother mentioned they would be, and he didn't switch the car off.

He got out of the car and opened the doors for me and then the boys "Boys, you did so well and I'm very proud of you. Enjoy your lunch, I'll come pick you up for school Monday morning, ok?"

The boys didn't look too happy about their dad leaving, but they accepted and gave their dad a hug. Matteo didn't even look in my direction and got in the car without greeting me and left as soon as he made sure we entered the restaurant.

I felt so bad but pushed it to the back of my mind as we walked inside masking my expression with a blank facade.

"Where did Matteo go?" Ervin asked as we reached the table.

"He had to leave" I said, while taking my seat at the table.

"Boys, why do you look so grumpy? You will see him again and besides; you won all your items" Chase said, trying to sound enthusiastic.

"We know" Dylan said, as he slumped down in his seat. Vivian had to leave early this morning to sort out some business and Chase looked like someone that didn't have a wink of sleep from all the unimaginable stuff they probably did.

"Chase, did you get any sleep last night?" I asked, trying to taunt him.

"Daniella, leave your brother alone" my mother said as the whole table bursts out laughter, already knowing what he did the whole night. In my mother's eyes, Chase can do no wrong.

"Guys, we can only leave on Monday and not tomorrow" Ervin interrupted.

"Why?" Elira asked, not looking happy about it.

"Hey, you can do without that silly boyfriend of yours for a minute. Enjoy your time here with the family" Aunt Drita reminded my cousin.

"We were invited to the opening of a club here in New York" Ervin said, getting back to the main topic.

"Who's we and who's club?" Daniel asked.

"The Shqiptarët (Albabians)" Ervin said, pointing to everyone around the table "minus the old people" he followed up, making everyone laugh again.

"I'm too tired. Count me out" I said.

"Nah little Sis, Vivian is also coming. You can't bail when it is our last good night to spend with the cousins. Who knows when we'll see them again" Chase said.

"I'll think about it" I answered.

After my tummy was stuffed, the tiredness started to seep into my bones. The boys went with the old people to watch a concert, so I decided to take a nap with the intention to skip on the night club and the hopes that they would forget about my existence in order for me to sleep in peace.

Bujar and Daniel came to wake me up a few hours later "Dr. Harris, get your but up and out of this bed. We are leaving in an hour" Bujar said as he pulled the the blanket off me.

"I'm.... so..... tired" I said in a sleepy voice and groaned as i rubbed my face in my pillow.

"Danny, unemployment doesn't look good on you" Daniel said, and I gave him the questioning eyebrow.

"Yeah, you were use to no sleep and now you sleep late every day" he said.

"What time is it?" I asked.

"22:00 and you better get ready. We will be leaving at 23:00" he said then held his hand up as I was about to protest "we're not leaving you behind. You have to live a little and before you ask about the boys, they are asleep in their grandparents bed" Daniel stated, then he pulled Bujar out of the room.

I groaned getting my but up before I procrastinate and make everyone unhappy by staying in bed.

I stood in the shower, allowed the water to caress my tired body and enjoying the last few moments before I head into a club with sweaty bodies and loud obnoxious music.

Clubs are so not my thing.

I wrapped my body in a fluffy white towel and did the same with my hair as I headed into my walk in closet to check what clothes I have that is club worthy.

Mom bought me a few dresses a few weeks ago because the only clothing that was in my closet were a few evening dresses from when I was a teenager that probably don't fit and all types of jeans, pants, t-shirts, and so on.

I decided on a black long sleeved dress with a plunging neckline that reached my mid thigh. I went for a ten inch black pointy heel. I love heels every blue moon, even though I'm not a girly girl.

Once my hair was dried and styled, I headed downstairs. Everyone was seated around the kitchen Island drinking raki. I can feel the hangover already.

"Hey sis, you look sexy for a change" Daniel said, as he held out his arm for me to join him next to the table. I obviously ignored his comment because my mind was still foggy from the little sleep I got and I didn't really care what he said.

"Hey guys, where is Vivian" I asked Chase because I didn't see her.

"Here I am" she announced as she came from the direction of the bathroom.

"Hey girl, where have you disappeared off to early this morning?" I asked her.

"I had a work emergency" she said out loud for everyone to hear, but whispered in my ear that she had to go to bed and slept the whole day. Making me chuckle.

We headed to the club in 3 black SUV's. Once we got there, there was a long line of people outside, waiting to get in.

I'm not someone that frequent clubs and only went to one in my life, so this will be my second time.

We walked past the line and headed straight in with the bouncer just nodding at us. You could see chrome everywhere and neon lights. It was kind of overbearing but in a good way.

We went upstairs as all the rich folk apparently only hung out on the second floor. The floor was packed once we got upstairs and you could see the swaying bodies on the dancefloor from above.

My brain ignored the stares of the people and admired how expensive and beautiful this place was.

I glanced across the floor and could see probably 150 people standing and talking to each other. Everyone did look like they came from wealth, but you could make out the easy companions that's only there for a good time, if you catch my drift.

We were directed to white couches in the corner and the table was instantly flooded with all kinds of alcoholic beverages.

A tall blonde guy made his way in our direction our direction. He had on a white shirt with the first three buttons opened, black skinny jeans and a pair of expensive white sneakers. He had a gold chain around his neck to top it off.

He was introduced as James, who was a business man originally from London. He kept giving me glances, but I was too good at ignoring said glances.

I decided to zone and and started to drink from whatever was on the table. They wanted me to enjoy, so I will make sure to do so.

After my 3rd rum and coke, I started to feel the buzz. Daniel got up from his seat and I could feel and smell the person. A woodsy, minty scent.

"Hey, are you enjoying your evening so far?" James asked, while placing his arm behind me on the backrest making.

I feel buzzed but I'm not blind "yeah, nice place you have here" I said.

"So, how long have you been friends with Ervin and the guys?" he asked.

I decided to be sarcastic "since birth" I said. He gave a questioning smirk "he is my cousin" I answered.

"I wasn't aware that he had such a beautiful cousin"

At that moment Ervin jumped in "Yes, this is my lovely cousin" he said, giving me a side hug, before continuing his conversation on the other side of him.

"So, what do you do for a living?" he asked.

"I'm currently unemployed" I said, as I started to giggle at the shit coming out of my mouth.

"I'm looking for staff at the club if your interested?" he said.

"My guy, she's a Doctor. Don't let Danny fool you" Bujar piped up.

"Really?" he asked.

I decided after my fourth drink that I needed to go and dance because that's what I felt like doing. I just wanted to escape my thoughts for a short time or for my mind to be blocked out from the world.

I further Ignored James and gave Daniel a look. He knew to followed me downstairs to where the normal people danced. These overbearing pretentious crowd were never my thing and I knew not to go downstairs alone.

I started to dance while stuck in my head as my body started to move with the rhythm. My heart dropping in my stomach again going over how rude I was towards Matteo.

I spotted Daniel at the bar talking to a dark haired girl, but his eyes remained on me. I loved my brothers for their protectiveness. They were always looking out for me.

I headed in his direction and got myself four shots of tequila. I downed all four glasses and made my way back to the dancefloor without interrupting Daniel, who was looking at me wide eyed as he continued to speak with the girl.

I don't know how much time went by, when I felt two hands on my hips and my heart instantly dropped. I faced Daniel to check if he still had his eyes on me and he did, but he was standing there with a smirk which made me frown.

I got a familiar smell as I slowly turned around and saw the one person that I thought wouldn't speak to me so soon.

"Matteo"

"Daniella, are you drunk?" he asked peering down at me, with his arms now wrapped around my waist.

"Maybe" I answered, as I looked into his eyes. Drunk and captivated by this man standing before me "what are you doing here?" I asked.

"I should ask you that. I didn't think you would be interested in places like these?"

"I'm not. It's the second time in my life coming to a place like this" I answered.

I placed my hands on his chest "I'm sorry about earlier today. I didn't mean to offend you. I don't like upsetting people" I said, but he stopped me before I could continue and bent down to bless me with a kiss.

I closed my eyes as the father of my children take another first from me. I have never kissed anyone and he could probably sense that, that was the case.

But the alcohol in my system didn't allow embarrassment to creep into the list of emotions I'm experiencing as he

Bliss, as his hands unwrapped itself from my body and moved towards my hair massaging my head. His tongue asked for entrance and I allowed it as he took control and showed my just how earth shattering his kisses ar.

He pulled away after a minute and my eyes fluttered open as I peered up into his gaze "let leave?" he asked and I gave a nod.

I glanced towards the spot where I saw Daniel last "he went upstairs" Matteo said.

"I have to get my clutch and let my brothers know I'm leaving with you" I said.

"No need. Already told them your leaving with me and your brothers will take your clutch home" he said.

He pulled me by the hand as we made our way to the door. It felt like the alcohol was affecting me more after stepping into the evening chill.

My feelings and actions are so unexplained but the alcohol allowed me to not care at this point in time.

It made me bold but will i regret this?

Chapter 33

Drinking two nights in a row has never been a good idea.

The tequila I consumed last night definitely made my liver quiver this morning. feeling like a dried-out prune on the inside. Like I haven't had a sip of water in days and my head was throbbing as I tried to lift my medulla off my pillow to check out my surroundings.

Definitely dehydration as I felt the drowsiness hit and my curtains drawn open this early didn't do my throbbing head any favors.

I frown as I stare at my curtains. I'm sure I closed them last night before I left for the club.

Last Night....the club... Oh my, what have I done? But I felt like I was alive for the first time. Like this is how life should be.

My mind is instantly flooded with the memories of last night as I rested my arm over my eyes, trying to rid myself of this dizzy feeling, as I over analyze last night in my constantly overthinking mind.

I danced and let loose, for the first time probably in my life and it felt so...good, but most of all freeing. A freedom that's inexplicable to explain with words after being held captive by my past. To not care about what people think of me or how they would perceive my actions or reactions.

But most of all, the guilt and burden of not knowing who the father of my children is, have been lifted. This made me realize the huge impact it also had on my mental health and that, that was a huge part that was holding me behind. I have truly come a long way in such a short timeframe with the help of the people that I love.

Mateo joined me on the dance floor last night and everything felt like a movie scene happening in front of my eyes.

He didn't dance, but stood there entranced whike watching me dance to my heart's content.

We kissed! My first in my 26 years of existence to be exact and I didn't freak out! The night at the club with him in it was just perfect and I wouldn't change it. I enjoyed every minute of it and then we left the club.

It felt good to be wanted in that way and not just as a daughter or sister, or am I reading his actions wrong?

I mean, he wouldn't have kissed me if he didn't feel some sort of way towards me.

I won't deny my attraction towards him. I don't feel any regret that he is the father of my boys anymore or that he took my first time. We already established that both of us were drugged and the only people to blame were the culprits that drugged us.

I am grateful that Matteo is such a genuine person towards me and ghat he wanted to be there for the boys without even having confirmation of them being his. Their faces were confirmation enough for him, aparently.

My family has been on a constant nag about me being stuck in a rut and I could never see the rut because I was too blinded by the past. They have always tried to push me to see past the things that happened and to become a better version of myself in order to enjoy my life and live for me so that I can live for the boys.

The past scared me so much that I became a version of myself I should never have become in the first place. I wasn't living; I was merely navigating safely through life and life is there to make mistakes in order for us to learn and grow.

How many people allow what others think of them to define how they lived life and the choices they make in life? Until you realize that person's life should be defined by the thoughts or actions of others, and that we should make the most of every day.

Instead of living to die, we should die to live.

I never knew I needed to come out of my shell until I gave it a try to prove my family wrong and shut them up and now, I'm thankful my eyes have been opened. This whole experience proved me wrong.

I don't feel an ounce of embarrassment, shame or regret.

I actually enjoyed the carefree feeling it evoked in me. After constantly having to check myself to play everything safe when it involved emotional attachments to people in order to not get hurt or let the past betrayal repeat itself.

I think the main reason I didn't care was because it was Matteo and he had shown me nothing but kindness and that he cares, not just towards the boys, but towards me as well.

I don't remember anything after getting into Matteo's car last night. I know i rested my head and that was it.

Lifting my blanket to check my attire, I saw that I was dressed in a pair of long-sleeved silk pink PJ's.

I cringe at the thought of him possibly seeing me naked.

I shoved the embarresing thoughts of him seeing me naked to the back of my mind. It has always been these kinds of intrusive thoughts that influenced my stagnant life. I was constantly playing life safe, but not anymore.

I'm going to put myself out there and live from now on. Not for the boys only, but for myself as well. I will do things that I've never done before and If I fail, I will pick myself up, dust myself off and move on to the next challenge and that pertains to as many facets of my life I can fit in.

I could see the miserable weather through my window, making my headache feel ten times worse. Snow should start falling any day now and the festive season is inching closer.

I was about to get up to check on the boys to get them ready for school, when I saw a glass of water and an aspirin on my bedside table with a folded note.

I took the aspirin and opened the note not recognizing the handwriting and a smile graced my face as I instantly recognized who the note was from.

"Good morning, Daniella

I hope you had a good rest. If you are wondering who undressed you, it was your mother and aunt who were still wide awake by the time we reached your house.

I took the boys to school so you can sleep in.

I hope you don't regret last night, and if you don't, then I will take you somewhere tonight. Be ready by 19:00 and dress warm.

Ps. I have already asked your mom to look after the boys.

Another Ps. If you don't accept me taking you out, then send me a message

xxx Matteo

I fell back on my bed with a huge grin on my face like a high school kid, giddy about her first date, but when I glanced at the small digital clock on the other side of my bed.

I can't believe I slept that late and no-one came to wake me up. It's 9:00 already.

I took a quick shower and got dressed in a pair of black skinny jeans and a white polo-neck and rushed downstairs. Everyone sat in the lounge in front of the fireplace, trying to stay warm.

"Ah nice to see sleeping beauty has finally decided to grace us with her presence" Mom said as I stood there with a bewildered look, thinking I'm late for our girl's date.

Yesterday, Mom mentioned that she wanted us to go for pedicures and manicures before my cousins have to leave for Albania.

Flamur and Elira sat there looking blue and hungover but gave me knowing smirks.

"Good morning, I'm sorry I'm late" I apologized. Mom just gave me a proper side eye. Clearly, she's not happy about something and I will sure hear about it later.

"Come on guys let's go spend the last few hours together before we have to leave" Flamur piped up, to get my mother's attention off me. I gave her a sly wink to thank her.

"Yeah, probably to get back to that man child" Aunt Drita mumbled under her breath. Referring to the guy Flamur is dating, but Flamur just pretended like she heard nothing.

We reached the Spa 20 minutes later. This is one of those fancy ones that has a restaurant and play area where you can drop your kids off and they will look after them. This is any woman's dream besides mine.

As I said before, I'm not a girly girl. I don't like doing extra nail stuff, but a good foot massage and rub is what I'm here for.

We were escorted into a private section where all the girls had pedicures and manicures, but I only opted for a Pedicure. They served some fruits and cheeses with champagne, but I stuck with water as I'm still dry to the bone and need my body to recover from these jitters before tonight.

The place was not crowded at all, probably because it was Monday.

When we were done an hour later, we decided to eat at the restaurant because I was about to faint from hunger.

We got settled and placed our orders, when mom decided that it would be the best time to bring up me being a drunken mess.

"Danny, why were you so drunk last night? You know I'm all for you guys enjoying life and all, but you arriving home, knocked out doesn't sit well with me" she stated as she rubbed her chest. I know flashbacks from the past must have crossed her thoughts when she saw me last night and i feel horrible about it.

"I'm sorry mom and thank you for dressing me. I was just tired" I answered while sipping my water. Trying to hide behind my glass as my mother glared at me.

"So, are you and Giordano a thing now?" Aunt Drita asked, referring to Matteo.

"No, we are not" I answered, making mom role her eyes.

"My vajza (daughter) is fast asleep, Drita. That man is totally head over heels in love with her, but I also understand why she can't see it" mom said making me feel a little uncomfortable with the conversation about my inexperience with men.

I decided to remain quiet because my head doesn't want to allow my mouth to rebel against my mother's comment at this time.

After eating our lunch in peace, we headed out, but saw people I was hoping to never cross paths with, ever again. Gina and her mother.

"If it isn't the putana (whore) in the flesh" she said under her breath as she walked past us with her mother grumbling next to her as they headed inside. My head snapped to my mother who instantly stood still, blocking us from walking any further.

Mamma was pissed by the looks of it, as she stood there fuming while balling her fists. Mom always had a short fuse even though she has a heart of gold. She does not take shit from no-one.

Mom turned around as all of us stood still looking at her "Excuse me?" mom asked, making Gina and her mother also stop and turn around "what did you just say about my daughter?" Mom asked, walking in the direction of Gina and her mother, taking slow maticulous steps.

It was like a lightbulb that went off in my head as I quickly followed suit. My mother will fuck the both of them up if I don't intervene.

So, i decided to stand near my mother, just in case she decides to beat them up.

"You heard me" Gina said, with eyes as red and puffy as the devil's booty-hole. Like she has been crying or something.

"I would keep quiet if I were you. Forcing a man to be with you, regardless of love, is what woman without dignity does. The apple surely didn't fall far from the tree" Mom said glancing from her to her mother "seeing that we are in public space, I will hold back but let me remind you that your last warning was when you fucked with my daughter's job. No chances left, so my only option is to come for you. Do you have anything to add, Dahlia?" Mom asked her mother, but she refrained from uttering a single word and just nodded.

Who is this woman scaring Gina's mother? Is it the same person I call Mom? I stood there shocked, but very relieved that I have a mother that stuck up for me.

"Thought so. Be sure to hear from me in the morning" Mom said as she turned around and walked to our car.

Once we got settled in the car, Elira was the first to break the silence with her giggling making all of us burst out in laughter "Auntie, I thought you left Ilir behind in Albania" Elira laughed, refering to my mother's name before she changed it to disguise her identity.

"You know, sometimes It's best to let her loose once in a while, to give these spoilt socialites a dose of reality" Mom said smirking while giving

Aunt Drita a reminiscent look. They were a menace growing up. Beating up anyone who stood in their way, from the stories mom told us.

"Mom, what did you mean with you 'they will hear from you in the morning?" I asked, really curious, because my mother never makes empty threats.

"Check the news tomorrow morning dear" Mom answered, making me frown, but I remained silent. I will interrogate her later today and try to get some info out of her.

A few hours later we bid my cousins a safe flight and we got back home by 16:00 in the afternoon.

I cornered my mother in the kitchen after Aunt Drita and Uncle Besim went upstairs to take a nap. The old people are going out to the Opera tonight and the boys get to go along.

Mom sat at the kitchen Island still looking so sad, but I decided that now would be the best time to talk to her about last night and at the spa.

Mom watched my every move, as I took a bottle of water out the fridge, opening it and taking a sip, while sitting across from her at the kitchen island meeting her gaze.

"So mother, why so upset?" I question, testing the waters.

"I just, I don't like people hurting you" mom said while wiping some new formed tears from her eyes, making me frown with concern but she continued "I wanted to destroy those fuckers when you told me what they did you that night at that party. I was so upset and would have probably destroyed their families as well if you hadn't stopped us. My precious beautiful daughter is so innocent and smart and i love you so, so much" she affirmed while stretching her hand across the island for me to hold.

"I know mom and i love you too" was the only response I could muster as I was trying very hard to compose myself.

"Seeing you depressed, barely eating, struggling to deal with the pregnancy and then with those precious babies I would give my life for if it meant you all are safe out of harm's way. That is something I never want to see you or any of my children experience again. That's why your dad, brothers and I, Uncle Besim, Aunt Drita and your cousins, will always have your back like we have each other's. If we don't make an example of that girl, she will continue to taunt and make your life miserable. I know you have never liked violence or retaliation, but It's time you stand up and not allow people to walk all over you" mom said the last part with anger "I also don't ever want to see you come into this house unconscious regardless who brings you through that door. Do we understand each other?" she asked, and i just gave her a nod, too coward to say anything in my defence cause i had none.

"What do you plan on doing mom?" I asked with concern lacing my tone but also changing the subject .

"Tomorrow when you wake up, you will know. It's time we start making examples of people who don't respect others" Mom said.

My dad came strolling in with a file, then placed it in front of me on the counter. He kissed my head and proceeded to make his way towards my mom and did the same before sitting next to her waiting for me to open the file.

As I opened the file, I saw the deed to a building that was transferred into my name. I glanced up looking at dad and giving him a questioning look.

"Happy birthday baby. I know your birthday is long gone, but that was your gift from all of us. We couldn't give it to you because of the shooting that night, but now is better than any other since it's now fully transferred"

I got tears in my eyes as I read through it. My parents are aware that I always wanted to start a clinic or Medical Centre. With that huge building in the city, I would be able to start a hospital, but I would have to start slowly. I first have to make a profit before opening different devisions and fields of expertise. I will be starting with Neuro because that's what I do and then work my way up, employing more staff. I don't have to rent or buy a place and this building is huge, but filling it in time won't be an issue.

I was crying like a baby as I got up and made my way towards my parents and gave them both a hug with a grateful heart.

They are and have always been the best, that's why I hate disappointing them.

"Thank you so much, but how much do I owe you for this" I ask dad, testing the waters knowing that building was bought when I was a todler, and he never had an idea of what to do with it, but knew it had potential.

"It's yours for free, baby" he said, reciprocating my hug "you make us so proud and we would do anything for you, even a few murders if it had to come to that" dad taunts, making me laugh.

"Silly old man with his silly old jokes" I said.

"You have to head upstairs and get ready for your date. Don't worry about the boys, I will dress them. You enjoy your evening with my future son In-law" mom said without one ounce of shame. I just shook my head at her giving me to Matteo that easily.

"What? Give the man a chance, honey. You never know, next year this time we might have a wedding or a baby if Chase doesn't beat you to it" she said giggling with my dad, who's still gave her crazy eyes while mirking at her nonsense.

I Got up and got ready by soaking in a tub for an hour. I spent a good few minutes with the boys. I didn't get to see them this morning and they gave me a rundown of their day, which i always love to listen to.

I got dressed in a pair of high wasted jeans with a knitted sweater and flat knee-high boot because It's freaking cold outside.

The old people left with the boys and a few minutes later I could see Matteo making his way up our long driveway.

Well, let's see what this night has in store for us.

I stood there staring through the window like a creep. He stopped and got out of the car, than made his way towards the front door.

I didn't want to make it obvious that I was waiting for him on pins and needles. I don't like not knowing how things will play out. Gosh! I just want this night to be over already.

My brothers were nowhere to be seen, so when Matteo knocked, I counted to ten then headed towards the door.

His face graced me with the sweetest smile as I opened it. Making my blood rush to my face instantly. He was also dressed in a pair of dark colored jeans, a white shirt and thick black jacket.

"Hi" I said awkwardly, sounding like an inexperienced schoolgirl as he approached me.

He came and stood in front of me as an icy cold breeze carried the scent of his perfume through my nostrils. Oh, I could literally eat him up just because of the way he smells.

"Hi, how was your day?" he asked, with his deep but mellow voice.

"Good" I said, with stars clearly written in my eyes.

He bent down and I froze as my body went rigid as he pecked my lips. I mean, I don't object to his advances at all. It's like I want to absorb him so he can be part of me. Oh, his lips are the softest. Now that I think about it, I know we kissed, but can't remember the exact feeling.

What is happening to me? All these foreign feelings I was allergic to a few months ago.

"Shall we get you in the car out of the cold?" he asked as he took my hand and proceeded to direct me towards the car. He held the door open for me and after both of us were in the car he took my one hand in his as we made our way down the long driveway to wherever this gorgeous man is taking me.

Chapter 34

We drove for about 15 minutes from where my house is situated, still in the same area from what I gathered, though. The property is also very secluded like ours, but still looked rough around the edges with the overgrown trees, shrubs, untamed hedges, broken fences, and gravel road leading to the house.

"Where are we?" I asked as I glanced around the darkness, trying to make sense of what I'm seeing, when a big unfinished house came into full view. It's not as big as ours but still huge.

"This is the property I mentioned I'm busy renovating which will also be my permanent home" he answered as the car came to a stop next to a fountain situated near the main door.

I gave a nod in acknowledgment as I felt his stare burning through my side profile "What's the story behind the property?" I asked, as my interest peaked after seeing the structure of the house that looks very unfinished.

"Sit, I'll open the door and I'll explain on the way" he said, while squeezing my knee. 'What a gentleman' I thought to myself.

He proceeded to get out and walked around the car, opened my door and held his hand out for me as support "after I saw your parents' property and the amazing work they did; I knew I wanted to live in this area and create something similar but according to my taste and style. The boys can freely take a bike ride or drive there when they are older themselves or even walk to their grandparents or from there to here if need be. They seem very attached to your family and I wouldn't want to take that away from them or spend any less time with them. I also like the privacy the property gives and it's so secluded and quiet and that's something I never knew I wanted until I saw yours" he said as both of us came to a stop in front of the house admiring the structure.

His explanation and thoughtfulness made my heart skip a beat. The fact that he has the boys included in his plans says a lot about the type of dad he is as well.

"How long before you move in?" I asked, because it doesn't look like it would be completed soon and last time we spoke, he mentioned soon.

"It would probably take two weeks longer than the estimated completion date before It's move in ready. We had a few setbacks with the roof today. We have to redo the whole thing due to the extent of the rot and we also have to wait for the specific slate I wanted. They were out of stock here in the city, but 3 to 4 weeks should be enough to finish inside, outside the house and the roof" he confirmed.

He enveloped my small hand in his huge warm one, sending tingles throughout my body, instantly giving my insides the warmth, I never knew existed or wanted.

We walked through the front door with him lighting the way holding a huge flashlight in his other hand, and I could instantly see the vision he had in mind even though everything was just framed and raw.

We walked upstairs on a floating stairway as he explained that the rail will be all glass and that the temporary planks that served as rails are just for safety and would be replaced soon.

I could picture his vision of the house, though I can't fully see the extent of the land due to the bad lighting, I know this house will be a dream for him to live in.

The upstairs boasted with 6 bedrooms with on-suites, a lounge with gas fireplace, huge floor to ceiling windows so you can admire the outside of the property and the vast number of trees.

We went downstairs and he took me through an unfinished cinema room, huge lounge with an adjacent dining room. The kitchen was still raw, so there was nothing I was able to imagine there. There were more spaces, but the doors were locked by the workers. He explained that downstairs in the basement was a huge garage to store all his cars, but there's nothing interesting other than a huge space currently.

The lighting in the house is currently non-existent due to issues with the electricity that should be resolved soon. If you asked me, I would say this house comes with more issues and resembles a hopeless cause, but I'm here to see the end result.

He escorted me with a huge flashlight towards another lounge area with a wood fireplace that was busy making a lovely crackling noise as it lit room. I'm not sure how many lounges there are in this house, but every space is huge.

My attention was mostly captured by the romantic setup in front of the fireplace, though. It was decked out with a huge soft blanket on top of a fluffy carpet. A picnic basket to the side with a bottle of champagne in a bucket of ice.

I stood there enamored with this man and how thoughtful he was to not take me to a crowded public space as a first date. The silence filled the room when Matteo cleared his throat, gaining my attention as I turned my head to look at him. He's probably under the impression that I'm not impressed because of my emotionless façade.

I should really work on my people skills.

"I hope you don't mind us having dinner here. I thought having it away from many people would make us both feel more comfortable" he said, as his eyes remained on mine.

I gave him a smile "It looks perfect. I love it"

"That's a relief" he said, while blowing an exasperated breath. Did I make him nervous? Nice to know that I held that much power over him.

We took our shoes and jackets off and sat cross legged as he took out food that was prepared by a restaurant one by one. It was still hot because of the thermal bag inside the picnic basket.

"I hope you like it. It is Chicken Cordon Blue on mash with more than enough sauce and a side of asparagus and some Greek salad as well. For dessert, there's some sticky toffee pudding with custard and top it off this lovely French champagne" he said while pointing to towards each item "to celebrate our first date" he ended off, gracing me with one of his gorgeous smiles while simultaneously giving me goosebumps as his eyes raked over my face as he's trying to figure out how I felt about the food.

"This looks lovely" I said in a squeaky voice which he instantly chuckled at. I could feel the heat rise on my face due to the embarrassment I felt in the moment.

"I'm happy you like it"

We ate in silence, and I loved every single bite of it. Matteo's phone has been buzzing constantly and you could see the frustration on his face every time he declined the call.

He placed his phone face down on the blanket in order to not see the flashing screen.

"Is something wrong?" I decided to ask. I don't want to be the reason he missed out on something important.

"What isn't wrong at this point" was his reply, instantly making me feel bad.

"I'm sorry, I didn't mean with us. It's just...no, forget about it. Let's enjoy the evening. I don't want to bore you with my issues and I'm really enjoying this break from my family life" he said, as he re-filled our glasses.

"I'm here for you if you change your mind" I said, giving him some assurance while reaching and squeezing his hand.

He took my hand and interlaced our fingers and looked down at how our hands fit into each other like a puzzle "I know and thank you for that, but I want to get to know you better and that's the most important thing for me right now, besides the boys. I will deal with the issues later" he said as he cleared the blanket and the both of us sat side by side looking at the crackling fire.

"You don't like interacting with people, do you?" he asked, changing the subject while taking a sip from his glass.

"Yup, I hate interacting with people I don't know"

"Yeah, but you are a doctor. How does that work?" he asked, while wrapping his one arm around my shoulders. I rested my head on the side of his chest as I gave an exasperated sigh.

"I stick to the issue at hand and discuss that without bringing emotion into things" I answered, while being entranced by the flames.

"Tell me more about you?" he asked, sounding interested in knowing who I am and how I became this person.

"Growing up, my family has always been very private and always tried send representatives on behalf of the company to public events. Only on certain occasions where they can't back out of commitments, dad or Chase would go out and attend or allow interviews, but very rarely minimal info is given out about who we really are. We try to keep a low profile at all times in order to get the best out of life. So, growing up I read a lot and schoolwork was something that has always been the easiest, so my parents did certain tests and discovered that I was gifted. That's why I was able to finish school earlier than my peers" I explained while glancing in his directions. He was looking back at me with so much interest.

I glanced back at the fire before continuing but giving him the short version "I was 16 years old and in the same grade as people who were two years older than me. Their lives always looked intriguing and fun. I wanted to be part of it so badly. I felt like I was missing out on life. If only I knew" I muttered the last part under my breath.

"What do you mean 'if only you knew'" he interrupted.

"I was set up by the girls in my grade. Normally the boys in the football team had a tradition to see how many girls they could bed and deflower"

"Well, that's a filthy tradition" he commented, whilst looking uncomfortable and not very happy about what he's hearing.

"Yup, that's how they did it. I always heard about it but never thought that I would become a victim om theirs"

"Don't stop, I want to hear everything, please" he said, while rubbing up and down my arm and sneaking glances at me now and then.

I continued "A few girls decided that I would be next and made friends with me exactly one month before graduation. They won my trust and in turn invited me to the party where it happened. They thought it was another couple on the bed that night and that I had escaped because they left me alone in the room. The next morning, I thought to leave before you woke in order to avoid the embarrassment" I ended off with a long sigh.

"I'm so sorry for my part in all this, but I refuse to apologize for the boy's existence" he said, as I smiled looking into his eyes. I just gave him a nod to indicate that I did understand what he meant.

"You know" I said, while holding his stare "I'm happy that it was you that night and that you are their dad instead of a duce bag that wouldn't recognize the boy's existence" I confirmed.

His penetrating gaze tugged at my soul, leaving me vulnerable and emotionally exposed to him but also igniting an inexplicable fire inside of me that I never knew existed. Like a moth drawn to a flame, his head lowered as the arm that was around my shoulders reached my head as he massaged the back of my head while his face came closer to mine.

I could feel his breath caress my face and I had no intention of pulling away. I wanted this as much as he did, so I allowed our lips to meet in a slow but passionate kiss that had me wanting more, even though I knew I wouldn't continue past just kissing.

I felt his other hand move to my hip, evoking tingles throughout my body. He took me by the hips lifting me onto his lap so that I was straddling him, now.

"Beautifull" he murmured, causing my cheeks that were already ablaze to feel extra hot.

"Thank you" I replied, making him smirk while his gaze lingered on my lips. He bent down and brushed his lips against mine and fireworks continued to explode in my mind and stomach at how content I was in this moment.

The emotions I was reading in his eyes, told me that I was where I'm supposed to be.

His soft lips connected with mine sending electric currents through my body. I had been going with the flow the night at the club and tonight I'm doing the exact same. I have no clue if I'm doing it right and I don't care, really. It just felt right in this moment, and he looked content with our current situation as his arms tightened around my waist.

I wrapped my arms around his neck as our lips moved in sync. Both our tongues fighting for dominance and enjoying the moment when the sound of a can or something falling over interrupted us, making both our eyes instantly snap open.

I gave him a questioning panicked look, too scared to glance around and kept my eyes focused solely on him. We silently got up from our positions and put our shoes and jackets back on at lighting speed as if we discussed this beforehand.

Matteo looked at me and gave me a smile and gave me a quick peck on the lips as he put his finger on his lips indicating for me to remain quiet. We made our way to one of the side doors with my hand nestled in his firm grip.

Matteo reached into the back of his jeans removing the gun I failed to notice this whole time we've been together. We could hear the grazing of footsteps hitting the tiled floor as it inched towards us.

My heart was beating in my ass at this point as I tried to stabilize my breaths to get rid of this panicked feeling without Matteo realizing it. Seeing the faces of my boys and family flash before my eyes was not doing me any favors.

We moved behind the open door blocking our bodies from the person entering's vision. Matteo held 3 fingers up giving me the indication that there were 3 people in the house. I don't know how I know that, but I just know.

It was like my world stood still. Should anything happen to us, they would grow up without parents.

Yes, that's the shit that goes through my mind before I gain hope for survival in any situation, I perceive every bad situation as the end of the world.

"Stay here, don't make any noise. No-one will notice you here. I'll come get you" he assured me and gave me a rough toe-curling kiss, leaving me breathless and with new regained hope that we would make it out of here.

I heard something or more like someone fall, then gunshots rang through the house as my heart dropped in my stomach. Sheer panic enveloped my senses as the last gunshot rung and a body could be heard falling.

Loud, quick footsteps made their way in my direction. I took shallow breaths and closed my eyes. I could feel the slight breeze of the door being pulled away from me, exposing me to whomever stood in front of me.

I refused to open my eyes until I felt a warm hand on my cheek. Upon opening my eyes, I saw Matteo standing in front of me and relief flooded my senses, calming me in an instant.

"Are you ok?" he asked, while checking my body for injury in this darkness.

"Yes, you?" I asked, with concern lacing my voice.

He gave me a curt nod as I could make out from his shadow "we should head out. Vito is almost here" he said, as he took my hand in his and gently pulling me out the same door we were hiding behind.

As we made our way outside, I saw a car approaching and I immediately hid behind Matteo.

"Don't worry, It's Vito" he said, pulling my head into his chest as the car came to a stop in front of us. Matteo opened the back door for me to get in. I got in wondering why we were not taking his car, but my thoughts were interrupted by Vito "hi there, Doc" he said, while gracing me with a huge smile regardless of the situation we were in.

"Hi, umh...Vito" I greeted him nervously as Matteo got into the passenger seat next to Vito. My hands were still shivering as I rubbed it together to warm it up while trying to relax in the safety of the car.

"Cleanup is on its way. How many guys were there?" Vito asked Matteo.

"5 Guys but I don't recognize them" Matteo answered.

"Did Alessia or Julian get hold of you?" Vito asked Matteo, changing the subject while I sat in the back still in shock while trying to make sense of what just happened.

"Your dad is marrying Alessia of to the Amato's. I tried to reach you the whole night to inform you, but I see you were busy yourself" Vito said, as Matteo rubbed his face clearly looking stressed.

On another note, who is Alessia? I thought to myself. Most probably his sister if his dad is to marry her off. If that's the case, then it's a shame.

"Where's Julian" Matteo asked, as he's busy scrolling through his phone and typing like a mad man.

"I don't know man. He left your parent's house very pissed after the news" Vito answered.

Vito drove down our driveway and stopped in front of my house. Matteo also got out with me.

"Bye Vito and thank you for the lift" I said, as I exited the car.

"Good night, Doc and It's my pleasure" he said back. He sounds like a nice guy.

"I'll be back in a few minutes. Wait for me here" Matteo instructed Vito and followed behind me.

I turned around, stopping him in his tracks "what's wrong Matteo and don't dare lie to me?" I warned.

"Is your uncle still here?" Matteo asked, making me frown.

I gave him a nod "yeah, the old people should be in the lounge in front of the fireplace. They sit there every night" I confirmed, leading the way towards them.

"Good evening, old people. You're up late" I announced as I made my way into the lounge. After all of them greeted and taunted me back for calling them old people, I informed Uncle Besim that Matteo wanted to have a word with him. They obviously put him on the spot to talk in front of all of them, cause that's just how they are. Even the women are as crazy as the men. I'm still trying to figure out how I fit into this family.

I excused myself because I don't really subscribe to mafia matters and I have a feeling that Matteo will be discussing something mafia related.

"I'll see you in a minute" Matteo assured, and I made my way upstairs.

I took a quick shower to calm and warm myself up, knowing the talk will be longer than 15 minutes and I only need 10 to get a decent shower. I got dressed and went to kiss my boys in their sleep and inhaled their scent.

I got back to my bedroom just in time when Matteo reached my door. I walked inside my room with him following behind. After he closed the door, he wrapped his arms around me and buried his face in my neck inhaling deep breaths.

"You smell so good" he muttered under his breath, making me chuckle.

"What's going on, Matteo? Please don't lie or hide the truth from me" I begged again, making him sigh.

"I need to leave. I don't have time to go into much detail. I need to save my sister" he said, instantly making me feel bad for her.

"The Alessia you were talking about?" I questioned him and he responded with a nod.

"I will sort this out and then, I'll crash at Vito's place. I'll come pick the boys up for school tomorrow morning. Do the school run with me and then we can go do breakfast after dropping them off?" he questioned.

"Yes, that's..."

Before I could finish Matteo's tongue was thrusted into my mouth as he held my face in between his hands. It was rough and intense, but I liked it like that. My hands wrapped around his torso and his hands gradually slid over my shoulders downwards until it reached my behind, making me jump at the foreign touch as I'm not accustomed to it.

He giggled while throwing his head backwards. He held me in his arms after coming down from his laugh and gave me a kiss on my head and lips.

He bid me goodbye, left my room and I immediately jumped into my bed, thinking about the night's events.

Chapter 35

- -

Daniella's POV

I woke up the next morning still feeling a bit tired, but I got up and got the boys ready for school. We discussed the upcoming school holiday while running around for socks and shoes.

They want to go to a warm place that has a beach so that they can snorkel and get away from the cold. My parents do the French Alpes every year and they wanted everyone to do it over the festive season. They mentioned wanting their dad to come along for both, but I told them that they had to ask their dad themselves.

"Grab your coat, Max" I reminded him, as he was about to exit his room without it. We headed downstairs so the boys could eat something before school. Luckily, they get school lunch from school, so there's no need to pack lunch.

"Morning everyone" I greeted, taking in my seat as everyone sent greetings back.

"How was your date?" Aunt Drita asked, just as Chase and Vivian made their way inside the kitchen greeting everyone. Vivian didn't look well, and Chase looked stressed. I wonder why?

I gave Vivian a huge smile accompanied by a questioning look. She mouthed that she would tell me later, already knowing that I spotted something was wrong.

"Did my sister go on a date, date? With whom?" Chase asked settling in his seat, as I pored myself a cup of coffee while rolling my eyes at him. That instantly made the boys' heads snap in my direction.

"Mom?" Dylan questioned. His facial expression almost made me spit out my coffee. I decided to taunt them a little.

"Yes boys, I went on a date with a man last night. What is the problem?" I question trying to sound serious while taunting them.

"What about our dad?" Dylan asked, with glistening hopeful eyes. The protector of the two that will fight an army for the people he loves but he will never disrespect his mother. He would rather cry than do so, like he's about to do if I don't put him out his misery.

"I Went on a date with your dad, guys" I said, as both their faces instantly lit up. Making the whole table laugh.

"Aunt Drita, the date was nice" I answered, not wanting to divulge any more details or mention the ambush. I'm also too shy to mention the kissing part and I don't think people share such personal info with family.

"How have you been, Vivian?" I asked, sitting back in my seat trying to move the point of conversation away from me, but Vivian had other plans and rushed to the bathroom. Alarm bells went off in my mind as my head snapped in the direction of my mother, who sat there smirking while sipping her tea. I swear this woman is a secret spy that knows everyone's business. Chase was following right behind Vivian.

"I guess the family will grow at least. This house won't fill itself" I said, making Daniel chuckle.

"Dan, are you very busy later today?" I questioned my brother who I haven't seen in a hot minute. I always enjoy his company and need a dose of Dan.

"I can always fit you in, what's up?"

"Will accompany me to...." I trailed off, listening to the TV playing in the background as the room fell silent. My mother increased the volume, while looking at me.

"Breaking news just in. Senator Morgan and his wife of 22 years, headed to divorce court after his affair with New York socialite Gina Russo has been exposed. Gina Russo, daughter of Millionaire businessman Victor Russo, has allegedly been in a relationship with the 56-year-old Senator for two years. According to sources, she had two abortions at the request of Senator Morgan. Medical documentation, financial statements and photographic evidence of their time together was submitted as evidence by Mrs. Morgan's lawyer. The couple has four children together and Mrs. Morgan is set to sue for sole custody. They had an iron clad pre-nup and she is set to cripple the Senator financially...".

I sat there looking from my mother to Aunt Drita, trying to figure out who these women really are, and I questioned if I really knew them at all. This was their handywork, obviously.

I don't know how to feel about this. I have never been someone that opted for revenge, but I'm also aware that If I stopped my mother this time, that I would never have heard the end of it and Gina wouldn't have stopped with her taunting and disrespect.

"That's madness" dad said, while Uncle Besim chuckled almost choking on his toast. That gave me an indication that all of them were in on it.

"See Sis, we try to live in peace, but there's always that one skank that underestimates this family that takes our kindness for being powerless and try to slip through the cracks. Hopefully, she'll lay down and rest with her 'sugar' from now onwards" Daniel said, confirming to that he has also been in on this, while buttering his bread.

"Were all of you in on this?" I questioned, glancing around the table.

"Well, we're family, aren't we?" Uncle Besim asked.

I just shook my head and got up from the table giving the old people kisses on their cheeks and left the table when Matteo said that he was outside.

Matteo was driving a different car than last night. He got out, meeting us halfway through the door.

"Morning Dad" the boys announced simultaneously.

"Morning Boys" he responded, ruffling their hair as he gave them some morning hugs.

He stood in front of me with tired eyes, giving me the indication that he didn't get any sleep. He pecked my lips "morning" giving me one of his sexy, panty dropping smirks afterwards.

"Good morning" I answered, smiling back at him while lost in my own fantasy about the father of my children.

The boy's giggles reminded us that they were still standing outside the car, watching us.

As soon as we got into the car, the boys bombarded their dad with their holiday plans, speaking over each one another.

"Boys, I know you're both excited, but can we talk one at a time, please" he asked, clearly enjoying their excitement and the fact that they wanted him to be part of anything they want to do.

I zoned out while they were having their discussion, my mind flooded with ideas for the new building and the fact that this man is making me feel emotions that I wholeheartedly welcome.

We reached the school and saw the boys off, then we left to have some breakfast. Before we got out of the car at the cafe, Matteo thought it would be a good time to give me a proper greeting by making out with me in full view of the passersby.

I walked into the Café with a reddened face and made our way inside and got situated at one of the tables at the back that's more secluded. Matteo just gave me one of his sexy smirks when he saw my embarrassment.

I was beyond hungry, so I ordered a cream cheese bagel with scrambled eggs and smoked salmon and my second coffee for the morning. Matteo went with an English breakfast and orange juice.

While we were waiting for our food, Matteo gave me the rundown of his whole family dynamic and the fact that someone had been actively targeting him. I was shocked to hear that there were previous attempts made to unalive him and that's after the restaurant shooting.

My main concern was the safety of the boys, but he assured me that he has men keeping an eye on them.

"Dylan and Max mentioned the holiday they want to go on in a few weeks? Where do you plan on going?"

That must have happened while I was busy zoning out in the car "yeah, they mentioned a beach holiday. I haven't thought about the details yet.

I know my family will go on holiday in the French Alpes for a week over Christmas, so it has to happen before or after".

"I'll check my schedule and make time for whenever you decide" he said, looking at me lovingly.

"Ok" I answered, while glancing at the Café that's getting fuller by the minute just as our food arrived.

"What are your plans for today?" he asked, as we ate our breakfast.

"I need to go look at the building where my new clinic will be. I can't remain unemployed forever" I said.

"That's great! On the other hand, I'm sorry about what Gina did with your job and car. If I refused my dad's proposal from the start, none of this would have happened to you"

"What happened, happened so don't beat yourself up. It's over now and I don't think she will bother me again after the news. Wait, did you see the news this morning?" I questioned.

He shook his head, so I took out my phone and showed him the latest news about her. His eyes grew wide reading the article about her, so I explained the spa incident to him and that it seemed to be my family's doing.

Matteo sat there smirking while continuing to read the articles, then shook his head "do you know how long I've been looking for some dirt on her to end the engagement? Unless..." he trailed off, deep in thought.

"Unless, what?" I asked him.

"Unless my dad made sure the guys didn't give the information about her to me and I never had any control of anything. They were the best at finding information, so it makes sense now" he said, as a grim look came over his face.

"How are things between you and your dad?" I questioned.

"Bad, since finding out about the boys. But I've come to realize there's so much my dad has been hiding from me and I don't understand why he doesn't like your family or the boys who are his own flesh and blood. I just have a feeling that there's something big going on with him" he explained, glancing up at me.

He probably thinks I would be upset hearing about his dad's dislike towards the boys.

"Did you find out who's behind the shooting at the restaurant?".

"Yeah, got that information, but I don't know these people well. I'm still trying to get more info on them and what their motive is for trying to hurt my family. Though now it seemed all their focus is on getting rid of me. Last night's attack was confirmed to be the same people. I need to eliminate this threat.

I gave a nod. A heavy feeling enveloped my chest as he spoke about his life being in danger. I just hope he can get more information on them in time to stop them.

"How's your sister?" I asked.

"I asked your uncle to hide her for me ....in Albania, until I find a solution to this madness" he said, waiting for my reaction, but I only nodded in response.

"I always thought arranged marriages happened in books or movies, never thought people still do that today"

"I agree, my dad is the only one in our family that feels his kids should also be punished like his parent's punished him. Luckily, I've got you now" he confirmed, making me blush.

Matteo got up bent over the table and gave me a peck on the lips in full view of the patrons. Why does he feel the need to do these personal things in front of people?

We sat there for an hour after we ate, just talking about life and the future we want for the boys. He also told me more about his family and then it was time to leave as he had to get back to work and I had to go have a look at the building.

***

Matteo's POV

3 Weeks later...

My mother gave me a call early this morning to meet her today. I decided on my restaurant 'Fiore' as I must check out a few things before picking the boys up from school.

As I came walking in, I saw mom having a conversation with Amber, who has been working here a few months.

"Mother, Amber" I said, as I approached them.

"Oh, hallo Son" Mom said with a smile, giving me a peck on the cheek. Her puffy eyes are cause for concern. She looks tired and It's making me feel guilty to know that I am part cause of her stress.

We got settled in a quiet corner. Mom gave me such a longing look that I felt bad for her, but I can't help her if she doesn't want to accept the truth and stand up for herself. She allows dad to control her and if she doesn't see an issue, then I can only do so much.

"Where's the boys?" she asked, glancing around. She tried to meet up with the boys and I at least twice a week without dad knowing about her visits.

"They are still in school. I'll go get them in an hour after their practice. What's wrong Mom?" I asked, cutting to the chase.

"Is there a way that you could talk sense into your sister to come back home, please" she asked, giving me a pleading look with tears pooling in her eyes.

I sigh "Mom, I already tried talking some sense into her. I've also tried to contact her but it's difficult. With dad forcing all his children to marry people they don't want; I don't blame Allesia for running away" I said, seeing the hope diminish in her eyes.

"I know" she trailed off, deep in thought "he hasn't been home much, or he gets home to just shower and then he heads back to work. He treats your brother horribly as well. I don't know what to do anymore. He blames me for giving birth to ungrateful children".

"You have been the best mother we could ask for and we know these requests are from dad and that you don't have a say in it. It is wrong of him to force any of us to give our lives away because previous generations did and Its tradition. That's just wrong to expect that from us"

"I know, but please don't stop the money you give to the family. Some of the buyers cancelled some deals after they heard you left. Business is not doing well" mom said, giving me a pleading look while wiping her eyes with a tissue.

I blew a frustrated breath and ran my hands through my hair a few times. I love my mother so much and I can see she's dealing with so much.

"Ok, but I will revise it in 3 months, so dad better get his cash flow sorted. I have a family now that is my first priority. I need to make sure my kids are set up for the future. I'm making up for lost time with them and they come first now and that includes their mother" I reiterate, so that my mother can understand how serious I am.

Mom smiled as she gripped my resting hand across the table "How is Daniella doing?"

"She's doing good. I'm accompanying her tonight to the Cancer Association Gala she was invited as an honorary guest".

"Yes, I was supposed to go with your dad, but he has become the old Isaac and said that It's best if I stay at home" mom said, referring to how dad was at the beginning of their marriage.

"Mom, I am here for you anytime you might need me, remember that. I just can't deny my own to keep dad happy and it took me a long time to realize that"

"I know and I'm proud of you. They are both the spitting image of you when you were their age. I admire you; you know?" she said, giving me a sad smile. It was like the life she knew had been slowly seeping away from her.

"I have to go" she abruptly said, glancing at her phone while getting to her feet "But you protect that boys and tell them that I love them and be the man to Daniella that your father failed to be to me. Don't let Isaac pull you down, ever" she demanded, as she made her way in my direction to give me a hug "I love you, Matteo" she said while giving my hand a death grip. She turned, leaving the restaurant in haste, like she was caught in the act.

I stood there with a look of concern as my eyes followed my mother leaving the restaurant onto the street. I always thought that they were happy, but her last statement tells me something is amiss, and I know my mother won't tell me the truth.

I left the restaurant, picked the boys up after practice and took them for an ice cream before dropping them off at home. Daniella wasn't home yet, so the boys stayed with their grandpa while I had to go sort a few things before the event tonight.

I have 1 week left before moving into my house and I can't wait to have some stability in my life. I've been crashing in between Vito, the hotel and Daniella's and I'm ready to settle in one place now and with Vito's new girlfriend Melissa in the picture, I feel like I'm intruding on their privacy. That's why I sleep at the hotel most nights and if I finish work early enough, I sleep over at Daniella's, which her family love.

I just finished taking a shower and getting dressed in a black suit with bow tie since It's a black-tie event.

As I made my way out to pick Daniella up, my phone started to ring and It's the person I'm trying to avoid, my dad.

"Hi Dad"

"Teo, I need you to come see me tomorrow. I need to discuss a few things with you" he demanded.

"Ok" was the only response I was willing to give that man that has disappointed me so much.

I drove to Daniella's house, damn exited to see her after this long ass day. He event starts at 19:00 and Its 18:00 now, so I still have some time to kill.

I got to Daniella's house 15 minutes later being welcomed by a quiet house. Everyone went out for dinner and the boys went with them.

I knocked on her bedroom door and walked in without waiting for her to open. She exited the bathroom dressed in a white silk robe and she looked naked underneath it from the shape of her pebbled nipples clearly visible through the material.

Fuck I'm horny!

I won't force myself, but it doesn't mean I can't tease her.

"Hey Babe" I greet, grabbing her by the wrist and swinging her in my direction into my chest as my hands glide from her back down to her ass. Yup, naked underneath.

"Good evening, Mr. Giordano" she said in a husky voice, clearly riled up just as much as I am from the moment my eyes caught her exiting the bathroom in this sexy silk robe that leaves nothing to the imagination.

Things between us are good. I love learning something new about her every day. I've come to realize, she's really, really intelligent. I've also come to realize she doesn't involve herself much in mafia business and will walk away or zone out when she's not interested in the conversation.

The way she blushes every time I mention me wanting to do things with her, but I don't want to overstep any boundaries if she's not ready to do more than kissing.

"How was your day?" I asked, stroking her back.

She pressed herself further into me as she slid her arms around my neck, pulling my face towards her lips. I stood there shocked at the fact that she was taking the initiative to start kissing me.

"The day was too long" she answered, pecking me everywhere on my face making me gulp trying to see what her next move would be.

"Mhm...did you miss me?" I questioned as I slid my hands down, taking both her cheeks into my hands, making her gasp and I used the opportunity to shove my tongue into her mouth.

My manhood instantly stood on attention as she pressed her front against mine. My hands slid up to her neck and into her hair as I started to pepper her with kisses on her neck making her moan.

Her face was scarlet as my open-mouthed kisses moved from her neck down to her bare chest as the top of the robe slid past her shoulder and revealed her beautiful chest.

She instantly snapped out of our make out session as if realizing what we were about to do.

"I'm sorry, I need to get dressed" she said, pulling the robe over her shoulder and heading into her walk-in closet.

I sat there on the edge of her bed trying to figure out what I did wrong. I decided to answer some e-mails I missed and responded to Vito on a few messages he sent.

My baby came out dressed in a beautiful black floor length sequined gown with her shoes in her hand. Her eyes on the floor were too shy or embarrassed to face me.

"Do you mind zipping me up, please?" she asked, turning her back towards me still seated on the edge of her bed.

"Sure, but can you tell me what's wrong or at least what I did wrong?" I asked, turning her back so she could face me before I zip her up.

Her eyes looked sad as she kept her eyes on the ground. I lifted her chin so she could face me.

"No more hiding behind sad eyes. Tell me what's wrong and be honest, please?" I asked, glancing straight into her eyes.

"I Scared"

****

Chapter 36

Daniella's POV

"I'm scared" I said, making him frown.

"I Don't understand?" he asked, pulling me in between his legs as he's seated on the edge of my bed.

"This" I said, waiving my hands between the two of us "I don't know what this is, and I'm just... scared that you might wake up one day and decide that this not what you want.

"What do you mean? Do you think I'm not serious about you?" he asked, grasping my hands in his.

"I mean, I don't know how this dating thing works and I don't want you to feel obligated to date me just because we have children together. I don't even know if you're seeing other people while you're dating me. I've never had a boyfriend, kissed or slept with anyone besides you, but I won't sharing a man with someone else. If you don't want monogamy, then I don't think we should continue with this" I said, blowing out an exasperated breath.

Matteo cleared his throat "Daniella Harris, mother of my two handsome sons, I wanted you from the moment you walked through that hospital door the day you operated on my father. I've had your face in my memory taunting me for the past 10 years and I only want you and no-one else" he stated, rubbing my cheek with the back of his hand "I can't picture my life without you. I haven't had a girlfriend or solid relationship in many years because I couldn't get you out of my mind. The night things happened haunted me around every corner thinking I've hurt such an innocent looking girl. You are 'it' for me, perfect in every way" he said, squeezing my butt, with stars in his eyes "you are my girlfriend or wasn't I clear enough?"

"When did you ask me to be your girlfriend" I asked, giggling at his playful shocked face.

"I thought I made it clear when I asked you to give me a chance a few weeks ago on our romantic date that turned into an ambush" he said, wrapping his arms around my waist, resting his chin on my tummy.

"I thought you meant you wanted to see where things go" I said, making him role his eyes.

"Ok, ok, now listen. Daniella Harris, would you do me the honor of becoming my girlfriend?" he asked.

"Yes, now help me zip up this dress so that we can leave, or we will be late for this stupid event" I said, rushing to put on my shoes after seeing the time on my clock.

"Or we could stay and continue where we left off. The kids are out, the house is quiet. Might as well make the most of it" he said, as he slid his hand up the side slit of my dress, sending shivers throughout my body, but I shoved his hand to the side.

"Matteo, we have to leave in 5 minutes, or we will have to walk in with everybody already seated and I don't want their attention focused on us. I hate attention from strangers"

"Give me a kiss to seal the deal first" he asked, looking at me expectantly with pouty lips.

I gave him a quick peck and finished getting ready and left.

We reached the event with 5 minutes to spare before everything was supposed to start, but people were still busy walking around, chatting and drinking champagne.

I internally role my eyes at these rich snobs in their overpriced designer clothes. I don't like fancy events or events that host rich people in general. They are too pretentious, power and money hungry, but I guess donating to the cause will help many people suffering from this horrible disease.

We checked the seating chart and I saw that we are seated at table number two. Now we need some drinks to make it through the night.

"Let's get some drinks" I suggested to Matteo who flagged down a waitress for two glasses of champagne on her tray "I see many people from the business world here. Who invited you again?" he said.

"You do? I was invited by my college professor, Mr. Charleston".

"Yeah, I also see the guy that has been targeting me. How lucky am I tonight?" Matteo said, as we weaved through the bodies, finally making it to a spot where we have a good view of the whole floor.

Nervousness flooded my senses at the mention of the person trying to kill Matteo, being here "show me so that I can know his face, please?"

"The guy that's standing next to the lady in the red dress near the statue. He the one with the curly black hair with a beard" Matteo explained. My eyes instantly caught them, and it also caught sight of Isaac, Matteo's dad. Who's busy making his way in our direction.

I lifted my glass towards my mouth mimicking taking a sip "your dad is making his way over to us"

"Yeah, saw him" Matteo said, placing a hand on my waist.

"Son, fancy seeing you here" he said, looking at Matteo a little panicked "Doctor, nice seeing you again" he said, without looking me in the eye.

"Good evening, Mr. Giordano" I greet back.

"Teo, what brings you here tonight, son?"

"I am accompanying my girlfriend, father and I'm a businessman, why wouldn't I be at an event like this?" Matteo asked, as his grip on my waist tightens. I placed my hand on his to remind him to relax, and his grip instantly slacked.

"I told you to end this" He stated, agitation clearly visible on his face.

Does this man have no shame to utter such nonsense in front of me, about me at that. He clearly has no shame. If he thinks that I will be offended, well then, he's in for a huge surprise.

"Dad, please. She's the mother of my children and I love her. Dylan and Max, your grandsons, are your and my flesh and blood. That's not something that can be ended or that I want to end....ever" Matteo said.

My heart started to slam against my chest. Not for his dad's utter disrespect, but for 'love' part. Did he just say that he loved me? This man is making my heart melt more, day by day.

"It clearly seems as though you've kept this from us on purpose. Why have you been hiding them from us, Teo? Why, if they are so important, did you pretend like they didn't exist? And you..."

His boring rambling has been interrupted by the announcer asking everyone to take their seats, ending the conversation midway. Which I was very thankful for.

"Well, the event is about to start so I'll see you tomorrow as discussed" Isaac said, pulling his suit together and went in the direction of his table, and we did the same. He was also seated at the same table the guy that is out to harm Matteo, is sitting.

We got some more drinks as we headed towards our tables with Matteo clearly unhappy with the interaction with his dad.

While the event was in full swing as introductions were made, I was on my 3rd glass of champagne already and fully ignoring the people talking on the stage.

The people at our table are all mature and, in their forties, or I would guess fifties at most. They were more interesting to look at as if i was able to read their minds.

My university professor was the one that invited me, and he was the next person to speak.

Matteo was sitting with his arm at the back of my chair "How long does events such as these normally take to be over and done with" I whispered in his ear.

"A few hours. It just started, baby. How do you now know how long these things take?" he asked back.

"Well, I always declined these types of events, but I thought I'd be adventurous and change my reclusive ways and partake in the activities of the so-called social scene".

"Really?" Matteo asked, rubbing circles on my shoulder with his thumb.

"Just kidding, my university professor that's currently on stage begged me since my return. He even made contact with my parents, and I couldn't say no to them. Dad also mentioned that he is willing to sponsor the program I want to start at the clinic where I help train new doctors and help them make their start while still learning.

"Your dad's a genius. So, you will need the professor to supply you with new doctors that's willing to learn"

"Bingo"

"Tonight, we would like to invite a special guest to the stage. This doctor has been a student of mine at Harvard University and has passed top of her class. She also became a world-renowned surgeon in the shortest time it would take many, saving hundreds of cancer patients' lives by performing surgeries that doctors with decades of medical expertise under their belts wouldn't attempt to perform. Her resilience and determination in performing lifesaving surgeries impacted so many lives for the better and tonight we would like to give the following award to a lady that's a Neurosurgeon called Dr. Daniella Harris".

"Why, why, why" I mutter under my breath. I didn't have enough to drink to face this crowd.

"Did you know about this?" Matteo asked noticing my slight panic.

"No" I answered, exhaling a deep breath.

"Dr. Harris, please make your way to the front" he announced from the stage.

Mateo gave my thigh a squeeze as I got up, hating every stare on my back as I made my way to the front.

"I sorry to spring this on you, but you deserve this. Congratulations Dr. Harris" Professor Charleston said.

"I shook his hand and thanked him thinking it was the end of it, but he insisted I give a word. I could have used this opportunity to promote my clinic but decided against it.

I stood in front of the podium trying to compose myself. I have never and will never be a public speaker, but I do know how to be someone I'm not in order to get through things.

"Good evening guests, I would like to firstly thank Professor Charleston for the heartwarming words. I would also like to thank the medical fraternity for exposing me to difficult cases that allowed me to learn and for the patients that put their trust in me. I salute you. Thank you" I said, making a quick exit back to my seat.

"Congratulations baby" Matteo said, sporting a huge smile on his face as he kissed my cheek.

"Thank you" I said, still trying to get used to his terms of endearment.

We sat there another minute then food was served. Matteo and I were busy throwing down glass after glass of alcohol and didn't eat much. I desperately needed to use the bathroom.

Matteo was busy observing his enemy from a distance while we sat and discussed the pettiness of his father while sneakily rubbing his hand up and down the side-slit of my dress, sending tingles through my core and this is not the time to feel anything down there with a full bladder.

I bent sideways as my lips reached his ear "I need to use the bathroom"

"I need to go too, I'll walk with you" he said, reaching for my hand and helping me get on my feet.

We walked hand in hand towards the bathroom and luckily no one stopped us. We headed down a dimly lit corridor and saw the bathrooms sign.

"I'll wait in the corridor when I'm done" Matteo said.

I went in and did my business. As I was about to exit the cubicle, I was shoved back in. I wanted to make a noise and protest, but when I saw it was Matteo, I let out a breath of relief.

"Why do you always corner me in the bathroom?" I asked, waiting for a response from him.

He gave me a sexy grin while pushing me up against the door. Luckily, the cubicles are fully enclosed, so no-one will be able to see us in here. His hands were placed on my hips keeping me in place as he bent down and pecked my lips, making me smile and peck his lips back.

Matteo started to lay kisses down my neck as his hands went up into my hair. We then started to make out as he pushed his front into mine making me instantly let out a soft moan.

Giving him a clear indication of just how horny he is making me. Our breathing started to pick up making the small space too tight.

Matteo's hands gripped my but "I can't get enough of you" he said, as he tried to devour my neck while sliding his one hand up the slit of the dress. Gliding his warm hands up the soft skin of my thigh. He was about to slide his hand further upwards when the door of the bathroom opened, making both of us snap our eyes open.

We couldn't make a peep, or we would be discovered doing unholy things in the bathroom. Matteo's hand was still rubbing my thigh as our eyes remained focused on each other's.

"Did you see him speaking to his son?" the one female said.

"Yeah, it seems the doctor is in a relationship with the son. I saw her joining him after she made her way off the stage.

Matteo immediately stopped his rubbing but his and remained on my thigh as we listened to the discussion these two females had about us.

"What do you think how long it will take dad to end things with that woman?" the first voice asked.

"I don't know, but I hope after tonight he will realize just how serious we are and that his empty promises mean nothing. Greg's just helping him expedite things" the one female voice responds. The both of them started to laugh and I have to say, it sounds ugly.

Both of them left while we waited a minute before exiting the bathroom into the corridor.

"What was that about?" I asked Matteo as we continued to make our way into the main hall.

"I don't know, but we're about to find out soon" he said, while typing on his phone.

"What are you doing now, Matteo?" I asked midway towards our table.

"I asked Vito to get someone to hack into the surveillance system and check who came into the bathroom at the time we were in there.

"We can head home if you want to?" I suggested.

"Yeah, I also think It's best if we head out" Matteo said.

"Ok, let me go bid the professor a good night. I'll be with you shortly" I said, not waiting for a response and headed towards the professor who was standing a few meters away from us.

My journey was interrupted by the curly headed guy Matteo was talking about earlier. He was not unattractive but he was a little chubby around the cheeks and mid section.

"Good evening, Doctor" he said, waiting for a response from me as If I knew who he was.

"Good evening?" I asked, giving him a questioning look, waiting for him to introduce himself.

He held out his hand "Stevenson, Greg Stevenson"

"Nice to meet you Mr. Stevenson" I said, starting to feel really uncomfortable under his stare. It felt like he was busy undressing me.

"Honey, who do we have here" a female voice said.

"Oh, mother. This is Dr. Harris" he introduced. She looked like a fifty odd year old spinster that loves to drink a lot of wine and dye her hair, but she's beautifully non the less. though, inner beauty is what we should measure people by.

The lady held out her hand as her scrutinizing gaze fluttered all over my body and face.

I held my hand out to her "nice to meet you Mrs. Stevenson" I said, trying to sound nice as she shook my hand.

"Nice to meet you too Doctor. We are impressed with your achievement" she said with a smile that's not reaching her snake eyes. Her son is a carbon copy of her but the male version.

I stood there awkwardly not knowing what their reason was for stopping me midway. I don't think the award has anything to do with them talking to me.

Luckily professor Charleston made his way past me, so I interrupted the non-existent conversation.

"Apologies, I'm about to head out and need to have a quick word with the professor" I said, politely excusing myself.

"It was good meeting you Doctor, hope to see you soon" he said. I just gave a nod and a half smile and left.

Greeting the professor, I made my way towards Matteo who had his eyes on me the whole time while busy with a conversation on his phone. He finished the call and took my hand in his as we made our way out the door.

****